" . . . for what passes for truth on one side of the Pyrenees is error on the other side."

—Blaise Pascal

Trouble crossing the Pyrenees

A NOVEL
BY
GAYLORD
LARSEN

Regal
Books
A Division of GL Publications
Ventura, CA U.S.A.

The foreign language of all Regal books is under the direction of Gospel Literature International GLINT. GLINT provides financial and technical help for the adaptation, translation and publishing of books for millions of people worldwide. For information regarding translation contact: GLINT, P.O. Box 6688, Ventura, California 93006.

Published by Regal Books
A Division of GL Publications
Ventura, California 93006
Printed in U.S.A.

Library of Congress Cataloging in Publication Data

Larsen, Gaylord, 1932-
  Trouble crossing the Pyrenees.

  I. Title.
PS3562.A734T76   1983   813'.54   83-3272
ISBN 0-8307-0880-4

Prologue

The solitary figure stood at the seaman's bowsprit leaning heavily against the railing and thrusting his head forward as if to suck in all the magic of the calm night at sea. The distant lights from a Mexican village off starboard seemed to dance in a midnight heat wave. He remembered the weather report indicated a mild santa ana blowing down from the California high desert. Perhaps that explained the warm and gentle mood of the ocean. Ideal for reflecting, for one last chance to tie in with the elements. Darwin had had his voyage of the *Beagle;* and now he had his own thought-wrenching voyage, the voyage of the *Inquisitor.* The lone man's face broke into a strange smile as he considered what lay ahead. Tomorrow they would be docking. How would his co-workers receive him? How should he play the scene? Should he let them make their own discoveries piecemeal or should he spring it on them all at once? It was going to be fun.

The reverie was broken by an approaching seaman.

"Howdy, I thought it was you, Doctor," he said. "I saw the moonlight gleaming off your . . . " He pointed.

The doctor smiled at him and passed his hand over his bald head. "Quite a night, isn't it?"

"Yup. Once in a while ol' mother nature turns balmy on ya, just to tantalize ya," the seaman declared, spitting into the bow's wake to demonstrate his superiority. "Glad to see you're up and about again, Doc. You had us worried for a spell there."

"Thanks, Kelly. I'm feeling much better."

With their spheres of common interest exhausted, the two men fell silent and watched the night, each lost in his own thoughts. Finally, Kelly checked his luminous wristwatch. "Well, time for me to be on the quarterdeck. Hope I don't fall asleep."

"What time is it, Kelly?"

"Comin' on four bells."

It was time, too, for the doctor to put his personal thoughts aside. He had a practical matter to attend to. He had been away from his cabin long enough for anybody on board who was interested in looking through his belongings to have done it by now. He edged his way slowly along the deck railing and went below.

At his cabin he drew back the running curtain, but instead of stepping inside, he stuck his head in and looked down at the rubber deck mat just inside the water chamber door. There was the 8½-x-11-inch sheet of white paper he had placed there an hour ago, but it now bore the unmistakable imprint of a sneaker. He began humming a nondescript melody, picked up the paper and tried to discern enough of a shoe pattern to identify it. Then he moved to his bookshelf and checked the line up of the twelve ledger books over the desk. Two of them were no longer touching the light pencil line he had drawn on the shelf. He checked the titles on the binders then smiled.

"Well, well. So that's what they're after," he said half aloud. "Looks like it's time to put out the bait."

6

Chapter One

Henry came back from the phone and folded himself into the chair opposite his wife at their patio breakfast table. She waited and watched as he absently stirred his already tepid coffee and scowled out in the general direction of their backyard garden. When she could stand it no longer she asked, "What did he want?"

"Oh, he's got a problem down San Diego way."

"Why is he calling you about that?"

"He wants me to go down. Any more sourdough toast?"

She got up, reached across the windowsill leading into the kitchen and dropped another slice of his favorite bread into the toaster. "Well, would you like to know what I think?"

"What's that?" he asked, as though he had a choice.

"I think he's got a good deal of cheek asking you to do anything for the department after what he did to you."

Henry smiled at his wife. Chapin did not have him fired actually, but the combination of meaningless assignments and the generous retirement offer accomplished the same thing. Henry's careers in three different U.S. intelligence agencies could not be called failures, but the last few years had been frustrating and the chance to be out from under was welcome.

"You turned him down, didn't you?"

"I told him I'd call him back after we'd talked."

"Oh," Valery said, then sighed to project her disappointment.

Despite the retirement settlement, Valery wanted her husband to get himself into a new job with a regular salary. The longer he put it off the more nervous she became. He had already had two offers with local accounting firms and, without her saying so in so many words, Henry knew Valery wanted him to settle on one of the offers. At fifty-two a man can't be choosy.

The toast popped up, and as Henry proceeded to carefully bury it under gobs of butter and orange marmalade he began methodically listing for her all the reasons for and against accepting the temporary assignment.

Henry doubted if Chapin was asking him to do this job as a backhanded way to make up for any past injustices. CIA department heads were not that susceptible to pangs of conscience. More than likely he simply thought of Henry in California because it would be cheap, it was Henry's kind of work, and they didn't have an agent they could release for such a small assignment.

The job itself was a rather mundane housecleaning task. Last year when a U.S. geological team was preparing for an extensive ocean floor survey in the Pacific (including the Bering Straits and the Kuril Trench, whatever that was) the Washington office had gotten the bright idea of surreptitiously piggybacking along on the trip with some of their supersensitive monitoring devices to do a little eavesdropping on some of the Russian ports.

Unfortunately, now when the trip was nearly over, the

geological team was not releasing the Precursor, one of the CIA's advanced monitoring devices. According to Chapin, the geologists had discovered an application for the machine that helped them in their work and they were not about to give it back. This latest turn of events Chapin learned when the company's two equipment operators left the ship in Mazatlán, Mexico.

As usual, the legal ownership of the machine had been compromised; because of the department's zealous efforts at maintaining their cover, they had listed the machine as being purchased by the geological association. Now the geologists said they were keeping it for payment for all the inconveniences the CIA had caused them.

This bothered Henry. There had been instances in the past when unscrupulous individuals had taken advantage of the department's need for secrecy and had taken equipment because they knew they would never be accused of theft in an open courtroom. But geologists? Or the geological association? They're reputable people. What were they doing taking equipment they knew didn't belong to them?

Henry told Valery only the basic outline of all this, but the whole messy scene went through his mind while his eyes were scanning the flower beds for spring buds.

"It would be a thankless task," Henry said. "About the only thing I could do is slap a few wrists. If they've got their minds set on not giving the equipment back, the department'll just have to live with it."

"Is the Precursor thing very expensive?" Valery asked.

"Yes, I suppose so. It consumes a lot of electricity, I remember. But Chapin is more concerned with keeping its operation a secret."

Valery watched her husband scowl for another moment, then she slapped her napkin down on the glass

9

tabletop with finality.

"Oh, Henry, why don't you just call him and tell him you won't do it? Put all that business behind you. It only makes you grumpy. We moved to California for a fresh start, remember?"

"The geologist in charge of the expedition was Dr. Ralph Pangbourne," Henry said.

"Are we supposed to know him?"

"He's the bigwig in the natural sciences at El Rio University."

"Oh." Valery started to rise but sat back down at this bit of news. "And you think he knows Philip?"

"No doubt he does. That's Philip's field of study," Henry said, nervously twisting his coffee cup in its saucer. "It would be a natural way for me to see him again. I'd be down in San Diego anyway . . . "

Valery put a gentle hand on his wrist to stop the noisy cup. "But you'll still be working for the CIA."

"It's a little different now. He'll certainly see that."

She leaned back and studied her husband. "He knows where we live. I think it's up to him to get in touch with us, don't you?"

"Valery. He's our son."

"And I remember the way he talked to you."

"He was just a kid."

"Kid? He was twenty-two years old. Twenty-three now. I just don't want you hurt again."

"I've forgotten all about it."

"Well, I haven't. I still say he was responsible for your breakdown."

"Valery, have a little understanding. He's a product of his time, just as we are."

"And when does he show some understanding? We raised him in a proper manner . . . " Valery went on repeating all the old arguments for a few moments, but then stopped when she saw Henry's slightly walleyed look that told her she wasn't getting through.

"He's been on my mind a lot lately," Henry said thoughtfully, "and I just feel with this little ownership tussle turning up right now—with the ship coming into San Diego Harbor and one of the main characters knowing Philip—I just think maybe the Lord wants me to take it."

Valery had promised herself she would not argue religion again, but her blood was up, "And is the Lord going to help us with the house payments? Remember, you're the one who wanted the big house with a garden. The children are practically grown and we've got an upstairs full of bedrooms."

"Oh, we have a long time before we have to worry about meeting bills."

"Well." Valery said for no particular reason, then started clearing the breakfast dishes. "When will you be leaving?"

"Thanks, hon, I knew you'd understand."

Early the next morning, with his bag packed for a four-nighter and a good-bye kiss planted discreetly on his left cheek, Henry aimed the Volvo onto the south ramp of the 405 Interstate and settled down for the long ride to San Diego. Once he was through the heavy L.A. commuter traffic he set the cruise control at fifty-seven miles an hour (there was a sweet spot at fifty-seven where the car seemed to hum nicely) and let his mind start wandering, as was his custom of late.

Perhaps it was a terrible thing to admit, but he didn't exactly feel badly about leaving Valery this time. Can you love a person and still not want to be with her? There was no doubt their marriage had greater strains on it now than any time in the past, and Henry cast about in his memory to determine what had changed. Or who had changed.

11

The current tensions, Henry decided, really hadn't surfaced until his conversion to Christianity. That was at the heart of their problems. What was it Jesus said? "I bring a sword that will divide the family." He and Becky were Christians, but Valery and the boys were not.

Christian was the wrong word. Valery used it as a synonym for "civilized" and saw herself in the forefront of that English-speaking world where truth, justice, and economic enlightenment were meted out to a dark and sinister world, and husband Henry was one of the leading torchbearers. Henry had felt that way too until the roof fell in.

Was it the diatribe Philip had laid on his father last year that triggered it all? Henry and Valery were stationed in Washington after a long stint in Europe and Philip had come "home" during a term break in his graduate school studies. It was one of those periods when the U.S. foreign policy was being raked over the coals of the fourth estate and the CIA activities were again suspect. To top it off, Philip had been monitoring a political science class taught by a political firebrand of communist persuasions, and he came laden with horror stories which he spewed at his father, complete with foul language and a vindictive attitude. It was apparent to Henry that Philip's teacher was privy to some inside information; although the stories were also laced with a good many falsehoods. But rather than argue points, Henry, like a good little well-trained agent, bore it all in silence and watched as his son forced the dangerous chasm between them wider and wider. Strange how the tongue can damage living tissue. Sarcasm truly tears the flesh; he could feel it, deep down where he lived.

Henry's star with the agency was already on the decline primarily because of his own loss of drive. It wasn't a fair statement to say Philip's outburst had triggered his breakdown. Or even that he'd had a breakdown. *Turning point* was the term he preferred. Henry was already well on his way to his new approach to life when all that happened. Long before he had begun to question the morality of some of the agency's actions—blunders, double agents unearthed, the demise of close friends on assignment in East Germany . . .

But all this was prelude and he knew it. He could spend the entire trip to San Diego thinking of reasons why he was dissatisfied with his old life. How could he expect Valery to understand what had happened to him when he couldn't explain it to his own satisfaction? How do you explain to a self-assured, confident person like Valery, who has all kinds of positive feelings about herself and her lifestyle, your sudden need to change? To put God in the center of your life and to make everything else—your decision making, your interests, your goals—subservient to His interests? To her the whole thing smacked of an admission of weakness and failure.

How could Henry talk of confessing his sins and shortcomings as though he were some evil person? Weren't they a good deal better than 95 percent of the people they knew, to say nothing of the rest of the world?

How could he respond to arguments like that? Each time he had tried the discussion seemed to degenerate into a restrained, tense silence. Perhaps the event that had happened in Henry's consciousness was of such a personal nature that it could never be successfully communicated to another human being. Henry remembered having been dragged to a religious movie several years ago, the plot of which dealt with the religious conversion of a successful businessman. It was supposedly based on a true event but all he could recall of the film was how dreadfully it failed. The whole thing smacked of unbelievability. To view a Christian conversion from outside the Christian experience has a phony ring to it. Who can look into another's heart and tell why a person does one thing and not another? Why one chooses to live for the dollar while another chooses the austere life of a missionary?

Since Valery had this same problem of understanding, she took the attitude that Henry's condition was a temporary one and, like a bad cold, it must be suffered for a time before things could return to normal. Maybe so. But Henry didn't think it was going to happen that way.

Chapter Two

It was a beautifully clear breezy day in San Diego; the whole town seemed to sparkle like the ocean it embraced. So bright, in fact, Henry had to make a one-handed fumble around in the glove compartment for his old, out-of-date sunglasses. The agency people had been discouraged from wearing dark glasses for fear of attracting unwanted attention. But Henry decided the rule didn't apply to middle-aged errand boys.

Since the *Inquisitor* had been scheduled to dock early that morning he thought he'd go directly to the ship and take a chance of finding most of the scientists still aboard. He wanted to take a good look at the Precursor anyway, to determine what would be involved physically in getting the contraption moved. The *Inquisitor* was temporarily berthed in the Navy shipyard. That was good. If push came to shove, the more government personnel he had around him to call upon the better he felt.

Apparently Chapin had called ahead for Henry because he had barely given his name at the main gate when a navy-grey escort car pulled out from nowhere and he was invited to follow along behind. After driving by the headquarters' complex and several empty slips they turned south toward a restricted area which fenced off an aircraft carrier that was undergoing extensive repairs. A cluster of civilians, apparently relatives and friends of returning sailors, were gathered near the guarded gate. Two deeply tanned bearded men were the center of attention, sorting duffel bags and warding off their clinging children.

Henry's escort called to the guard on duty; the guard pushed the driveway gate open and Henry and the escort hurried on through.

As they rounded the bow of the aircraft carrier, Henry spotted the little research vessel docked next to it. There was such a difference in the comparative sizes of the two vessels it appeared they didn't belong in the same ocean. The *Inquisitor* was a twin-hulled vessel with a good deal of deck space and top rigging. Plenty of rust spots showed but to a landlubber like Henry it seemed to be a functional ship, considering its purpose.

They pulled up near the passenger gangplank and a young officer with a shore patrol arm band got out of the escort car and approached Henry. "I'm Ensign Shirley, Mr. Garrett," he saluted. "I've been ordered to give you any assistance I can."

"Thank you, ensign," Henry said, getting out of his car. "Do you know why I'm here?"

"Yes, sir, I understand it's an ownership problem about a piece of government equipment."

"Yes—" Henry started.

"The captain of the vessel is already over at the dispatch office, but I believe the scientist in charge of the expedition is still aboard. His name's Pangbourne. Will we be seeing him?"

"We? Well, I'd like to. Yes—"

"If I may say so, sir," the ensign interrupted, rocking

16

confidently on his widespread legs, "they made quite a tactical error accepting our docking facilities."

"How's that?"

"Tug service," he smiled. "They can't get out of there without it and we're not about to order it until this matter is cleared up to our satisfaction. Shall we go, sir?"

"Uh, tell you what. I'd like to keep this whole thing low-key if possible. Why don't I go aboard and see if this can be cleared up without hostilities, okay?"

The ensign seemed hurt but agreed to stand-to until needed.

Henry went down the gangplank and approached two young men in cutoff jeans who were cleaning a cable in a milk-white solution. They chatted with Henry in the friendly, easygoing manner of people just back from a long ocean cruise, and gave him directions for finding Dr. Pangbourne. Henry went down a long metal companionway, turned to his left and groped his way through a dark narrow corridor, stumbling over a couple of the raised hatchway sills in the process. Then he came to the sun-drenched space between the two hulls of the ship and found himself looking down on a small blue submarine resting on a series of support girders between the hulls.

Sitting on the rounded prow of the sub was a baldheaded middle-aged man with a faraway smile on his face. Humpty Dumpty sat on a wall . . . Assuming it was Pangbourne, Henry stood in the shadows for a moment to get a better visual reading on the man. He was tanned and heavily wrinkled about the face but still a good physical specimen with muscular arms and legs, a flat stomach and a broad hairy chest. Here was a man in good command of himself who no doubt lived life to the hilt.

Henry changed his lookout angle to see if there was anyone else about; there didn't seem to be, which was a surprise because the bald man's face was so animated and

17

expressive. It was the kind of expression one wears when talking to someone. Then Henry saw that something was scrawled on the submarine near the man's left thigh. He was examining it, then in turn looking up, smiling as though enjoying his own private joke. And as he smiled, the muscles of his cheeks pushed his eyelids up at an angle, giving his expression an evil twist. *What sinister thoughts must be going through his mind,* Henry wondered.

"Hello there," Henry said, stepping out onto the catwalk. "Are you Dr. Pangbourne?"

"That's right," Pangbourne said, without bothering to change his expression.

"I'm Henry Garrett. Mr. Chapin asked me to come down and—"

The doctor raised his arms. "Don't shoot! I surrender."

"What?"

"You fellows don't let any grass grow under your feet do you?"

Pangbourne rolled deftly to his feet, sidestepped along the top of the boat's backbone and swung up on the catwalk. Meanwhile, Henry leaned forward to see what had held the doctor's attention; he saw that someone had scrawled "Old Score" on the sub with a broad yellow chalk or paintbrush.

"You're here about the Precursor, right?" Pangbourne said, extending his hand to Henry.

"Yes, that's right. I understand your association feels it has some claim to the ownership—"

"No. Not the association," Pangbourne interrupted. "It was my bright idea." He smiled, watching Henry's face which held passive. Then he laughed. "Don't worry, I'm not going to pursue it."

"You mean you'll release it to me?"

"Yes, I will, just as soon as you prove to me you're

18

from the CIA."

"We don't carry badges around, you know."

"Yes, I know," Pangbourne said, putting a friendly but heavy hand on Henry's shoulder and walking past him into the corridor. "Why don't you have this Chapin fellow send a telegram to you including the serial numbers on the Precursor?"

"Fine, I'll see to it right away."

"Sorry to have to ask you to do it this way," Pangbourne said, "but we've already had a few problems on the expedition of people misrepresenting themselves."

"You mean someone else has tried to claim the unit?"

"Not sure. It seemed to be regarding another matter."

By now they had moved into the doctor's living quarters and he was looking with a critical eye at the suit, shirt, and tie hanging above his bunk.

"Well, I guess I can't put it off any longer. It's back to civilization." He started to take off his dirty work shorts.

"Should I wait for you on deck?" Henry asked.

"Oh, we're all one big happy family around here. I suppose you're wondering why the switch on giving the equipment back."

"As long as we get it back in good shape I think the company will be happy."

"Yesss," Pangbourne said with a pregnant smile. Then he pulled his dress shirt free from its hanger and slipped it on. "It's probably just as well."

"I am curious to know what application you made of it though," Henry said.

"Do you understand plate tectonics?"

"You mean the theory of sections of the earth's crust moving—"

"Oh, it's more than theory now," Pangbourne interrupted. "The major purpose of our trip was to map the movement history of the Pacific plate. You see, when the

19

new material is formed from the earth's molten zones and oozes up to the ocean floor and hardens, a magnetic pattern is formed . . . "

Pangbourne, like a true teacher, stood in his small living space in his shirt and undershorts, gesturing with rolling and waving hands how the molten lava forms new crust, how it packs together to form mountains, then how, in other places of the world, it folds back into the earth's inner crust to be recycled into molten rock. " . . . and your machine can detect the very slightest shift in magnetic balance in this new material. It saved us drilling a lot of samples we ordinarily would have had to drill."

"Well, that's fine," Henry said. "Maybe a modified version of the Precursor can be declassified so this application can be used in the future."

Pangbourne smiled, "That thought had passed my mind."

"I take it it's been a good trip."

"Yes, yes it has. We have quite a few numbers to run through our computers yet, but I'd say we're going to blow the lids off a few old theories." Again, the odd smile.

"I was wondering, doctor, if you knew my son Philip? He's studying—"

"Philip Garrett?" Pangbourne asked, studying the father's face for signs of similarity. "Of course. He was one of my teaching assistants last semester. Yes, I certainly do. He has a very fine head for research."

"Thank you . . . "

"He never mentioned his father was in the CIA."

"That's understandable. I don't think he's any too proud of it."

Pangbourne laughed. "Ah, these kids. The morals of angels. Wait'll it's their turn. They'll sing a different tune."

Henry smiled, but it still hurt to hear his old agency roasted on such a subtle fire. Did he have to grasp Henry's

20

meaning quite so quickly?

"There, how do I look?" Pangbourne asked, turning in front of his small dressing mirror. "Will I pass muster?"

"Fine," Henry said. The doctor pushed up his tie knot and indicated approval of what he saw with a smirk. In spite of his bald pate he was still a handsome figure with a vital, energetic presence that women probably found attractive.

"The Precursor is in the number two radio room down the—"

"Dr. Pangbourne!" a woman's voice interrupted. Henry turned to see a beautiful young woman standing at the hatchway trying to give an impression of a scolding mother.

"Hello, Tracy," the doctor said. "This is Mr. Garrett. You remember Philip Garrett, don't you? This is his dad." Pangbourne smiled at the girl a bit more than the moment called for.

Tracy seemed totally disinterested in the Garrett family tree. "You know, of course, we're late. The whole team is waiting."

"Yes, yes. They've waited six months already. A few more minutes won't kill them."

Tracy scowled, which looked incongruous on her tanned creamy smooth complexion, then left with a gruff, "We'll be on deck."

Pangbourne chuckled. "Hell hath no fury like a woman scorned.

"Listen, Garrett, I'm going to be socked in with meetings at the university the rest of the day and most of tomorrow. Could I ask you to drop by out there when you get your telegram? I'll keep the manifest clearance papers with me and I'll sign 'em and give you your 'ok' right on the spot."

"Yes, I suppose—"

21

"Again, I'm sorry to do this to you. We're having a national conclave of geologists at the university this summer and the program is yet to be worked out, which doesn't speak very well for the initiative of our committee I'm afraid. Everybody waits on the old man. And our new catalog listings for the fall term . . . " He rubbed his brow. "Rats." He started gathering his briefcase and a small suitcase for his disembarkation, bemoaning his return to the world of mundane responsibilities.

"So all you need then are serial numbers?" Henry repeated, to make sure Pangbourne was committing himself.

"Yeah, that should do it. You want to take a peek at the contraption? It's right down that passageway," he said gesturing. "Can we drop you someplace?"

"No thanks. I've my own car. I thought I'd go by and see my son."

"Of course. I'll probably be seeing him myself a bit later. Well . . . " He looked about wistfully at the small compartment that had been his home for the last half year. "I'm just taking my personal stuff now. The school will be picking up my papers— We'll be talking, I'm sure."

"Of course," Henry called and watched as the retreating figure gracefully maneuvered its way down the narrow passageway.

Later, when Henry rethought their parting comments, he mused philosophically about how easily we all asuume a permanence to that which is really temporal. How glibly we make our plans and plot our little schemes, seeing events only from our own limited angle. His main goal during their talk had been to humor the doctor and avoid anything that might change his mind about relinquishing the government equipment. But Henry was destined to reconstruct their casual, chatty conversation again and again in his mind, searching for hidden nuances and fresh

22

meanings, because the element of violent surprise which the best laid plans can never anticipate was about to be heard from, echoing its alarm throughout the hallowed halls of academia. Henry would not be seeing Dr. Ralph Pangbourne alive again.

Chapter Three

Henry walked down the passageway Pangbourne had pointed out and found the room he was looking for. Radio room number two had a red and yellow stenciled sign on it, indicating it was off limits to the ship's regular crew, and a government seal Henry recognized as a company mark was attached to the heavy metal latch on the hatch.

No doubt the seal was affixed by the company operators before they left the ship in Mexico. Peering through the clear patches of the porthole where the grey paint had started separating, he could see the familiar dials and gauges of the Precursor. He understood now why Pangbourne would not be afraid of Henry finding the serial numbers on his own; the entire operating console, some six or seven feet wide and standing four feet high, had been anchored into the side of the room as if it were destined to be a permanent fixture. Any serial numbers were no doubt out of sight against the bulkhead.

He stood with his hand on the latch for a moment but

then let it go. Although authorized to enter the room he decided against breaking the seal. Ship security seemed lax enough already. Why extend someone an invitation? He would have to check about security with the ensign.

As he stood quietly listening for other signs of life a little shiver went up his back. Except for the sounds of a bilge pump and the drone of a fifty-cycle generating engine reverberating somewhere deep in the ship's metallic bowels, Henry could be totally alone. Although not a large ship, it did seem to generate a powerful presence all its own. Perhaps its own personality: "I search out the world's secrets. I am relentless. I am modern science, so beware, beware."

He was shaken out of his reverie by someone calling his name, then he heard the unrhythmic clomp of heavy sandals drawing closer. He turned in time to see a large slender figure hurry by the opening at the end of the corridor.

The large figure had apparently caught a glimpse of Henry as it raced by, but like a character in a movie cartoon it took several strides to recover: *clop, clop, clop.* Then a head reappeared, extended on the end of a long looping neck.

"Oh, hi. Mr. Garrett?"

"Yes?"

"Oh, hi. I'm Jeremy Bruce," the young man said, approaching Henry in his own inimitable way. His height, Henry estimated, was somewhere between six-eight and six-ten, although it was hard to say because there were so few spots in the ship's pipe-filled narrow passageways where he could stand erect. And he had worked out a unique way of navigating the short waterchamber doorsills. He would extend one long gangly leg into the chamber ahead, then skew his body around so that his rear end appeared next, then his upper torso and finally his head

25

and other foot. The whole maneuver was done quickly, which seemed to make it funnier still. He was a deadly serious, eager young man in his mid-twenties, pressing his fingertips together in a supplicating manner as he closed in on Henry.

"Dr. Pangbourne said you'd be down here. Hi."

"Hello."

"I was wondering if I could hitch a ride with you."

"Yes, I suppose so. Where are you headed?"

"Oh, I thought maybe Philip told you about me. I'm his roommate. We share the apartment together. Dr. Pang said I might be able to hitch a ride with you if you're going there now. I got all my gear ready to go."

"Fine," Henry said. "I'll be making some phone calls on shore, then I'll be ready."

Jeremy bobbed his head forward twice which Henry took to mean agreement. "This is great. I really appreciate it." He smiled and bobbed some more.

Then followed a series of false starts as the two men went into an Alfonce-routine to see who would go first back down the passageway. Henry finally took the initiative with a smile. He was a bit too tall for most modern structures himself, so he could empathize with the gangling Jeremy who never seemed to know what to do with his body. But after passing through the hatchway he couldn't resist looking back to watch as Jeremy went through his contortionist act once more. He wondered how many weeks of the expedition it took to get that move down pat.

As Henry watched, his angle of view also allowed him to see the entrance to Dr. Pangbourne's quarters just down the passageway behind Jeremy. Almost as if on cue, a tall blond man in seaman's work clothes stepped out of Pangbourne's room. He glanced in Henry's direction, started to turn away, did a quick double take at Henry, then quickened his pace in the other direction and was gone.

If it hadn't been for the double take Henry would have thought nothing of it, but it seemed to be a glance of recognition. If he knew Henry perhaps Henry knew him. Henry tried to see the man in his mind's eye without the dirty work clothes and the blond stubbly facial hair. Unfortunately as he did so he slowed down his pace and Jeremy, who was close on his heels anyway, didn't notice this and proceeded to plow into him, sending the two of them into a heap.

"Upff. Excuse me. Are you all right?"

"Yes, I think so," Henry said, rubbing the spot on the back of his head where he had just tested the firmness of the ship's angle-iron bracing. If he was going to maintain his personal health and safety Henry would have to learn to keep his distance from Mr. Jeremy Bruce. The incident was not without its benefits, however, because he remembered where he'd seen the man before: the image of a clean-shaven blond courier the company employed in Amsterdam popped into Henry's mind. This was a long way from Amsterdam. What was a courier doing in the cabin of a researcher on an exploration ship docked in San Diego Harbor, *USA.?*

Once on deck, Henry hurried up the gangplank and watched from relative safety as Jeremy collected his suitcase and two large duffel bags. The ease with which he hoisted his heavy loads to his shoulders and reconnoitered his way about the ship's rigging and up the gangplank was surprising. Perhaps the young man only needed to be so burdened all the time to function like a normal human being.

While they were loading the gear into the trunk of the Volvo, Ensign Shirley approached, field-stripping his cigarette butt as he walked. He stopped some twenty yards away and waited for Henry to separate himself from his young passenger. Henry went over and explained what had transpired between himself and Dr. Pangbourne. Clearance for the Precursor was just a phone call away. This news seemed to disappoint the young naval officer; perhaps he had visions of rescuing the prized secret weapon after a suicide charge with fixed bayonets. But he agreed, as Henry instructed, to seek out the captain of the *Inquisitor* and ask to post a temporary guard in the passageway outside radio room number two.

They then got in their cars and drove to the shore patrol office so Henry could make his calls. Chapin could not be reached immediately so he left word for Chapin to return his call at Philip's apartment. He then called the local number for the nationwide household mover the CIA and other sensitive government agencies used for their moving requirements. Chapin had alerted them and Henry briefly ran over again what they would be moving and what would be needed to get the job done: three antennas, two wave generators, and the guts of the unit Henry had seen in the radio room. If needed, they had the necessary steel cutting equipment and were only waiting to hear from him to start the operation.

This all pleased Henry. So far so good. As he headed back toward his car he was already making plans in his mind for his return trip home around noon the following day.

He found Jeremy thumbing through the old Bible Henry usually carried with him when he traveled.

"That didn't take long."

"No, it didn't," Henry agreed.

"You a Christian? I found this on the seat here."

"Yes, I am."

"Well, praise the Lord. So am I. What church you go to?"

28

All the directness discussing such personal matters with a relative stranger was not something Henry could handle gracefully. He mumbled something about not having time to find a church home yet.

Jeremy babbled on, "I was raised in the church. I mean I've gone to Sunday School and stuff all my life. My mom and dad were missionaries and I hope to make Christian work a full-time thing, too."

"Oh?" Henry said. "You were on the expedition, weren't you?"

"Sure."

I thought all the students aboard would be going into the sciences full time."

"I am. I'm in the doctoral program at the university just like Philip, only I'm a creationist."

"Creationist?"

"You know. We believe man was created by a Supreme Being instead of evolving from lower forms. Don't you?"

Henry laughed at Jeremy's directness. "I don't know. I guess I haven't given it much thought. I suppose I've always assumed that God used evolution as His way of creating mankind."

"Oh, no. Oh, no way. You haven't thought that through."

"I haven't?"

"No. You see, your thinking is the product of scientific atheism that permeates our educational system. Turn left up ahead there."

They passed the last gate of the Navy base and Jeremy was directing them to the fastest route to the university east of town. As they drove, Henry learned more than he cared to know about the creationism theories—that there was a big effort afoot, especially in California, to have creationism taught on an equal basis with evolution in the school system; that creationism, according to Jeremy at least, was a sound and reasonable theory strictly from a scientific point of view; and that there was really no scientific basis whatsoever to indicate man or any of the other animals had evolved from a lower form of life.

Henry cast a suspicious glance at his passenger. There seemed to be two Jeremy Bruces. One was a confused, uncoordinated, eager-to-please youth, likeable but not a person to be taken seriously. But once on the right subject, he became an intelligent, highly motivated zealot for the cause. He could rattle off his statistics and scientific terms with authority as though he could close the discussion on the entire matter of man's origins with one devastating sentence. Henry was in no position to argue data or the reasonableness of theories with him so he took another tack.

"I take it you take your faith quite seriously."

"Oh, sure. I mean, yes, I do."

"Excuse me for saying so," Henry said good-naturedly, "but aren't you more or less missing the whole point of Christ's ministry?"

"What do you mean?"

"I mean He gave us two primary commissions for our walk in this life: to preach the gospel—the good news that He is the Son of God and our salvation is through Him—"

"Right," Jeremy bobbed in agreement.

"And secondly, that we should care for and nurture one another."

"Right."

"So isn't this what we should be doing? I mean I've got all I can handle just now, learning to love my *family* the way I should. I realize it's none of my business but I think arguing over scientific theories is missing the boat."

Jeremy shook his head. "No, you don't understand what's involved here. Where's your authority? If someone tells you they reject this gospel business and loving one another as just another story to be put on the shelf next to the Bobbsey Twins and Rebecca of Sunnybrook Farm," he waved Henry's Bible in front of him, "what do you say to that?" Jeremy's voice was rising in pitch and volume. "If evolution is true, we owe our existence to chance—to a series of meaningless events. So why should we even think of considering anything as asinine as a God in heaven? He didn't create us. Chance did." He sat rocking and shaking his head sadly, oblivious to the rapid traffic outside. "What are morals? What's love . . . or conscience . . . but a recent development in a chain of mutations that we can use or ignore as we see fit.

"You know who was the perfect product of the evolution theory? Hitler. Think about it. The superior race. Triumph of the will was just another term for survival of the fittest. And weed out all inferior races and deformities without any show of conscience, because conscience is not a gift from God but an unnecessary mutation that can be bred away in the future like a useless appendix.

"Of course, now all the world rushes to condemn Nazism, not even realizing it was a natural product of their own theory of evolution—the theory they still embrace today. They don't even realize—I swear we're headed for another Hitler."

Henry watched Jeremy clench his fists. And he noted the venom in his voice as he spat out the pronoun for evolutionists—"they"—as though referring to a dark and sinister enemy. Henry *was* developing a very healthy respect if not a fear toward the young brooding giant next to him. Could it be true that they were both members of the same religious club? It hardly seemed possible. What a sharp contrast between this dark troubled scholar and the quiet considerate congressman who had been instrumental in Henry's own conversion. But it wasn't long before the cloud lifted and the other side of Jeremy's personality

31

emerged again.

As they approached the university, Jeremy's gloom dissolved into excitement and he started pointing out some of his old haunts to Philip's father. A spring fair the students sponsored was still going on and some of the local stores across the street from the free speech area were decorated accordingly. Apparently, the theme was an Old English or Elizabethan cultural "faire." A group of students in costume were manning some of the makeshift booths where handcrafted articles were on display.

"Oh, look," Jeremy called. "Pull over here a second, can you?"

Henry eased his car to the curb in a red no-parking area next to some of the fair activities.

"There's Dr. Teague," he laughed and pointed to a cage that held the soaking-wet professor. He was sitting on a small perch and taunting several students outside. Above the cage was a sign reading "Dunk a Dean— $1.00."

The students were laughing and egging on one of their own who was throwing baseballs at a target. A bull's-eye apparently would release a trap door and send Dr. Teague splashing into the water in the bottom of his cage. Jeremy laughed and called to his caged mentor, but the man was much too occupied to see or hear him.

When a university parking officer on a three-wheeler rolled up behind them, Henry took the hint and pulled away from the curb. Jeremy explained that each year the school put on the fair in order to raise money for the charities which the sororities and fraternities sponsored. They helped a lot of people and everybody had a good time before the spring finals.

As they drove across the grounds some of Jeremy's excitement wore off onto Henry. It was nice being on a university campus again—the tall clean buildings, citadels

32

of learning, with well-manicured landscaping, and people in casual clothes walking about with purpose and a spring in their step. It had been a long time away for Henry and he marveled at how young the students all seemed.

The apartment they were headed for, Jeremy explained, was one of those originally built by the university for their married students, but since the number of married students had shrunk, several of the units were now rented to graduate singles. Parking around campus seemed to be a mess. The street in front of the apartment building and the parking areas were all jammed with small late-model cars, most of them of the expensive variety.

Where does all the money come from? Henry wondered. Full tuition at El Rio had to be about ten thousand. How can parents afford to send their youngsters here plus give them $25,000 Porsches to run around in? Philip was on a scholarship or grant program now, plus his maternal grandparents had set aside a nice amount in their wills for their grandchildren's education, so Henry and Valery had never really felt the pinch of supporting their two college students. But the arrangement also had its drawbacks. Henry had felt for some time that the college money gave the children an independence he was not ready to grant them. Perhaps that feeling of financial freedom had contributed to Philip's argumentative stand against his father. Perhaps, perhaps . . . these thoughts and the expectancy of seeing his son again made Henry's heart beat a bit faster.

With no parking places available, Jeremy found a familiar car and told Henry to pull in behind it. He knew the owner and would tell him where to find them in case he needed out of his slot.

They unloaded the Volvo and made their way up to the second-floor unit Jeremy called home. Philip was not there. Jeremy busied himself with putting his gear away, pushing aside some of Philip's things which had spilled into his domain, and making himself at home again. Henry took some time rubbernecking about the apartment, looking for familiar signs of Philip's presence. But it was as if he were looking over the personal effects of a total stranger. There wasn't so much as a picture of his boy to reassure him he was in the right place.

Philip had been in boarding schools for two years before he started at the university, so it seemed logical, Henry decided, that he would not recognize articles Philip had accumulated over such a long period. And the thought occurred to him that Philip *was,* to a great extent, a stranger. The natural science college texts that lined his orange-crate shelves, the girly magazines on the end table next to the old sofa, the strange names and faces that looked out at him from the record jackets stacked next to the hi-fi, all told him what a small influence he now was to Philip. True, early impressions are important and perhaps more lasting, but even then the mother played the major role in the formative years. Was there really anything of him that Philip would be carrying on? For the first time Henry felt a little foolish in his quest to become reattached to his son.

The phone rang. Jeremy stopped sorting his dirty clothes long enough to answer it and turn it over to Henry.

"Got your message," Chapin began. "How'd everything go, old man?"

"Better than I expected. Apparently they'd had a change of heart about the ownership thing. The head man, Dr. Pangbourne, assured me it's all ours as soon as we can prove who we are—"

"And just how do we do that?"

"Didn't you get the word about the serial numbers?" Henry asked.

"Oh, I getcha. I didn't understand that part of the note.

I told my girl, Florie, about them and she'll call them in to you first thing in the morning."

"In the morning?" Henry checked his watch.

"Sure. It's eight-thirty back here you know," Chapin said. "What's the big need for all this? Didn't you tell them I'd sent you?"

"Yes, but apparently there'd been some trouble on board. What about I don't know. Say, what's our man Steckman doing on board?"

"Our Steckman?"

"Yes. Tall, blond, kinky-haired fellow we used to use as a courier in Amsterdam."

There was an unusual lull from Chapin's end so Henry continued, "American, I believe."

"No, Canadian," Chapin intoned slowly.

Chapin was a sharp cookie. If he wanted to mislead Henry or keep him in the dark about an operation he'd have no difficulty developing the right flow of language to do it. But the silence was another matter. Henry was certain Chapin knew nothing of Steckman's activities. Was there another CIA branch involved in this? Things would be humming in the fir trees of Virginia tomorrow.

"Did he recognize you?" Chapin went on.

"Yes, I'm sure he did. He was dressed like the other seamen aboard. It would be my guess he was on the expedition," Henry volunteered.

"See if you can find out what name he's operating under—"

"Right."

"And what he was doing aboard."

After that Chapin flipped into a lighter tone; he asked about Valery and their new carefree life on the beaches of California. Henry thought this was at least partly intended to play down the importance of the Steckman matter.

Before they hung up, Henry told of his own indefinite

35

plans. There didn't appear to be room for him at his son's apartment so he probably would be getting a motel room near the campus for the night. What about getting the telegram to him? Chapin, the logistics expert, directed that he'd have it left with the downtown San Diego FBI office under Henry's old code name.

"No," Chapin quickly corrected. "We better use a new one. Any preferences?"

"How about Charles Q. Darwin?"

"All right. You got it."

Jeremy finished stuffing the last of his whites into a duffelbag and stopped to give Henry a quizzical look after this last comment.

Henry hung up the phone and asked Jeremy if he knew one of the seamen and described Steckman.

"Oh, you must mean Duffy."

"Duffy. Is that a nickname or a last name?"

"Gee. I don't know. We just called him Duffy. The scientific team really didn't have a whole lot to do with the regular crew members."

"What were his duties?" Henry asked.

"Just regular crew. They were pretty interchangeable. He took turns in the wheel house and night watch and stuff."

Henry nodded a thanks and wandered over to the window overlooking the street and spent a few minutes waiting. Since it didn't look like Philip was going to show before the dinner hour Henry suggested the two of them go out to get a quick bite to eat.

"Oh, thanks, but I can't," Jeremy explained. "I got a meeting with Dr. Pang tonight at 9:30 and I got a lotta stuff to get ready. But you can drop me at the Laundromat down the street."

With Jeremy delivered to the Laundromat, Henry checked in at the Campus Life Motel, and after ordering

36

the businessman's special in the coffee shop, decided to try the apartment again. No answer. Then he dialed his home number to let Valery know he'd arrived safely. Becky, their college junior just home for the summer, answered the phone.

"Hi, Daddy. We just sat down to our soup and salad dinner. You wanna talk to Mother?"

"Oh, it isn't necessary if you're eating. I just wanted to let you know I'd arrived safely but I haven't seen Philip yet."

"Oh, well, I hope things go well for you when you do," Becky said. "I mean I'll be praying for you."

"Thanks, honey. I appreciate that."

Henry didn't know that Becky knew about Philip's blowup. He was learning that Becky and her mother were keeping no secrets these days. That made him feel good.

"How come you're only eating soup and salad?"

"Mom said with the big eater out of the house this would be a good time for us to start our diets."

Henry laughed. Then Becky went on with the happy news. She had landed a summer job helping a physical therapist, something she'd always been interested in doing as a career.

Her dad wished her well, then finished up their conversation with more light chatter. In spite of a lack of substance to their brief talk it gave him a warm glow. There was a sense about it he could not put into words, a sense of rightness, perhaps.

Chapter Four

He finished his dinner alone, and rather than try Philip again he decided to stroll across the campus and soak up a little atmosphere and maybe end up over at the apartment.

Twilight was just settling in and it seemed to have affected the mood of the school. Gone now were the cocky shouts, the Frisbees, and carefree banter of the younger students of the day. Now there was a larger number of senior citizens and people from the business community rushing to their evening classes. Sprinklers were on in some lawn sections, forcing the night students to stay close on the sidewalks. Henry watched the serious, drawn faces as the students hurried by. Even the "regular" students seemed withdrawn, almost as if the presence of outsiders on their turf put a crimp in their style. A bell tolled in a distant tower and very quickly Henry was alone, except for the last few scurrying truants. He headed toward the apartment once again.

About a block away the wail of an approaching ambulance wiped out the haunting memory of the bells. Alarm before education. Then the flashing light and sounds of a gathering crowd drew Henry to the apartments behind his original destination.

These units were in a Spanish motif with a heavy wooden balcony giving access to the units on the second floor. A campus police car was up over the curb with its spotlight trained on the balcony. Several second-story tenants, looking as though they'd quickly come out of their quarters, were at the railing looking down at something on the ground and buzzing with their neighbors. A crowd was gathering at the foot of the banister, but someone was trying to keep it all orderly with shouts and pleas for breathing room.

When the ambulance finally got into position the attendants hopped out and prepared a gurney for a patient. From force of habit, Henry slipped behind the attendants as they made their way through the small gathering and he soon found himself in front of a girl who had apparently fallen from the balcony. The attendants moved to her side and started assessing the extent of her injuries. Most people, trying to comfort the girl, moved aside quickly but the young campus policeman near her head seemed unwilling to move.

"Now listen to me," he shouted, "we have three witnesses. Three people saw him do it—"

But the girl was shaking her head no between sobs of pain.

"Why won't you press charges?" he bullied. "Just tell me why."

But she only shook him off without explanation. An attendant finally got the officer to move so he could examine her head and neck. As he did so he brushed her hair away from her bruised, tearstained face. Henry felt sure he had seen her before. Yes, the girl in Pangbourne's cabin, her beautiful complexion turned to a series of red blotches. Henry studied her face with a scowl. *What was she doing here? She must be a graduate student like Jeremy and Philip. Some homecoming,* he thought.

But Henry's evening of surprises was not over yet. As he started to withdraw, a pot-bellied man in pajamas began calling and pointing at someone on the balcony, "That's him, folks. That's the creep that hit her."

Henry looked up to see his son Philip come out of a second-story doorway and walk to the railing. "How does it feel, creep? You know you coulda killed her, don't you?" the fat man yelled.

Several others in the crowd picked up on the jeering now, but Philip seemed oblivious to their taunts. He had eyes only for the injured girl. Henry, in turn, stood watching his son watching the girl. There was an intensity in Philip's eyes he had never seen before. A combination of heartbreak and hatred were etched in his tortured face and Henry's heart went out to him. Where had this anguished stranger come from? Is this the same person he used to rock in the old leather rocker? Who used to laugh until he wet his pants when they wrestled on the living room floor? *Think, son, don't you remember where you came from? Maybe it will help the hurt . . .*

Henry's thoughts were unreasonable, he knew, but the expression on his son's face seemed to transcend rational words. The crowd seemed to pick up on it too. They quieted down as though they now understood the real injured party was not the girl at the foot of the balcony but the young man at the balcony rail.

Attention shifted to the girl again as the attendants clumsily tried to attach an immobilizing splint onto her broken left arm. When she cried out in pain, Henry saw his son cover his face and disappear into the apartment. The girl got to her feet, refused the gurney and was led by the

40

attendants into the back of the ambulance.

Once the ambulance was underway the crowd started to disperse, except for a few diehards who gathered around the fat man to hear him repeat his version of the affair. He had been watching TV when the shouting on the balcony brought him to his window. Looking up he saw the young bearded fellow punch poor Tracy right in the face and send her over the railing.

Henry went slowly up the stairs. Should he try to talk to him now or not? The door was ajar and he pushed it open. Philip was standing over the girl's open suitcase which was on the bed. It looked like she'd been unpacking.

"Hello, Philip."

He gave a slow, red-eyed look over at his father, then back down to his fumbling in the suitcase. Apparently he had seen Henry in the crowd.

"I thought maybe some of her things needed hanging up," Philip said, unconvincingly, his mind elsewhere.

Henry closed the door behind him and watched in silence. Philip had lost weight. In spite of his tousled hair and well-trimmed black beard he looked more than ever like his mother. He was wearing a corduroy suit and a thin, nondescript tie, which was dressy for him—college had turned him into quite the Bohemian, much to his mother's consternation.

"How's the new house coming along?" Philip said to the suitcase.

"Oh, just fine. You'll have to come up and see it."

"Mom doing okay?"

"Yes, I think so."

"What brings you down here?"

"Oh, a little work—mostly to see you though . . . " This drew no response so Henry went on, "Feel like taking a walk?"

"What for? To lay a little fatherly advice on me?"

41

"Well, if any came to mind I suppose I would. Lovers' quarrels didn't begin with your generation you know."

"Yeah, but *your* generation . . . " He glared at his father but didn't go on. He finally found a dress that needed some hanging out and hung it in the closet, then in a calmer voice he said, "You still working at your old job?"

"Not exactly. I'll be getting into accounting in private industry eventually, but the company wanted me to do an errand down here," Henry said in a casual tone. "I won't be overthrowing any South American Marxist governments or torturing any Iranians this week. Just picking up some hardware the company misplaced."

"Company hardware. I can imagine what that might be."

"Well, your Dr. Pangbourne developed an attachment for it. It was on board the *Inquisitor* you see, and—"

"Dr. Pangbourne is another illustrious member of your generation," Philip said, his voice dripping with sarcasm.

"Look, what's this 'my generation' business?" Henry said with a nervous smile. "Am I supposed to feel some sort of collective guilt for the sins of my generation? If so, the connection escapes me."

"Skip it."

Another uncomfortable pause followed. Henry resisted the temptation to tell Philip he was only making more of a mess of the suitcase of clothes.

"Son, a lot of things have been happening in my life, spiritually, philosophically . . . and I was hoping we could just talk. Get reacquainted and so on."

"Look, spare me the gory details, will you? Becky wrote me all about it. I'm sorry if anything I said made you flip out or whatever, but I stand by what I said."

"I don't care to argue the matter, if that's what you're thinking," Henry said. "Affixing blame is not a major concern—"

"Look," Philip interrupted, "I'm in a lousy mood right now. Okay?"

"Somehow or other I sensed that," Henry said, hoping to coax a smile out of his son. "I rather think you left that impression on your audience downstairs too."

"You embarrass me. You know that, Dad? Coming in here with your rinky-dink jokes . . . "

Philip stared tensely at his father for a moment, then picked up some of the girl's toilet articles and disappeared into the bathroom.

That night in his motel room as he readied for sleep, Henry tried to analyze his strange meeting with Philip. He felt very frustrated, yes. But embarrassed? No. Not for himself or for his son. Perhaps Philip was expecting him to play the more traditional role. Perhaps he should have come in with, "I never thought I'd see the day when a son of mine would strike a woman . . . " or the more subtle, "Son, son, what would your mother say?" Yes, that's always good for a few twangs on the old conscience fibers. But would it have brought about the desired results? And what are the desired results? What did he really expect of his son? Did he want him to be a carbon copy of his parents? No, he did not honestly feel that to be the case. What then? To be a "good boy"? Well, of course, but was that really primary? The more he thought about it the more elusive the answer became. He really didn't know what he was expecting from this unusual quest he was on. Unless it was simply to have communion with him.

Perhaps his son was right. Perhaps such a desire was, in fact, too much of an embarrassment for him to bear.

Once in bed and with the lights out, Henry's mind snapped back in time to a scene in their temporary home in the Philippines when Philip was a three-year-old, some twenty years ago. It was a scene Henry had dreamed of

43

many times, and he fully anticipated having the dream reoccur now after his confrontation.

The actual event was simple enough. Henry was baby-sitting with Philip for the afternoon while Valery and her mother, who was visiting, took the baby with them into Manila for some shopping. It was a warm day and Philip was enjoying the coolness of being rocked in the big leather chair. He sat on his daddy's knees, holding his hands and rocking happily back and forth, creating his own cool breeze. When he begged, "More, Daddy. More. Higher, Daddy," Henry obliged, until finally the rocker's balance point was passed and father and son fell over onto the rocker back. It was an old overstuffed rocker and they rolled harmlessly back onto the rug. But for the three-year-old it was panic time. His wide blue eyes pooled up and his lower lip started to give way. To counteract this, Henry put on a surprised smile and laughed, "What happened?" This changed everything; if Daddy thinks it's all right, then it must be all right. The tears quickly switched to surprised joy and they happily giggled in each other's arms. It was a moment of oneness Henry had reflected on many times and it never failed to give him pleasure.

In the dream version of the event they would sometimes rock back into a shallow pool of alligators; but at other times they fell on a hillside of daisies next to Ferdinand the bull and his cork tree, as featured in one of Philip's childhood books.

During Henry's breakdown/turning point, the government psychiatrist examining him had asked Henry to tell of any recurring dreams. When Henry mentioned the rocker sequence, the doctor quickly suggested the bull Ferdinand was very significant; he explained the docile bull from the story represented his son's latent puberty, the traditional time of tension between father and son, as he explained it. As long as Philip was small he offered no threat to his father's position, but once grown with all his "male juices" working, independence and a subtle or subconscious struggle for "pack leadership" followed. Henry's subconscious understood and pointed this out to him in the dream. As to the alligators, the doctor had no such integral explanations.

But this night the expectant dream never occurred. Instead Henry visited a grassy shack in the heart of darkest Africa. In the shack sat young Jeremy Bruce with his missionary parents huddled about a table working on objects they would soon be distributing to the destitute natives of the region. This scene was repeated ad infinitum as though they were part of a film company reshooting a scene until a certain elusive nuance would finally be captured.

Henry was relieved to be out of the frustrating dream even though it was a phone call at 5:10 in the morning that brought him back to reality.

"Hello."

"Is there a U.S. Twilligar at this address?" a strange woman's voice asked."

"What? Uh, wait, yes. I'll take it. Yes," Henry sputtered. It took him a moment to recognize his old cover name. Chapin came on the line in a voice more agitated than usual."

"Sorry about the hour, old man, but I had to reach you."

"How did you? I didn't tell you where I was staying."

"Simple. It's the only motel close to the college and I remembered your penchant for convenience."

"But I used a phony name as you suggested."

"Ah, but you were the only new tenant who stands six-four and walks like he has a sore back."

"Very good," Henry said. "Now I know why I'm an accountant and you are a director."

Chapin didn't bother to laugh at the compliment but got right to the point. Henry was to forget about the new cover name and the telegram. Chapin gave him the necessary serial numbers over the phone, and he was not to use the moving company he had contacted yesterday. The phone number of a new firm was given to him. Then he was given a complex series of instructions on how to recontact Chapin as his work progressed. The object of all this, Henry figured, was to avoid using Chapin's office phone for fear of bugs.

"What's all this about?" Henry laughed.

"Please. Just do as I ask, okay? Have you found out anything more about Steckman?"

Henry told him what little he knew, then asked, "Have you got problems back there? If so I better know about it."

"I honestly don't know. I just don't want to take any chances."

They double-checked the serial numbers, ran over the communication plans again, and hung up.

Knowing sleep was doubtful, Henry lay in bed pondering the call. The cloak and dagger business of secret names and double-back phone calls always made him feel foolish, and he could not recall an instance when it had proved of value. Had something happened to change their original plans or was Chapin just getting jumpy? It didn't sound like he knew any more about Steckman than Henry did. Could be just departmental jealousies or—did he dare think it—the possibility of a double agent? But why would a mole be concerned about picking up some five-year-old hardware? He jammed his fist into his pillow to restore its buoyancy, rolled back over on his stomach and contemplated counting sheep.

Sheep! Yes that was it. He sat up so quickly he nearly threw himself out of bed. It finally dawned on him why Chapin called him in the first place. Henry had been out of the service for three months and before that, for nearly six months, he had not been given any meaningful assignments or been privy to any briefings of substance because of his "condition." That made him a virtual outsider, yet an outsider Chapin could trust. So here was Henry obeying orders like a blind sheep. Like a robot, as the company referred to such operatives. But what for? For what purpose?

He got up and showered, then sat down with his Bible for the morning devotional time he had started on his own. But this morning it was hopeless; he found himself reading the same verses over and over without comprehension. *Oh, Lord, still my heart and let me know that you are God . . . but what about this Chapin business?*

Henry was an "anxiety eater." He found a twenty-four-hour restaurant nearby and methodically downed a ham and cheese omelet, hashbrowns, a small stack of wheat cakes with maple syrup, three cups of coffee and a large order of sourdough toast with orange marmalade. It helped. The thought of being caught up in a major company "event" slipped a little further away.

He stepped out of the restaurant and checked his watch. A quarter to seven. What time, he wondered, did Pangbourne come into his office? It was going to be another sunny day. There didn't seem to be anyone around so Henry put his back firmly against the warm stone facing of the restaurant and wiggled his arms and shoulders about in a manner that sometimes relieved pressure on his tender lower back. It was a funny looking little maneuver and he normally did it in private. He wouldn't have been caught dead doing this while he was still in service, so why do it now? The difference had to be his conversion experience. Of course! When you live your life for God you don't really care what the world thinks of you. He was playing to an audience of One. Good heavens! Does that mean he'll be losing his normal social graces? Would he be slurping his soup next? He smiled to himself at the thought and pressed his back all the harder like a giant cat getting scratched on the sweet spot.

Finally he ambled across the street and headed up the campus mall, hoping to meet someone who could direct him to Pangbourne's office. As he approached the fair booths he noticed there was already a crowd gathering. It was a strange crowd, made up of early morning joggers, ground maintenance people, and a few students. Whether it was because they were so silent and stood so still he could not say, but somehow he sensed there was something very wrong. Moving closer he saw the object of the group's attention. As part of the fair's money-raising activities the students had erected their own version of the old seventeenth-century public humiliation stocks. Situated in the kneeling position, with hands locked securely in the wooden stock holes, and head thrown unnaturally back, was a dead body. A plastic bag had been placed over its head and secured tightly about his neck by several winds of masking tape. Henry felt a weight in his chest and he instinctively drew in an extra deep breath of air, in part as a reaction to the thought of a suffocating death and partly because of the disgust of recognition. He stepped slowly closer and stopped. Moisture had condensed on the inside of the bag about the face so the features were unclear, but the bald head and the suit told the story. It was Dr. Ralph Pangbourne. In a knee-jerk response Henry put his hand over his hip pocket and the serial number list.

A uniformed police officer he hadn't noticed before stepped toward him. "Please step back, sir. We're roping off this whole area."

"What happened?" Henry asked.

"You know as much as we do. We just got the call," the officer said.

48

As he stepped back into the circle of spectators he couldn't help thinking how much like a group of art aficionados they all were, standing at the prescribed distance of twenty feet to properly view the piece of art. But the object was somehow too lifeless. Better to see a good marble. What strange little tricks the mind plays on one when reality becomes too raw.

More police arrived with cameras and cases of paraphernalia for examination of the crime scene. First they methodically went to work setting up flimsy wooden standards and stringing a yellow rope about the area as though this were an everyday occurrence.

A late-model Ford came screeching into the nearby parking lot and a white-haired man got out and started quickly toward the group. His hair stood wildly on end and he still wore his striped pajama tops under his coat. A young girl broke away from the group of spectators and raced toward him.

"Oh, Dr. Mumford, it's Dr. Pangbourne. It's awful . . . "

But he hurried on by her, over the low-hanging rope and up onto the little platform. A policeman called to stop him, but before anyone could act he had ripped open the plastic bag by the dead man's face and leaned forward to give him mouth-to-mouth resuscitation. But their lips had barely touched when he drew back staring dumbly at the dead face. By now two police were at his elbows drawing him back and pleading for him not to touch anything more.

"But that's Dr. Pangbourne, don't you understand?" the man said repeatedly. "That's Dr. Ralph Pangbourne," as though the name itself carried with it the claim to immortality and there had been some terrible misunderstanding. The two officers and the female student tried to calm him.

"Oh, Lord, here comes the press." One of the uniformed policemen moaned. Henry turned to see two scruffy looking people approaching. The bearded one in the plaid shirt headed straight toward the older policeman in civilian clothes, pulling out a notebook as he came.

"Who the devil called them?" the same officer near Henry asked in disgust.

His partner said, "Probably picked it up on their police band radio."

"But it hasn't been broadcast yet."

The other member of the fourth estate headed straight toward the body and started taking flash pictures. After the third quick shot the white-haired professor started swearing at him and demanding the police cover the body. A policeman put his thumb into the camera lens and started backing the cameraman away amid shouts of "police brutality" and "constitutional rights." It was done in a good-natured way as though they'd both been through this dance routine many times before.

"C'mon now, c'mon," the officer said. "You know your tame rag isn't going to run a shot like that anyway."

Henry moved closer to the plainclothes officer being interviewed to see if he could learn anything more.

"What does the sign mean?" the reporter asked, pointing at the front of the stocks.

"Probably left up from yesterday's activities," the officer said.

"But you're not sure?"

"Of course, we're not sure. Look, why don't you go talk to the prof over there? Maybe he can answer your questions."

On the front of the stocks hung a placard intended to describe the offense of the prisoner being punished. Several others, all printed in an old English style, were scattered about the front of the platform. Some titles read, "Boring Lecturer," "Cheat," "Giver of Unfair Tests," and

"Parsimonious." But the one hung on the stocks simply read "Liar."

By now the body had been covered with an old brown-red blanket and the crowd had dwindled to only a few. Henry was about to follow when the walkie-talkie the older policeman had in his coat pocket started squawking.

"Go ahead, Jimmy," the officer said in the mouthpiece. "Do you have something?"

"The pen name is paying off," the amplified voice said. "Our man's a graduate student right here on campus."

"Did you get an address?"

"Yes. Uuh, 133 Campus Way, apartment 227."

A chill went up Henry's back. That was Philip's apartment.

"All right, that's close by." the officer said excitedly. "Get down here as soon as you can."

Henry started off across the grass toward Philip's at a slow pace at first, then started picking up speed until he was running with a long slow stride. Pangbourne's words from on board ship came back to him, "Hell hath no fury like a woman scorned . . . a woman scorned . . . " Did Pangbourne "scorn" the young graduate student? With the ship back in port did he jilt her after a shipboard romance? Did Philip find out his girlfriend had an affair and . . . ? He physically attacked the girl. Did he do the same to her lover?

Henry was halfway through the parking lot at the apartment complex when he found he had to slow up. His breakfast was sitting like a giant lump in the middle of his chest and he had to gulp air several times to keep everything in its place. After several more deep breaths he recovered enough to attack the stairs two at a time.

With the second loud knock Philip answered the door. He was already up and dressed in a golf shirt and slacks.

"Dad! What are you . . . Come in."

51

"Have you heard about Dr. Pangbourne?"

"What about him?"

"He was just found dead over on campus."

"Dead? Pangbourne! You're kidding?"

"No, of course I'm not kidding."

"I didn't mean . . . It's just that it doesn't seem possible. Was it a heart attack or what?"

"It appears he's been murdered."

Philip's jaw fell open. "Ho-ly sa-mokes!"

Henry watched him carefully as he walked over to the table where he'd been working; he picked up a red pencil and started turning it end to end in his hand.

"I wonder if my eight o'clock is even going to meet now? I'm T.A. for an oceanography survey class," Philip said, indicating the papers on his desk.

"T.A. What's that?"

"Teaching assistant. I'm supposed to be handing back these tests this morning and I haven't finished grading them yet."

"Son, listen to me. This is important. What were you and the young lady arguing about last night?"

A flash of understanding jarred Philip's expression. "You think that I . . . you think that because of Pangbourne that I . . . " He didn't finish but the slow sad shake of his head obviously meant "my own father."

Two cars hit their brakes hard in the parking lot. Henry went to the window and looked out.

"They're here. That's the police. I wanted to warn you. Now, Philip, this could get rough. I don't know any lawyers in the area but I—"

"What are you saying?" Philip shouted. "You think I killed Pangbourne?"

"It doesn't matter what I think. Now keep your wits about you—"

Philip backed himself against the wall away from his

father. "What are you talking about?" he shouted. "No. This is crazy."

Footsteps sounded in the hall, then a knock on the door. As though in response to the outside knock the door to the bedroom opened and Jeremy looked out. His rumpled pajamas and wild uncombed hair made him look bigger than ever.

"What's all the noise about? Hold it down will . . . Oh, Mr. Garrett. I didn't know you were here."

A second knock at the door—a little louder this time, but nobody moved.

"Why don't you answer the door?" Jeremy asked. Philip still didn't budge. "Well, I'll answer it."

""No, don't," Philip blurted, but too late.

"What do you mean, 'don't'?" With three quick strides Jeremy crossed the room and flung the door open to the plainclothesmen.

"Yes?"

"Are you Jeremiah Bruce?" the older of the two asked.

"Yeah?"

"I'm Lieutenant Smithson with the San Diego City Police," he said, presenting his badge.

"Yeah?"

"It's my duty to inform you that you are under suspicion of murder and—"

"Who is?" Jeremy laughed.

"You are."

Father and son stood in shocked silence as the officer read Jeremy his rights.

Chapter Five

Back in the motel room it took nearly a half hour for Chapin to return Henry's call. The news of Pangbourne's death brought on a torrent of questions for which there were no ready answers.

"What kind of case do they have against this Bruce boy?" Chapin asked.

"I haven't the foggiest," Henry said. "My gut feeling though is he didn't do it."

"I was afraid of that."

"You still feel there's something going on in the company?" Henry asked. Chapin hadn't said so in so many words but he felt getting the implication out in the open might help clear the air.

"Yes . . . " Chapin pondered. "The last I have on Steckman was that he was still on our call sheets and living in Ottawa. But he packed it all in last January—about two weeks before the *Inquisitor* sailed."

"Can you justify bringing the FBI into the investigation?"

"Not yet, not yet. I don't want 'em. They make too

many footprints. And this Pangbourne was something of a national figure."

"Well, you better send somebody out to look over the shoulder of the local police then."

"What's the matter with you?" Chapin asked.

"I'd rather not be officially tied in with this business."

"Why not?" Chapin shot back.

"I'd rather not go into that."

During the ensuing pause Henry could almost hear Chapin's brain clicking. Then, "All right, I'll get someone out there as soon as I can. In the meantime you get the ball rolling with the local people. You owe me that much."

"I owe you?" Henry asked. "How do you figure that?"

"Look, how many people you know can afford to retire at fifty-two?"

"Henry could tell him a thing or two about the inflation rate, fixed income and nebulous company loyalties, but decided to hold it. "Okay, I'll get the ball rolling. What about the Precursor?"

"I don't think the Navy's going to let it walk away. Put it on the back burner. But zero in on this Steckman. We gotta know what he's up to."

"You'll send the usual telegram?" Henry asked.

"I'll see that it's sent."

"Has the thought occurred to you that Pangbourne was killed so he couldn't sign the Precursor release papers for us?"

Chapin sighed, "Yes, Henry, I know, I know."

Another phone call to the San Diego police told Henry that the central division and a Captain Orvil Blanchard would be heading up the Pangbourne investigating team. Assuming the telegram would have arrived by then, Henry made a 9:30 appointment to meet Captain Blanchard.

But he mistimed it by a few minutes. Instead of being ushered into the captain's office as he expected, Henry found himself at a four-foot-high information counter fencing words with an overweight female desk sergeant.

"If you'll tell me what is on your mind I'll see to it the captain gets your message."

"You mean he's not available?"

"I mean the captain is very busy this morning."

Several people were talking and moving about in a corner office. "Is that the captain's office?" Henry asked.

"If you'll tell me what's on your mind I'll see to it the captain gets your message," she repeated.

"Yes, I'm sure. But if you'll give him my name and tell him I'm waiting, it—"

"If you'll tell me what's on your mind I'll see to it . . . "

Henry studied the woman's face. "Did your mother ever teach school in Keokuk, Iowa?"

"No, why?"

Henry squinted an eye and wagged a finger at her. "You're a dead ringer for a teacher I had in the sixth grade."

"Very funny. Now please be seated."

He sat and pondered the humor of teaching sixth grade in Keokuk, Iowa. After a few minutes another female officer came in with what looked like a telegram in her hand and made straight for the corner office. Henry checked his watch. In exactly twenty-seven seconds a round red face appeared at the office window and squinted out at Henry, then slowly turned aside again to reread the message. Henry checked his watch again and smiled to himself; remembering the message nearly word for word he knew what must be going through the poor man's mind. It did not merely introduce Henry by name but went on, in legal double-talk fashion, to hint at grave national implications to the investigation and to imply serious legal consequences

56

if full cooperation with the "federal agent" was not forth-coming. Nothing concrete, of course, but plenty of valid threats and innuendos splashed into rambling sentences, sentences from which the joy of a simple declarative statement was forever hidden.

After two minutes and fifty seconds by the clock, a young detective came out of the office and received Henry. He rose and walked by the desk sergeant without winking and into the corner office. Other people were just filing out the two other doors to the office and he found himself alone with the round-faced Captain Blanchard.

"You're Garrett?"

"That's right."

"I suppose you're with the CIA. Don't tell me, I don't even want to know." He paused to light his dormant cigar but didn't bother to ask Henry to sit down. "You people know, of course, you have no legal standing in the states. All you can do is observe."

"Yes."

"And if you think we're going to let this case leave local jurisdiction, you got another think coming," he said in a gruff voice.

"We just want to know what you know when you know it," Henry said.

"What's your interest in the case?"

Henry briefly mentioned the squabble about the secret listening device on board the research vessel Pangbourne was heading up, Pangbourne's concern that all was not as it should be on board, and the fact that Steckman, alias Duffy, had been on board and may possibly be linked with Pangbourne's murder.

Blanchard blinked thoughtfully and puffed his cigar. "Sit down."

Henry sat, and asked, "What kind of a case do you have on the Bruce boy?"

57

"It's coming along. I was going down to question him now. I suppose you want to come along."

"I'd like to," Henry said, "but I'd also like to locate this Steckman for questioning too."

Blanchard puffed two more thoughtful drags on his cigar, then punched a button on his intercom, "Mickey, are you in a holding pattern with your robbery?"

"Yeah, we're still waiting for IDs on the two necklaces," Mickey squawked back.

"Come in a minute."

Mickey came in in shirt sleeves and with a writing pad and sat down.

"Try to locate a Richard Steckman for us. May be going under the alias *Duffy*. Description . . . " Blanchard pointed to Henry who filled in the description. Then Blanchard went on, "Probably came in on the *Inquisitor* berthed in the Navy yards. Start with the captain." Then, turning to Henry, "Anything else?"

"There were several scientists aboard from many different universities," Henry said. "I'd like to speak to anyone from Nebraska, like the University of Nebraska or Creaton University."

Mickey looked to Blanchard who nodded an OK, then he finished his notes and left.

"What's with Nebraska?"

"Oh, just an idea. Shall we talk with Mr. Bruce?" Henry said, rising.

Blanchard stared coldly at Henry a moment, then got a ring of keys out of his desk drawer, slammed the drawer shut a little harder than necessary and started down the hall to the interrogation room, Henry following his broad powerful back from a discrete distance.

Jeremy Bruce was sitting at the middle of a long table facing two plainclothesmen.

"How's it going, boys?" Blanchard asked.

The older arresting officer looked up at his superior, "He still maintains he didn't see Pangbourne last night and he—"

"Why don't we let him tell it," Blanchard interrupted and sat down directly opposite Jeremy.

"Oh, hi, Mr. Garrett, what are you doing here?" Jeremy smiled.

"Hello, son. Just looking in," Henry could feel the captain's glare on his right cheekbone. "You getting along all right?"

"Sure."

"Called your folks or a lawyer?"

"Shoot, no! What do I need with a lawyer? I haven't done anything."

Blanchard cleared his throat vociferously. "Now, Mr. Bruce, why don't you tell us what you did last night."

"Again?"

"Again."

"Well, Mr. Garrett here gave me a ride from the ship to my apartment about 5:30—"

"Why'd you ride with him?" Blanchard asked.

"Gee, I don't know. Dr. Pang said he was comin' our way and since the college van was crowded—"

""Who's Dr. Pang?"

"Pangbourne. Dr. Pangbourne. Don't you know about him?"

"Of course we know about him," Blanchard blared.

Henry grimaced and scratched his cheek, hoping his smile wouldn't show. Jeremy went innocently on, describing how he had taken his dirty clothes to the Laundromat—he had not washed them on board ship because they ran low on fresh water the last week of their trip—and then had gone back to his apartment to work on a report for Dr. Pangbourne.

"What kind of a report?" Blanchard asked. It appeared

59

he was the sole interrogator.

"He was letting me give a paper for the geological summer conference and he asked me to prepare an outline to be included in the conference program. It's just five weeks away and he needed the information for the printer right away."

"How long did you work on it?"

" 'Til I finished. About 9:00. Then I changed my clothes and went over to Dr. Pang's office."

"What time was that?"

"I got there at 9:25. I remember looking at my watch because I had a 9:30 appointment with him."

"How'd you get in the office?"

"He'd left it open. He had some other evening meetings and we were going to get together at 9:30."

"All right, you're in the office. Then what happened?"

"Nothing. He never showed up. I waited 'til around 10:15, 10:20 and then I left. I put my outline on his blotter with a note and I went home to bed."

"Did anyone see you in the office or on your way home?"

"Um, no, I don't think so."

"Did you lock the door after you?"

"No, you need a key to lock those doors and I don't have a key."

"Who else was the doctor meeting with last night?"

"I think it was some of the other professors. He said there was an emergency curriculum meeting about the fall catalog. He'd been involved with that for sure."

"Why do you say that?"

"Are you kidding? He ran that place. Nobody did anything without his say-so."

"He's not the head of the physical science division."

"No, but Dean Hazard never did anything without Dr. Pang's okay. I went by the conference room they usually use and there was nobody there. It was all dark."

"The only record the administration has of an extra meeting was in the life science building, called by their dean. Mr. Bruce, there was no meeting of the natural science people. How do you explain that?"

"Just because administration didn't know about it doesn't mean there wasn't one. Maybe they were meeting with the life-science people."

"All right. You went to your apartment around ten-thirty, or a quarter to eleven . . . "

"I think so, yeah."

"And did your roommate see you?"

"No, he wasn't in."

"What time did he come in?"

"I dunno. I was dog-tired and I didn't see him again until this morning when these guys were knocking at the door."

"So when these officers knocked on your door and woke you up that was the first time you'd seen your roommate in five or six months?"

"Oh no, he came in for a minute when I was folding my laundry last night and then he went out again."

"What time was that?"

"Oh, I guess about seven o'clock."

"Now you see, you didn't tell us that before, did you?"

"You didn't ask me."

"There's no need to get smart about it."

"Smart? Who's getting smart? You asked me a question, I gave you the answer."

"How'd you get the cut on your head?"

Jeremy's hand went to the very slight cut over his left eyebrow. Henry hadn't noticed it before.

"Oh this. I bumped my head on the door of the dryer at the Laundromat."

"Did it bleed?"

61

"Yeah, a little. Why?"

"If you're telling the truth there's probably a trace of blood left on the door. What Laundromat did you use?"

"Mission Cleaners and Laundromat by our apartment.

Blanchard nodded at the older detective and he made a note of it.

"Which dryer did you use?"

"Golly, I don't remember. Second from the wall, I think."

"Mr. Bruce, do you own a silver ballpoint pen with your name on it?"

Up until then Jeremy had clipped off his answers as quickly as the questions were asked. But with the mention of the pen his answers became more measured and hesitant.

"My mother gave me a pen and pencil set a coupla years ago for my birthday."

"With your name 'Jeremiah Bruce' embossed on the side?"

"Yes."

"Where is the pen now?"

"Well, the pencil is at the apartment. I hardly ever use it."

"And the pen?"

"I had it aboard ship. I suppose it's in some of the stuff I haven't unpacked."

"No, I don't believe it is."

"Oh well, then . . . " Jeremy fidgeted. "I guess I don't know where it is."

"I do," Blanchard said, and sat quietly looking at Jeremy, testing his nerves.

"Well, okay, then you do."

"It's right here in my pocket. Would you like to tell me how it got there?"

"No."

62

"Why not?"

"Because I don't know how it got there."

"Oh, I think you do," Blanchard relit his dormant cigar, taking his time at it.

"I don't like the cigar," Jeremy scowled. "Put it out."

""That's too bad—" Blanchard began.

"I consider that vile thing cruel and unusual punishment. Either you put it out or I'll call my father and he will call Jonathan Babcock the Third, who is a very famous Christian lawyer who has successfully negotiated with the Russians for the release of no less than twenty-seven persecuted Christians from behind the Iron Curtain. Now I've cooperated fully up to now with everything you've asked, but I'm not going to sit here and—"

"All right, all right," Blanchard laughed and handed his cigar to the younger detective who held it between his thumb and index finger and walked it out of the room.

Jeremy's voice had suddenly risen in shrill indignation about the cigar and it cleared the air in more ways than one. The docile "golly-gee-whiz" college boy had given way to the indignant zealot and tobacco hater. The change took everyone by surprise.

"Are we happy now?" Blanchard said, trying to regain the psychological advantage he had lost. "See how anxious we all are to accommodate you?"

"Where did you find my pen?"

"We found it under the left pant leg of the dead man."

"Oh!"

Henry felt for the young man. His darting eyes and flushed cheeks seemed to confirm his guilt. Gulliver under siege before his lilliputian captors.

"Now would you like to tell us how it go there?"

"No. I don't know how it got there. Honest, I don't. As God is my judge, I don't."

"Oh, come now," Blanchard said, and waited without

moving a muscle. But his little game didn't seem to be paying dividends; Jeremy was regaining some composure. Blanchard went on, "We're glad you told us about being in the professor's office, but then we already knew that."

"Sure, you saw my outline and my note so you—"

"There was nothing on the professor's desk."

"Sure there was. There were some other loose papers on the upper corner of the desk. I tucked my outline on the corner of his blotter. It was in a green folder . . . "

Blanchard was slowly shaking his head, then he held out his hand to the older detective who pulled out his note pad, flipped it back a few pages and handed it to Blanchard so he could read the information he needed.

"Do you own a book titled *Life After Life*?"

"Yeah."

"Do you know where it is?"

"I know where it's supposed to be."

"And where is that?"

"Well, when the expedition started we were all invited to loan some of our own books to the ship's library. You know, you spend an awful lot of time on board with nothing constructive to do and it's kind of nice to have something to read—"

"And you thought the shipload of scientists would be interested in reading your religious book."

"Sure, why not? I mean, it is scientific in a way. It's testimony of different people who've technically died and had a glimpse of the afterlife. I mean, cumulative testimony about a common experience is scientific . . . "

Blanchard smiled, "Quite the little evangelist, aren't you?"

"Is there a law against that?"

"All the books you contributed to the library religious?"

"Oh, about fifty-fifty."

"Did you have any converts?"

"Oh, you never know about the human heart. The Lord moves in mysterious ways—"

"I think we're getting sidetracked here. Did you take the book home with you when you left the ship?"

"No. All our books—there were five people aboard from our university and we all had quite a few books—and Dr. Pang said we could ship them all with our other scientific gear back to the university in the school's truck and pick 'em up out there. I just assumed that book was with the others."

"So you didn't see it on the truck?"

"No. I haven't even thought about it since the trip started."

Blanchard studied Jeremy with cold eyes, then got up and left without further comment, the other detectives following at his heels. Henry lingered and let the door swing closed behind them.

"Mr. Garrett," Jeremy semi-whispered, "what's going to happen now?"

"I'm not sure."

"They don't think I killed Dr. Pang, do they?"

"Well, it looks like they have some circumstantial evidence. But they need more than that to build a case. Motive for instance. You'd have no reason to want to see Dr. Pangbourne dead, would you?"

Jeremy glanced quickly at the closed door out of the corner of his eyes, then back to Henry. It only took an instant, but it was long enough to plant a doubt in Henry's mind.

"I loved Dr. Pangbourne, Mr Garrett," he said softly. "I wouldn't want to see him killed."

"I better go," Henry said, moving toward the door. "I still think you'd better get in touch with your folks."

"Dad's at a denominational meeting in Detroit and

Mom's . . . Mom just couldn't handle this."

"I see." Henry started to leave again, then turned, "Jeremy, was Dr. Pangbourne having an affair with the Tracy girl?"

Jeremy blushed noticeably, then nodded his head yes.

"Did that bother you?"

"Of course, it did. Dr. Pang's a married man. He's separated from his wife, but still, how does it look? A reputable scientist and all and students on board."

"Did you tell Philip about it?"

"Yeah. He used to go with Tracy and I thought he'd want to know."

"I see."

"Why?"

Before Henry could respond, Blanchard burst through the door.

"You're conducting your own investigation, are you?" he demanded of Henry.

"I was just coming, captain."

Back in Blanchard's office the two detectives and Henry sat and watched as the captain paced behind his desk. He stopped and asked the older detective, "How did he act when you brought him in?"

"Cooperative, I'd have to say."

"Did you have to tell him Pangbourne was dead or did he know?"

"Scottie told him," he said, pointing a thumb toward his partner.

"How'd he take it?"

"He started praying," Scottie said, "right there in the squad car."

Blanchard scoffed and paced some more.

"What are we going to do with him?" the older man asked.

"Put him in the tank for now," Blanchard said, then reached in his pocket and peeled off four one-dollar bills and handed them to Scottie. "Here, see how many cheap cigars this will buy and hand them out to his cellmates. Then release him before the evening meal with the usual warning."

The two detectives shuffled out of the room and Blanchard sat, avoiding Henry's eyes.

"Well, what do you think?" he asked.

"The case against the boy?" Henry asked.

"Yes."

"I think it's a little too pat."

"What do you mean?"

"I mean the pen with his name on it found at the scene, and the book, which I assume also had his name on it, found on the professor's desk."

"It was under the corner of his desk," Blanchard corrected, "like it might have been kicked there in a struggle."

"Perhaps," Henry granted. "But both of those articles could have been stolen on the expedition. Stolen by someone who had this murder planned far in advance and needed someone to blame it on."

"You mean someone like your Steckman?"

"Exactly," Henry said and waited for the captain to digest it. Then went on, "and what possible motive would the boy have for killing his professor?"

Blanchard shrugged, "Who knows? Maybe Pangbourne gave him a low grade or maybe he promised him something and then reneged on it. Remember the 'liar' sign on the stocks? Not much, I know; but for that matter, what motive would your Steckman have?"

"I still feel it's got to be tied in somehow with our equipment on board the vessel," Henry said.

"May I give you a little advice?"

67

"Of course."

"Too much conjecture this early in a case and you end up wasting a lot of time. Let's just collect facts for now."

"Fine."

"Here's the preliminary coroner's report," Blanchard said, shoving a manila folder across his desk toward Henry. "They're not scheduled to cut him open until tomorrow or Thursday. Due to a food poisoning problem in La Jolla at a senior citizen's rest home the coroner is backlogged. But this might give you some ideas."

Henry was not familiar with the form or the technical jargon employed by the medical team. "E.T.O.D. is . . . ?"

"Estimated time of death," Blanchard explained.

" 'Between 9:00 and 12:00 p.m.' Not much help is he?" Henry read on, " 'Light contusion in hairline near left temple.' Is that the only mark on the body?"

"Only noticeable mark."

"Strange . . . "

"Why strange?"

"If someone had put my hands in the stocks and tied a plastic bag over my head, I'd have struggled like the devil to get free. I'd probably try to scratch a hole in the bag by rubbing my face against the wooden stock or make a Herculean effort to wrench one of my hands free. That certainly would have ripped some skin or broken some bones in my hand."

Blanchard grunted an agreeing noise.

"Was the blow to the head enough to knock him unconscious?"

"It's in a delicate area. My guess is it could," Blanchard said.

"So he may have been killed or knocked out and then put in the stocks."

"Yes. He may have been killed elsewhere then brought

68

to the stocks for public display. But for what purpose? That's what puzzles me. Somebody went to a great deal of risk to make a point. They could very easily have been spotted by night custodians or some college kids making out."

"What were you telling me about too much conjecture early in a case . . . ?" Henry jibed.

A trace of a smile crept across Blanchard's face, "I was about to send Scottie out to the university to corroborate some of Bruce's story. Want to tag along with him?"

"What'll you be doing?"

"Playing politics," Blanchard said, checking his watch. "I have to sit in for the chief at the mayor's luncheon at the press club."

Chapter Six

Scottie McNeil turned out to be an easygoing chap who was moonlighting in the construction business. On their way back to the university Henry heard all about his efforts to get transferred to special night duty so he could spend his days more profitably. He and his father-in-law owned a parcel of land they were anxious to get subdivided for condominiums.

"You can't get ahead on salaries these days," Scottie explained. "You gotta be in business for yourself if you're gonna have a fighting chance."

Their first stop at the university was to call on Dean Hazard, the chairperson of the natural science division. But the division's secretary curtly explained that he was in class and how tight the dean's schedule was and he could not possibly see them until after his meeting with the associated student officers at 3:00. Scottie picked the appointment calendar out of the lady's hands and looked it over.

"What's this 'lunch with maintenance super'?" he asked.

"We're having some safety devices built into our labs for the new laser equipment . . . "

"Well, I suggest you call the 'maintenance super' and tell him the dean will be lunching with us today."

The secretary batted her eyes in surprise, "I beg your pardon?"

"That is," Scottie went on, "unless the dean would rather talk to us downtown. Tell him when he gets out of class, we'll meet him in front of the cafeteria at 12:15."

The lady's mouth had still not drawn closed when Henry and Scottie exited. Once in the hall, Scottie put a hand on Henry's shoulder to make sure he noticed he was doubling up in mock laughter.

"I woulda made a terrific tyrant. I just love to make people squirm. Especially when they think they're better'n me. Only fun I have left in this job. Hey, kid" he hooked the arm of a passing student. "Where's your school printer set-up?"

"It's in the new media services building next to the library," the student said and pointed the way.

As they headed in that direction Scottie made a point of ogling several of the young coeds as they bounced by. A discreet glance was one thing, but holding your heart and stopping dead in your tracks as the girls passed was quite another. Henry felt embarrassed and did his best to show a discouraging frown at each of the detective's displays. None of Henry's efforts had the desired effect though, as Scottie continued to grab at Henry's sleeve and perform his display of overwhelmed ardor with each passing morsel. When a girls gym class came on the scene Henry separated himself from Scottie by hurrying on ahead to the doorway of the media building. As he suspected, the ogling display had been mostly for Henry's benefit because, once Scottie thought Henry was not watching, the detective calmed down. There was a lesson in human

71

nature there which Henry would have to ponder at a later date.

The manager of the printing services was a heavyset man with ink stains on his hands which he was busily trying to clean up.

"What can I do for you gentlemen?" he asked, but went on before Scottie could get started. "Never change the ink color on a 17-20, let me tell you. It's easier to buy a new machine. They use a new fine ink that is unbelievably porous."

"I understand you are doing, or were doing, a printing job for Dr. Pangbourne," Scottie asked.

"Yeah, too bad about him, isn't it?" the man tisked and kept working away on his hands. "I didn't have any love for the man, but still I hate to see him die like that. You're investigating his death, are you?"

"Will you show me what he was having printed?"

"All I got is the original work order; I had a telegram Pangbourne sent two weeks ago but he took it with him yesterday." He dried his hands enough to pick out his work order from the counter-top file and hand it to Scottie.

"As a matter of fact, I'm changing ink colors to do a three-color cover for his brochure. We had already run the cover once but he wasn't happy with it." The man went to a large wastebasket and pulled out a heavy 8½x11-inch sheet to show them. The front half of the unfolded brochure was a black and white picture of the *Inquisitor* at sea with the catchy title "The Thirty-Seventh Annual Summer Conference of the American Scholastic Geological Association" burned across the rolling sea.

"That looks pretty good," Scottie said. "He didn't like this?"

"No, he said MIT did a slick three-color job last summer and we weren't going to be outdone by MIT. Well, that's all fine and good, but they got all kinds of federal money back there to work with. But," he shrugged, "what am I gonna do? I only work here. I crossed him once before and really got my tail burned."

"We're trying to check out a story," Scottie finally got in, "that the doctor was meeting last night with one of the graduate students that supposedly was going to be presenting a paper at this conference. You sure you don't have any old copy lying around that might verify this?"

The printer brushed back some wisps of his thinning hair and thought. "Just a minute," he walked over to a glassed-in cubicle where a girl was typing and opened the door.

"Flo, do you still have the old copy we set up for Dean Hazard?"

Flo went to her file drawers and quickly came up with the folder he requested.

"Now this is an early schedule," the printer explained, "that Dean Hazard put together. What's the student's name?"

"Jeremiah Bruce."

"Jeremiah? You mean like the prophet?"

"I suppose," Scottie said, looking over the pages of the printed schedule of events. "There's no Bruce here . . . In fact, all these presenters are doctors from different schools or research institutions. There aren't any graduate students on the list."

"Yeah, I think you're right," the printer said. "Course now, this is the old list put together by the dean. Pangbourne was making some changes in the second schedules so this Jeremiah could have been added or he could have been listed in the second schedule, but I don't remember seeing that name *Jeremiah.*"

"Hmmm. I wonder how likely it would be for a graduate student to be making a presentation to this group," Scottie mused to no one in particular. "This is an association of educators, isn't it?"

"Yes, it is," the printer said, then read from the logo under the mailing address on the back side of the old brochure. " 'An Association of Natural Science Educators.' "

Scottie looked at Henry, "You think a student would be lecturing teachers?"

"Could be, if he had some new discovery or new knowledge."

"Hmmm."

Henry had been looking over the original work order, "It says here the job was scheduled to be completed yesterday . . . "

"Yeah, I know," the printer groaned, "and mailed out today. But Pangbourne just got back, you know, and he ran the show. I had to put all my other work aside to finish this. Summer class schedules, everything. I came in here this morning at 5:30 expecting to find his finished copy in that mail slot. I get here and no copy. Well, you can imagine what I was thinking and saying out loud about Dr. Ralph Pangbourne. Then the campus police comes by around 8:30 telling us he's dead. You can imagine what I felt like . . . "

Scottie moved over to the mail slot and looked into the large box that was affixed to the inside of the door. "Pangbourne told you he'd drop his copy in here?"

"Yeah. His rough copy. Flo was to type it up right away and I'd start running it."

"When did he tell you this?"

"Yesterday afternoon when he picked his old telegram up, around 3:30."

"When is the conference?" Scottie asked.

The printer checked the old brochure cover, "July twenty-first through the twenty-sixth."

"What was the big rush? That's more than a month away."

74

"School year's ending. A lot of the teachers will be leaving their institutions and we only have school addresses for the conference participants."

Scottie slowly scratched at his cheek, then turned to Henry, "You got anything to add?"

Henry asked the printer, "I'm a bit confused. Are we talking about three different versions of this program schedule?"

"Yeah, counting this one," the printer said, pointing at the dean's schedule.

"And you received this one—?"

"We stamp copy when we get it. Here it is, 'May 2.' "

"And there was a second copy—"

"Yes, Dr. Hazard brought that in too. Said he'd received it from Dr. Pangbourne, telegrammed from one of the coastal towns in Mexico."

"When was that?"

"Oh, I'd say about two weeks ago."

"And then Dr. Pangbourne came in personally yesterday and said he was making changes again on his second draft?"

"Right."

"How did Dr. Pangbourne carry the papers away with him?" Henry asked. "I mean did he have a briefcase or anything?"

The printer stared at the exit door as though trying to visualize Pangbourne standing there. "You know, I don't remember."

"If the copy of the second or third schedule turns up would you call Captain Blanchard's office of the city police?"

"Yeah, I guess I could do that."

Back outside on the steps Scottie checked his watch. "Well, that was a wild goose chase."

"Oh, you never can tell," Henry corrected. "At least we know Pangbourne had some papers with him late yesterday afternoon and now they're missing."

Henry caught Scottie shooting a condescending smirk his way. Was he being too pedantic for the experienced policeman? Never mind. He could only be himself. "It might be a good idea to talk with the school's cleanup people and the lost-and-found . . . "

"Whoa, now," Scottie said, "let's not get carried away. He probably took the stuff home with him."

"Did he go home?"

"Why wouldn't he?"

"He told me on board ship that he had a heavy schedule through the evening."

"Well, he hadda eat sometime," Scottie shrugged. "Look, this is a defense attorney's work. I'm not gonna knock myself out proving Bruce innocent."

"I thought we were looking for the truth—"

Before Henry could continue, Scottie slapped him on the chest and stepped aside so another coed could walk by. This one was particularly well-proportioned and a soft whining groan escaped from Scottie. "Now there is truth, man. There is truth for you.

"Come on, it's 12:15."

Chapter Seven

Dr. Wendel Hazard was waiting for them, as ordered, outside the cafeteria. He looked out of place on the casual southern California campus. His well-tailored, vested, pin-striped suit, complete with highly polished wingtips, modified four-in-hand tie and wavy steel-grey hair would look more appropriate in a high finance board-room. He greeted them formally and led the two men in through the noisy cafeteria, already reverberating with students, and into a small quiet faculty dining room complete with red tablecloths and candles. The doctor selected a corner table, called a student-waiter over and made sure everyone understood they would be ordering on separate checks before he passed out the menus.

After each had ordered, Dr. Hazard took off his rimless glasses to clean them and leaned back. "Now then, gentlemen, what can I do for you?"

"Hey, this is pretty plush," Scottie said, rubbing the arm rests of his captain's chair. "You guys eat like this every day?"

When Hazard's only response was a vacant stare,

Scottie plunged ahead, "I mean rank does have its privileges, doesn't it? None of this rubbing elbows with the lowly students."

"In lieu of adequate salaries the school does make some accommodations," Hazard intoned. "This is part of our hotel management program."

"I usually lunch in a squad car on a stale sandwich and cold coffee," Scottie sulked.

"Now then, I really am on a busy schedule."

"Yess . . . " Scottie got out his notebook.

Henry was gaining the impression that Scottie played the buffoon for an ulterior motive. Whether it was to spice up an otherwise boring job by antagonizing people for the fun of it, or whether it was a calculated measure to throw people off guard, he could not tell. Certainly there had so far been no flashes of brilliance that might justify the latter. Or maybe he'd seen too many Columbo reruns.

Scottie cleared his throat and started, "We understand you had a meeting with Dr. Pangbourne last evening. Would you tell us about it?"

"Certainly," Dr. Hazard said, readjusting his glasses. "I saw Ralph three times yesterday. I presume you're referring to the evening meeting we had with Dr. Mumford."

"What time was that?"

"About 8:45. Dean Mumford came in a bit late."

"And where was this?"

"In a space we euphemistically refer to as a conference room. It's just off our large biology lecture hall—originally designed for the preparation of demonstrations.

"Does it have a name or number?"

"I think it's 16-C in the Harrison building. Don't hold me to that number though. I'm not in the building often."

"And what time did the meeting break up?"

"I would estimate nine-thirty. I dropped John off at his

78

home very near the campus, then I went directly home where I noted the time was ten-to-ten. I live twenty minutes from the campus."

"So everyone left at the same time?"

"N-no. Dr. Pangbourne left first. John Mumford and I chatted a few minutes then left together."

"No one else at the meeting?"

"Just the three of us."

"Did Pangbourne say where he was going then?"

"No. Home to bed I assumed. He looked quite tired."

"He didn't say anything about meeting someone at his office?"

"Not to me."

Scottie smiled across at Henry. Their food arrived and their attention turned to lighter things for a moment. The spring fair and the fast approach of a pleasant summer were touched on lightly. Then, while Scottie was busy working on his ham and swiss cheese on pumpernickel bread, Henry took the initiative, "Dr. Hazard, did Dr. Pangbourne have any papers with him?"

"Papers? He had his old black leather briefcase with him, but I don't recall him taking anything out. In fact, I'm quite sure he did not. It wasn't that kind of meeting."

"What was the meeting about?"

Hazard paused to touch the corner of his mouth with his napkin. "May I assume this information is strictly for police use and I won't be reading my comments in tomorrow's newspaper?"

"As long as it has no direct connection with Pangbourne's death," Scottie said between chews.

"Very well. Ralph had called a meeting to settle a dispute over the fall catalog. Dr. Mumford is dean of the life-science division and had taken it upon himself to take over instructional control of a new class the school will be offering in the fall."

79

"What class is that?" Henry asked.

"Put simply, it's a new approach to paleontology, the study of fossils. Fossils, as you no doubt recall, are impressions of living organisms that have been preserved in sedimentary rock, et cetera. This study traditionally has been in the domain of the geologists but, because of this overlap of disciplines, where it belongs has become something of a moot point."

"So did you reach any decisions?" Henry asked.

Hazard gave a cool smile, "We certainly did. Ralph explained the facts of life to John and he agreed the fossil class will remain under the aegis of the natural science division. He agreed to so inform the dean of instruction."

"Just like that?"

"Just like that."

Henry frowned, "What kind of power did Pangbourne have that he could settle the issue so quickly?"

"Power—" Hazard mused. "Yes, that's the right word. Ralph did have a unique kind of power. It's a shame he was known only in the scientific community. Political scientists would do well to study him. Next to him Machiavelli was a novice."

"Who's he?" Scottie asked. "Another teacher?"

Hazard raised a condescending eyebrow for him. "Our fencing instructor," he deadpanned. "Ruthless chap."

Henry coughed to hide a smile. "What did he say to make Dean Mumford change his mind?"

"Oh, dear, this gets a bit complicated." Hazard put down his soupspoon. This explanation apparently required gestures with both hands. "Ralph, as you know, was in charge of the expedition from which he had just returned. It was quite an honor to have been included on his trip. Only an august few were selected, and Ralph did the selecting, of course. And one of the understandings to which the entire team had to subscribe was that Ralph

80

would be in charge of any and all press releases pertaining to scientific 'finds.' Now it seems there were significant 'finds' in the biological area. They discovered hot spots on the ocean floor along the edges of the moving plates. Do you understand plate tectonics?"

"I have a vague understanding," Henry said.

"Well, anyway, ocean water seems to go down through these cracks in the ocean floor, become very warm, perhaps from contact with the molten lava beneath the crust, and return to the ocean floor. And in the spots where it returns myriads of biological organisms, heretofore unknown to us, seem to thrive—tube worms over twelve feet high, not the little variety we're used to, no bigger than my finger—how they got there we don't know. What their source of energy at that depth, we don't know that either. It literally opens up a whole new field for the life science people."

"So Dr. Pangbourne threatened to withhold the findings from Mumford unless the fossil class remained with natural science," Henry said.

Hazard nodded agreement, "The announcement rights—along with all the specimens—he threatened to turn over to the Scripps Institute people."

Henry shook his head. "I always think of scientists as being totally objective. Above political intrigues in their search for truth."

"Ah, yes, yes," Hazard paused for emphasis. "But whose truth?"

"And yet he was respected in his area, wasn't he?"

"Respected . . . and feared. Please don't misunderstand me. I don't mean to disparage the man. I owed him a great deal. But he did run matters with a firm hand."

"How did he come by such a position?"

"He had a unique set of talents. He was a scientist of the first order as well as a good administrator. No one took

81

the plate tectonics theory seriously until Ralph documented the movement in the mid-Atlantic rift. Then eventually everyone acquiesced, and with the prestige of that, plus being a reserve brigadier general in the U.S. Corps of Engineers, he soon began to dominate our geological associations. He had a special knack for getting money out of both the government and private industry for his pet projects. This latest *Inquisitor* trek was entirely underwritten by private funds. It was almost to the point that researchers in this area needed his blessing in order to undertake a project of any magnitude. I personally recall the instances in which oil firms were considering underwriting survey projects. They called Ralph for advice, and when he advised against them the projects got dropped."

This seemed to catch Scottie's attention. "A man like that must have developed a lot of enemies."

Hazard smiled. "I would have to call that an understatement. Professionally, it was not healthy to cross swords with Ralph Pangbourne." He laughed spontaneously, "I must tell you this one story because it so aptly exposes the man's genius. Several years ago now—five I think—Dr. Keven Thornton, a brilliant young chap from one of the big-ten schools was compiling a book on earth movement. Somehow Ralph got wind of the thrust of the book before publication and found out the young man was challenging some of his own pet theories."

When Hazard paused to savor the story again with a chuckle, Henry tried to anticipate the next move, "So, Dr. Pangbourne got the publication stopped . . . "

"Oh, no, no," Hazard laughed. "Nothing as gauche as that. We're dealing here with a man of style. A man with infinite resources." He shook his head in wonderment. "Somehow or other he got one of his gremlins at the publishing firm—I think a former student—to send the book out with the wrong library of congress card, so university libraries all over the country got their copies with the L.C. cards saying that the book should be filed under PZ 24." He enunciated the number as though it was the punchline of a very great joke. When neither Henry nor Scottie reacted as he expected, he had to explain, "PZ 24 is the call number for children's fairy tales. You can imagine what it did for the prestige of the book when it appeared. The publisher himself thought it should . . . " He broke off when this explanation still didn't generate a good response. "I guess one must be in the business to understand the humor of it all. To this day I can't attend a conference without someone referring to some inferior piece of research belonging to the children's fairy tales department. It never fails to get a laugh."

"Quite the practical joker, wasn't he?" Scottie said.

"Yes, that he was." Hazard agreed. "But he could get pretty rough with this idea of fun. On more than one occasion he went well beyond the bounds of good taste."

"Such as?" Scottie put in.

Hazard suddenly grew coy. Should he really be bad-mouthing the great man when his body was hardly cold. Scottie assured him it was his civic duty to tell everything he could about the dead man. After all, this was a murder investigation. This was all the justification he needed. He went into his story quite willingly.

"Last year we had an exchange teacher from Israel with us. She taught math and she was one unbelievable beauty. Dark hair, deep blue eyes, the most striking woman I've ever seen, I believe. Well, she had barely gotten on campus before she and Ralph Pangbourne became an item. Clandestine meetings, the whole bit. They used to drive off campus in separate cars around noon, meet in the Broadway parking lot north of the school where he'd get into her car and they'd drive over to her apartment. That is until one noon when there was a bath towel special at the Broadway and Ralph's wife thought she needed some new bath towels." He smiled and pushed the croutons into his soup while Henry and Scottie waited.

"So what happened?" Scottie finally asked.

"His wife, a strict Roman Catholic, wouldn't put up with this. I also had the feeling it wasn't the first incident. Anyway, she left him to rumble around in the big house by himself. Veronica, on the other hand—that was the Israeli math teacher's name, Veronica Weiss—thought it was just ducky. She started hinting at a permanent staff position and talking about redoing the house. I imagine Ralph had made some rather rash promises to her in the heat of passion, but he only wanted an affair. He wasn't interested in any permanent arrangement."

"He told you all this?" Scottie asked.

"He confided in me. Most I learned after the fact when we both could see the humor of it all."

"So what did he do?"

"Ralph performed one of his famous pirouettes and landed gracefully on the balls of his feet. It seems many of Veronica's ancestors were victims of the Nazi holocaust and, needless to say, she had some pretty strong feelings on the subject. Ralph saw his opening. He started surreptitiously planting racist threats and Nazi propaganda about where she couldn't help seeing it—in her fresh laundry, under the blotter of her school desk. How he got the little swastikas into her sealed paycheck from the university he never did tell me. But it worked. She was convinced the entire city of San Diego was a hotbed of neo-facism and she barely lasted out her first semester. I remember Ralph took her to the airport himself, no doubt crying great crocodile tears all the way. He could do it, too."

"What a crummy trick," Scottie mumbled. "Messing up the city's good name like that."

Hazard looked at him and laughed his superior little

laugh, "The *city's* good name?"

"Yeah, the city's. There's lotsa ways of getting rid of a woman that's getting too close. Why make such a big deal out of it?" Scottie snorted.

"Oh yes. Spoken like a true xenophobe."

Scottie frowned, made two starts at a response, but then gave it up.

"Dr. Hazard," Henry said, "do you know Jeremy Bruce well?"

"Bruce? Bruce. Oh, yes, Jeremiah Bruce. N-not well. Good grade point average as I recall—3.91—something like that. He was on the *Inquisitor* team."

"Did Dr. Pangbourne mention anything to you about his making a presentation at this summer's geological conference the school is hosting?"

"Bruce? He's just a second-year graduate student. Good heavens, no."

"You mean it would be totally inappropriate?"

"Mr . . . . "

"Garrett," Henry reminded him.

"Mr. Garrett, this is a rather important conference. We can't be opening it up to every thesis jockey who needs a forum. There just isn't time."

"The boy swears up and down that Dr. Pangbourne asked him to prepare an outline for him . . . "

Hazard shrugged, "What can I say? I'm sure he would have mentioned it to me. I'm coordinating the event for him."

"Did he show you his third version of the program schedule?"

"Third version?"

"Yes."

"You have me there. I don't . . . "

Hazard's blank look told Henry to jump in with an explanation, which he did, recapping their earlier conversation with the printer.

Hazard nodded, "So that's why you asked about any papers Ralph might have been carrying."

"So you don't know anything about a third version?"

"That's correct. I certainly don't," Hazard insisted.

"Dr. Hazard," Henry pressed on, "how did it make you feel to have Pangbourne telegram in a new program schedule after you had put together your own program?"

"There was no problem there. My selections of speakers were all people I knew Ralph would approve of. It was simply a matter of convenience for him."

"I know, but then just a week ago he surprises you with another program schedule—"

"Two weeks ago," Hazard corrected.

"All right, two weeks. But it still meant you had to call up your selections and tell them they were no longer on the program. No doubt they had made many preparations by that time. It must have been quite an embarrassment for you."

Hazard smiled, "There was a total of five people involved. They were all quite understanding. Especially when I explained it was Ralph's idea to include important new *Inquisitor* data."

"I see," Henry said, without conviction.

"My dear friend, let me explain the facts of life to you," Hazard said with his superior air. "I neither resented nor was jealous of Dr. Ralph Pangbourne. My role was not that of a competitor. I was the museum curator, Ralph was the artist. I was Boswell to his Johnson, if you will. I was well-suited for the role and I must admit I enjoyed it. We all knew Ralph was the real dean of the natural science division, but my name was on the door because Ralph didn't want to be bothered with all the housekeeping details involved. So you see, his demise is my loss; what's a Boswell without a Johnson?

"There is another matter which you must consider as well. We are now living in an era of declining university enrollment and there is stiff competition for students. This is particularly crucial to a private institution such as El Rio where we are heavily dependent on lots of warm young bodies whose daddies have lots of cold hard cash. I'm sure with the loss of Ralph Pangbourne many of our potential students will be matriculating in Stanford or USC, come September.

"So you see, my friend, if you can think of a series of circumstances in which the death of Dr. Pangbourne will somehow benefit me I would be most interested in hearing them."

Henry looked across at the silent Scottie and for a few moments could think of nothing except how much Scottie reminded him of an Iowa cow chewing its cud.

"I'm sure you understand the need for the questions," Henry said rather apologetically, "especially since you seem to be the last person to have seen Dr. Pangbourne."

"Aren't we forgetting Dr. Mumford?" Hazard said, "Oh, speak of the devil. Here he is now. John. John!" he called.

Henry turned to see the white-haired gentleman he had seen that morning at the stocks. He had just entered with three other teachers wearing white lab coats. At Hazard's call he came toward their table rather gingerly.

"Yes, Wendel?"

"Why don't you join us, John?"

"I am . . . I'm with my committee . . . "

"Oh, they can do without you, John. These gentlemen are with the police, here about the Pangbourne murder."

"Murder . . . yes, well, I . . . ah . . . "

Hazard pushed out the odd chair for the confused professor and introduced him to Scottie and Henry. He had to shuffle the books and paper sack he was carrying before he could extend his hand for the handshakes. He was older than Henry estimated that morning, either that or he had been doing a lot of aging during the intervening hours. Probably pushing seventy. He was a pudgy man with a slight tremor in his right hand whenever it wasn't locked into carrying something of substance. Traces of yellow chalk dust smudged the sleeves of his old herringbone suit coat and, with the soiled, poorly-tied bow tie, the white unkempt hair and the sagging horn-rimmed glasses, he appeared a caricature of exactly what he was, a doddering old absent-minded professor.

"It's hard for me to think of food at a time like this . . . " he began.

"But you've got to keep up your strength, John," Hazard consoled.

"Yes, I suppose you're right. Is there a waiter—"

"Aren't you brown-bagging today, John?"

"What? Brown b . . . oh, yes," he patted the paper sack in his hands. "The wife packed it before Pangbourne was . . . " He sat clutching the sack as though its contents were going to be consumed by a new osmosis process known only to elderly biologists.

"The gentlemen were asking about our meeting with Ralph Pangbourne last night," Hazard went on in a light tone. "Do you recall him saying anything about rearranging the speaker's program for the geology conference this summer?"

"Am I a geologist?" Mumford asked with an edge on his voice. "Why would he be talking to me about that?"

"Easy, John. I merely thought I may have missed something."

"Well, now you know."

Hazard quickly changed the subject, "Tell me, Mr. Garrett, do the police have any idea who did this?"

"We're working on it," Scottie cut in. "We found a very

good clue and it won't be long now."

"Oh? What kind of a clue might that be?"

"We found a pen with a student's name on it right next to the body."

"Oh, really? What do you think of that, John? What student was it?"

"Jeremy Bruce."

"You mean our Jeremy?" Hazard said, overplaying his surprise just a bit, in Henry's estimation.

"You call that a clue?" Mumford said. His right hand started trembling so much it slipped off the lunch sack, then he covered it with his left and went on. "Dr. Pangbourne was a notorious pen thief. He was always borrowing pens to sign something, then pocketing them . . . "

"Dr. Pangbourne?" Hazard asked with a surprised smile.

"Yes. It got so if he borrowed my pen I'd make a point to hold onto the cap so he couldn't—"

"John, that's nonsense," Hazard interrupted. "I knew him a good deal better than you and I've never known him to make off with a pen."

The two professors exchanged hostile glances, telegraphing more animosity than the pen argument alone would justify. Mumford turned to Scottie and went on, "The Bruce boy was on the ship with him. He no doubt borrowed the boy's pen and had it in his pocket last night."

"You'll have to excuse Dr. Mumford, gentlemen," Hazard said. "He's still smarting from his skirmish over the fossil class with Dr. Pangbourne last night."

"That has nothing to do with it."

"You will also be interested to know, John, the new associate professorship has been awarded to the natural science division."

"They can't do that," Mumford sputtered. "We need

that position. It was promised to us. Our selection committee is already working . . . " He pointed at his three colleagues seated at the other end of the room. "Why, I'm teaching five units myself."

"Sorry, John, but without the fossil class you don't have the upper divisional units to justify the position and we do. Sorry."

"Who says? How do you know?"

"Ralph told me last night before our meeting. He talked to the dean of instruction. I just didn't have the heart to tell you after the beating you got from Ralph."

"You knew it all along," Mumford fumed. "You just kept your mouth shut and waited for Pangbourne to come back and do your dirty work."

Hazard smiled at Henry and Scottie, "Gentlemen, I put it to you—is that the face of a murderer or is it not? Those bulging eyes, the heavy breathing. Anger enough and to spare—"

"What are you doing?"

"I can see it all now. With one telling blow he did Ralph Pangbourne in with that wicked right hand of his."

"What are you saying?" Mumford rose, completely rattled. "Are you out of your mind?"

"Oh, sit down, Mumford; everyone's staring at you."

"Staring at me? Staring at me? You. You're the one . . . "

"John, can't you take a joke? These gentlemen know I dropped you off at your home last night. They're not accusing you of anything."

"How can you sit there and joke like that? Don't you have any feelings? Don't you care?"

"Care? Yes, I care. I care about the quality of the science program of this university. We've just lost the diadem jewel of our institution and we have a life science division that is rapidly atrophying into a second-rate program—"

90

"Atro—at—at—atro," Mumford stumbled. "We'll see . . . we'll just see about that." He snatched up his burdens and hurried from the room.

"Sorry to subject you gentlemen to our little problems, but that exchange was a long time in coming. A very long time," Hazard said with a satisfied look in his eyes.

For a few minutes everyone's attention returned to what was left of their lunches. Watching Hazard savor the last of his soup, Henry had the uneasy feeling he was watching another first class manipulator at work. But why not, after years of studying at the feet of a master. Was the confrontation with poor old Mumford contrived in their presence in order to embarrass him? But why? To shame him into a resignation perhaps? The machinations and political intrigue of the academic world seemed to rival anything he'd seen in his former work, with the possible exception of a more subtle form of bloodletting.

Scottie scrubbed the front of his face with his rumpled napkin and started making noises about leaving. Henry was not quite ready though.

"Dr. Hazard, you said you left Dr. Mumford off at his home . . . "

"That's correct. Right after our meeting."

"Do you have any way of proving that you went straight home?"

"No, I don't. My wife's out of town. Our daughter is expecting her first child and Millie is helping out."

"How can you be so sure of your time when you got home? You said it was ten to ten."

"Yes, I wanted to watch the ten o'clock news on the local station. I don't generally watch the local news, but Ralph said they were covering the arrival of the *Inquisitor* and I wanted to see what they did with the story."

"What was the first news story they covered?" Henry asked.

91

"You mean at the start of the program?"

"Yes."

"Let me see . . . I think it was a food poisoning incident at a rest home in La Jolla. Yes, there was a loss of life due to some bad turkey dressing, I believe. Oh wait, my wife called up during the news. There's no doubt a record of the phone call from Phoenix. No baby yet. Just false labor. How's that for an alibi?"

"Not bad," Scottie said, "if the news story holds up."

"What about the phone call?"

"Maybe she phoned your record-a-call machine and not you."

"Oh, yes, I see," Hazard smiled. "But I don't own a recording machine."

"What time did she call?" Henry asked.

Hazard hesitated. "You know I can't make an association there at all . . . some time before the story on the *Inquisitor*."

"Then what did you do?"

"After the news? I did some paper grading and went to bed."

"I didn't think the dean of a division would have to teach a class," Henry said.

"University policy. Our school founders, in their infinite wisdom, required all divisional directors to teach at least three semester units just to keep their hand in."

"I see."

"Well, gentlemen," Dean Wendel Hazard said, rising, "If that is all, I have a meeting . . . "

Back outside again on the cafeteria steps, Scottie rapped his chest and waited for a belch that never came. "Oh, boy, would I like to pin the rap on that guy. That guy thinks he's pretty smart, doesn't he?"

"You don't think so, I take it," Henry said.

92

"Oh, he's smart with the words all right. That doesn't mean he's got common sense. Him and his 'facts of life.' "

"He orchestrated our interview with him very well, I thought."

"What do you mean?"

"The man didn't tell us a thing he didn't want to. But he did give us one more question to add to our list."

"Which is?"

"Why didn't Ralph Pangbourne tell Hazard about the new changes in their summer conference? I realize their meeting wasn't on that topic, but still it would seem to me he would have made mention of the change."

"Doesn't look too good for the Bruce boy," Scottie hummed under his breath for about the fifth time.

"But the printer says there *was* to be a *third* version," Henry said. "And maybe the Bruce boy's name was to be added . . . If we could only find Pangbourne's briefcase."

Scottie checked his watch. "The captain will be back from his luncheon pretty soon."

But Henry persuaded him to take a little more time on campus. They spent twenty minutes checking the three lost-and-found locations but nothing resembling Pangbourne's black briefcase had been turned in. At the maintenance office a very eager young secretary said she would alert the night cleanup crews to the importance of finding the article. Henry asked to talk to the person who had cleaned Pangbourne's office last night. He was told Rene didn't come to work until three, but the girl was able to reach him by phone. A young sleepy voice with a strong Mexican accent told Henry he only emptied the waste basket in Pangbourne's office; he didn't do anything to the top of the desk and he didn't remember if there was anything on the desk or not.

"Was the wastebasket filled or what?"

"Golly, I don't know. Just a little bit in it, I think."

93

"And you don't remember seeing a green folder on the desk? Dr. Pangbourne had been gone, you know, so you probably hadn't been cleaning the office. Didn't you glance at the desk to see if he'd come back?"

While the young custodian searched his mind, Scottie stood in the doorway telling Henry to hurry up by spinning his finger. When the custodian could think of nothing to add, Henry asked, "Was the office open when you came in?"

"Yeah, the light was on."

"Is that the way you left it?"

"No. There was no one around so I turned out the light and locked up, like I'm supposed to."

"What time was that?"

"Oh about ten or ten-thirty."

"You can't be more specific?"

Then, as Henry started fishing for more details on the wastebasket contents, Scottie's eyes rolled skyward and he pressed his forehead impatiently against the doorsill.

Finally he got Henry back into the car and heaved a sigh of relief. But Henry was already looking through a staff address book he had gleaned from the dean's office.

"Why don't we stop off at Pangbourne's home and see if he left his briefcase there?"

Scottie groaned, "I think we're doing just dandy building a case *against* the kid."

"Aren't you interested in finding the truth?"

"Yeah, but whose truth? as our learned friend Hazard would say?"

"Come on, Scottie, let's make like real detectives. It's supposed to be an unusual house. Maybe you'll get some ideas for your condominium complex. It's not too far out of our way, if I'm reading this map correctly."

Scottie moaned again and slid the car into gear.

Chapter Eight

The house turned out to be a reconstructed or recondi-
tioned Victorian mansion set on the crest of a knoll in
an older section of town and overlooking the original harbor area. Henry expected it to be rundown a bit because of
Pangbourne's long absence, but the yard and hedgework
all looked well-manicured. The only thing missing was a
group of turn-of-the-century picnickers with straw hats
and long white gowns playing croquet on the front lawn,
over by the iron deer.

Scottie pushed the ornate wrought iron bell and a five-
note chime sounded someplace deep inside. He laughed.
"If Mary Poppins answers, I'm leaving."

"You're not expecting anyone to be home, are you?"

"No, I guess not." He got out his set of master keys
and had the door open in no time.

Inside they split up and started looking for a study or
anything that looked like a work area Pangbourne may
have used. Henry's route led him through the dining room.
Everything looked neat as a pin, but when he ran his fingers over the dark rosewood of the dining room table he

realized that a thin layer of dust must be covering everything. The kitchen had been modernized—trash compactor, built-in microwave, a refrigerator that gives crushed ice through the door. Again, everything spotless, no dirty dishes in the sink or the dishwasher. The back porch produced the only signs of life. Just inside the back door a real estate sign was propped against the wall, "Geiger Realty, For Sale, Do Not Disturb the Occupants." The dirt on the tip of the stake flaked away easily under Henry's thumb. It hadn't been there long.

Doubling back through the dining room, Henry was startled to come face to face with a middle-aged woman in a white slip and stocking feet. Her nervous hands held an ancient twelve-gauge Parker shotgun leveled at his chest. It was a toss-up as to who was the most frightened. Henry watched her hands and automatically raised his own. "Hello, please be careful with that weapon."

"Who—what, what are you doing in my house?"

"Are you Mrs. Pangbourne? I can explain this if you'd just point the gun away—"

"Who are you? What do you want? Speak!"

Each time she spoke the gun seemed to wiggle a little more in her hands. For some dumb reason, Henry, for a moment, could think of nothing but the first time he had seen his wife in a slip.

"I'm with the police, Mrs. Pangbourne. I'm Garrett. Harry Garre—Gar—Henry Garrett—"

"What? Which is it? Where's your badge? Police badge?"

Out of the corner of his eye Henry saw Scottie with his handgun drawn coming through the hallway behind the woman. Henry started slowly to reach for the nonexistent badge in order to give Scottie time. Henry nodded toward him.

"There's my partner. He has identification."

As Scottie started to hurry around her back, the wooden floor squeaked. She looked in the direction of the squeak and Henry's head nod, but by then Scottie was on her other side. He put the cold muzzle of his service revolver against her right armpit.

"Drop it, lady, police," he started to yell, but she shrieked and pulled her hand off the trigger mechanism. The butt of the gun dropped against a dining room chair and the weapon fired with a deafening noise into the air. This was followed immediately by the sound of glass and metal crashing on the dining room table. With one unerring shot she had successfully bagged the dining room chandelier.

For a moment no one moved but stood stark still in the reverberating house and watched as the room filled with lovely white particles of acoustical ceiling and shell packing. The woman started crying and bemoaning the loss of her 1880 ceiling piece.

Henry sat down at the table as if it were dinner time and waited for his heart to finish playing a tattoo on his ribs. Scottie broke the shotgun open and nonchalantly examined it.

"Both barrels. You see, lady, that's what happens when civilians have guns."

"Who are you? Who are you? What are you doing in my house?" the woman said in a loud clear voice, with hands on hips. Anger over the dining room mess seemed to wipe out her nervousness.

"Easy, lady, easy," Scottie said as he fished out his badge. "I'm Officer Scott McNeil and this is Harry Gargare," he smiled, "operating under the alias, Henry Garrett. Now who might you be?"

"I'm Sylvia Pangbourne and this is my house."

"Oh . . . " Scottie said in genuine surprise. "I thought . . . we thought you weren't here anymore. That you'd left. Left your husband."

"So you come waltzing into people's houses because you think there's nobody at home?"

"No, of course not—"

"Look at that tabletop. That chandelier. One hundred-and-fifty-year-old Chippendale. My husband's going to have a fit."

"Ma'am . . ."

"You'll pay for this. You really will. Those scratches may be so deep they can't be repaired."

"Mrs. Pangbourne, your husband's dead."

For a moment she kept on shaking her finger at the table without speaking. "What?" she said, in a blunt voice.

"Your husband's been killed. That's why we're here. We thought the house was empty and—"

She bumped against one of the chairs and slid down heavily onto the edge of the seat. Scottie halfheartedly tried to help her.

"You okay?"

She didn't respond. Henry got up and left the room in search of her bedroom where he might find a dressing gown. He found the room where the bedspread had been turned back and the pillow slightly mussed as though she had been lying down for a quick nap. He found a Pendleton robe just inside the crowded closet and pulled it free.

Back in the dining room Scottie was telling what he knew of her husband's death, but she gave no sign of recognition. She seemed to be aging right before their eyes; everything about her was sagging.

"Would you care to slip this on?" Henry said, extending the robe. She studied it a moment. Her lip quivered and she pulled it to herself in a ball.

Henry sat opposite her at the table and waited as she struggled to compose herself.

"Do you have some friends nearby we could call?
98

Would you like us to call a relative, Mrs. Pangbourne?"

"No, I'll be fine. We were separated, you know. It's not as if we were . . . " Her voice trailed off in a high musical note, but her expression didn't break. "There's a four-thirty mass at St. Joseph's. I'll go early and light a candle. Pang always hated it when I prayed for him. Maybe this time he won't mind."

She looked at the robe as though she finally figured out what it was for. She stood up and put her arms into it. Henry started to rise too, but grimaced in pain.

Scottie noticed it. "You all right?"

"Just a moment . . . "

"You weren't hit were you?"

"No, it's my back." He pushed hard against the table with his arms to get the weight of his upper torso balanced on his spine. "There, it's okay."

"You look kinda funny," Scottie said, his head at an angle.

"Thanks," Henry grunted and started easing toward the door, particles of ceiling still floating from his head and shoulders.

"Well, this has been some visit," she said. "Quite some way to wake up."

Scottie mumbled an understanding and put the shotgun on the buffet.

"You people still haven't said what you came here for."

Henry turned to her, his back against the room's entrance arch. "We're looking for your husband's brief-case. We think its contents might shed some light on his death."

"Oh? Well, it isn't here."

"You mean you've been looking for it?"

"I mean I was looking for him. For any sign that he'd been home. He always carried the case with him and it isn't in the study where he normally puts it."

99

"Mrs. Pangbourne, the house doesn't look like it's been lived in for awhile. Don't you, ah—"

"Just a minute," she said and disappeared into the bedroom. She came back unfolding a telegram and handed it to Scottie. "Maybe this will explain. I've been living in Santa Barbara with my mother. The telegram came night before last. I have a job at the university there and I just couldn't get away before five yesterday. I drove down after dinner."

Scottie handed the paper to Henry. It read, "Wonderful news. Must see you soonest. Ship docks 9:00 a.m. tomorrow. Accomplished the impossible. Will miracles never cease. Much to explain. Love Pang."

"What does all that mean, you think?" Scottie asked.

"You mean 'accomplished the impossible'?"

"Yeah."

"I suppose he sold the house and needs my signature. I noticed he brought in the sign from the front yard. We have so much money tied up in this old place, reconditioning it and just keeping it up. And he was holding the price so high; the agent probably latched onto another antique enthusiast with plenty of money."

"So you hadn't seen your husband at all?" Scottie said.

"No, I didn't. I got here about one-thirty this morning. Some lights were on and he'd left a note on the hall table."

"Could we see it?"

"I don't know what I did with it. Let me see . . . All it said was he had called my mother to find out about me. He had some meetings at the university but should be back by eleven. I think he wrote it around the dinner hour yesterday."

"And he still wasn't back at 1:30."

"No, of course he wasn't back."

"I mean, wasn't it unusual for him to be that late?"

"I hadn't kept track of my husband's comings and

goings for some time, Mr. McNeil," she said, rolling up the sleeves on the robe that must have been her husband's. She folded her arms and stood opposite Henry in the archway between the dining room and the hall, apparently in complete control of herself. "I waited for him until 2:30 or so when I fell asleep in the downstairs bedroom there. I didn't know anything until I woke up and saw the back of your head going by the hallway," she said, pointing at Henry.

He smiled, "We're very sorry about that."

"Oh, it's not so bad," she sighed. "I always hated that dining room set anyway. It'll be fine with me if I never see another antique. He was the one who . . . " She rubbed her arms and tried to smile. "If I find that note would you like to see it?" She was heading them toward the front door.

"Yes, if you could," Scottie said. "I'm sure the captain will be in touch. Captain Blanchard. He's in charge of the investigation."

"Are you a scientist too, Mrs. Pangbourne?" Henry asked.

"Me? Heavens no."

"I heard you say you were working at a Santa Barbara school . . . "

"UCSB. I'm in the humanities. Just a part-time teaching position in their women's reentry program. Rather appropriate now, isn't it?"

On the way back downtown Henry rode supine in the backseat with his long legs jammed up against the door.

"She certainly seemed to recover well from the shock, didn't she?" he called to Scottie.

"Yeah, some people are like that. Brave front. She's probably bawling her head off about now."

"I wonder . . . "

"Boy, what's with you anyway? You start suspecting

101

everyone but the guy we got the goods on."

"Doesn't it disturb you at all that she came after us with a gun?"

"Look, we broke into her house—" Scottie began.

"But why didn't she assume we were with her husband? Maybe we were friends he'd brought home for lunch. Did she already know he was dead?"

"Look, she'd been sleeping. She woke up and got scared—"

"That sleeping is another thing that bothers me. Assuming she fell asleep at 3:00 this morning and we broke in around 1:45 P.M. . . . " Henry said, checking his watch, "that means she was sleeping for a solid ten hours and forty-five minutes. I can't sleep that long, can you?"

"Women got better bladders than men. Maybe she didn't get much sleep the night before. Maybe she took a pill. There's no law against sleeping ten or eleven hours, you know," Scottie yelled in frustration.

They rode in silence for awhile, then Henry asked, "How long does it take to drive from Santa Barbara to San Diego?"

"There's no way she coulda made it by 9:30 or 10:00. She left after dinner—"

"But suppose she didn't. Suppose she left at 5:00, or maybe she let her class out early, say 4:30—"

"Oh, brother," Scottie groaned. "You seem to keep forgetting that Pangbourne was a good physical specimen. He was up in years but he could handle himself."

"Not if he was hit from behind."

"Oh, brother. Then why didn't the body have a lump or bruise on the back of the head?"

The remaining ride to the station seemed to contain more than its share of quick turns and fitful stops and starts, forcing Henry to brace himself between the front and backseat several times. Apparently, Scottie's head was made up. But oddly enough, the vibration of the car helped to relax Henry's back muscles enough so he could walk at a normal gait again.

"Where you fellas been?" Blanchard bellowed from his doorway, not really expecting an answer. "This thing's getting bigger all the time."

"Be right with you," Scottie called to his boss. "Gotta fill out a gunshot report."

"What's he talking about?" Blanchard asked Henry.

Henry eased himself into the only straight-backed chair in Blanchard's office. "You ought to keep that lad away from Clint Eastwood movies, captain."

"What's that supposed to mean?"

"I think you'll prefer his version."

"Listen, Scottie's all right. Anytime I find myself between a rock and a hard place, Scottie's the guy I want with me."

"Mmmm, how'd your luncheon go?"

"Unbelievable. The speaker was a hotshot city manager from Philadelphia and the press didn't ask him one single question."

"Why not?"

"They zeroed in on me right away. Did we have any leads? Was anyone at the university under suspicion? Did I think having a usable humiliation stock on campus like that dangerous? And did I have any more pictures of the deceased in the stocks? A reporter from the Associated Press asked me that. They wouldn't run a gruesome picture like that in the *New York Times,* would they?"

"I don't know. He was a very big man in his field and it's a pretty dramatic way to die. Very photographic."

"What did the students have those stupid stocks out there for anyway?" Blanchard fumed.

"Dean Hazard said it was a flop as a money-maker for the fair because they couldn't get any teachers to participate. Once you're locked into those things you're at the mercy of the guy with the peg. The teachers didn't seem to mind spending their fifteen or so minutes in the dunk-a-dean tank—they could get out, take a shower and it was over with—but with the stocks, the more money the students put in the kitty, the longer the teacher had to stay and be heckled and they wouldn't stand for it."

"Mickey is on line three, captain," the intercom on the desk barked. Blanchard picked up the phone and grunted a few times between pauses. Then, "Mickey, the federal guy is here. I'll put on the speaker so he can hear this," Blanchard switched Mickey's voice into the room.

"Got a couple things for you. This Steckman fellow, alias Duffy, has been back on board the *Inquisitor* this morning looking for something."

"Looking for what?" Blanchard asked.

"Well, he said it was a book when the guard found him nosing around in the ship's library. But later they caught him going through a wastebasket in the chart room."

"Did you see him?"

"No. This was all before I got here. When the guard started asking more questions he took off."

"Have you talked with the ship's captain about him?"

"Yeah. Nothing there. He said he'd been an adequate crew member and that's about all he knew."

Henry asked, "Was he ever near the number two radio room?"

"Where the Precursor is? No. They think he was confined to the front part of the ship. The chart room, the library, and the officers' sleeping quarters."

Henry quickly reran the image of Steckman coming out of Pangbourne's cabin through his mind again. Whatever he was looking for that first time must still be missing.

"I don't suppose he was kind enough to leave his address," Blanchard said.

"No such luck."

"Okay, we'll get an APB out on him. He's probably still in town. Anything else?"

"Yeah," Mickey said, flipping his notebook pages next to the receiver. "We located a professor from the University of Nebraska, like you said. A Professor Beauchamp. He told part of the skeleton crew here that he and his family were headed for Disneyland. I called the state police and they found his car up there. He's on his way back down. Should be dropping in on you this afternoon."

"Great work, Mickey."

"Thanks. You want me to stay on this or go back to my robbery?"

"Oh, go back to your robbery but stay where I can reach you." Blanchard cradled the phone then shot a worried glance across at Henry. The prospect of working an investigation under the close scrutiny of a national press audience seemed to be chipping away at his gruff exterior. "Where's that Scottie? How long does it take him . . . ?" Blanchard said, charging out of the office. He soon returned with Scottie, then sat at his desk again and rubbed his ample forehead. "All right. What have we got?"

For the next fifteen minutes Scottie gave a nuts-and-bolts account of what he and Henry had been up to, including a slightly doctored version of the gunshot incident. Blanchard sounded the familiar alarm about search and seizure rules and the increase of lawsuits being levied against the police. Scottie nodded agreeably through it all, but the knowledgeable observer could see visions of new condominiums dancing in his mind's eye.

With that out of the way, Blanchard returned to rubbing his forehead and his question, "Now what have we got?"

"That story the kid gave us sounds phony," Scottie said. "Nobody thinks he was there in the prof's office to

105

talk about making a presentation like he said."

"Why would he lie about that, though?" Henry asked. "If he planned to kill the professor why would he make up an elaborate story about meeting with him at 9:30?"

"Oh, I don't think he lied about it," Scottie put in. "The prof was a practical joker, remember. I think he got the kid to make up a big paper like he was gonna be a bigshot. Then he pulled the rug out from under him."

"For a joke?"

"Sure. That would explain the 'liar' sign on the stocks too. The kid wanted to expose him for a liar. And who else would be strong enough to handle the professor? Not only bump him off but haul him the 200 yards across campus to the stocks? I'll bet the kid is strong as an ox."

"And you think because of a practical joke the boy got mad enough to kill?" Henry said, then shook his head.

"The boy does have a temper," Blanchard put in. "We saw him blow up this morning, remember?"

"But he released his hostilities verbally," Henry said.

"What's he gonna do? Poke a policeman in a police station?"

"Okay, let's say for the sake of argument, Jeremy kills Pangbourne. What does he do with the body? Pick it up and carry it across campus at 9:30 when the evening classes are starting to let out?"

"He leaves it in the room and comes back for it later," Scottie reasoned.

"When?" Henry asked. "The custodian was there at 10:30 and didn't see a body. And according to the maintenance people the campus lights are not turned off until 12:00 on nights they have night school. And why would he move the body in the first place? He would no doubt be scared. Why wouldn't he just take off?"

"Your turn," Blanchard said looking at Scottie. But Scottie had no answer.

106

Henry went on, "I think it makes much more sense that someone like Steckman was waiting for Pangbourne perhaps in the bushes between the natural science office building and the lecture hall where he had his meeting—"

"Is there such an area with shrubbery?" Blanchard asked.

"Yeah, there is," Scottie admitted. "But why would Steckman be after Pangbourne?"

"Maybe he was after the briefcase that's still missing. Captain, I'd like to go out and go over that area very carefully—" Henry began.

"No, you're not," Blanchard said. "We can do that later. You're gonna stick around and talk to this Nebraska guy so I can find out what that's all about."

During the hour they had to wait for Professor Beauchamp the two policemen busied themselves with what seemed an endless task of paper shuffling. This freed Henry to wander about on his own, thinking and making lists of loose ends he'd like to get tied up: *Mrs. Pangbourne's note from husband; check Pangbourne's mailbox at univ.; recheck lost-and-found; was Pang. house sold?; check realtor; who's in charge of vessel now?; Hazard's alibi—check TV station.*

Next he put in a call to son Philip asking him to go out to dinner with him that evening. Philip was reluctant, begging school responsibilities for an excuse. But he did agree to a quick dinner when Henry explained he wouldn't be in town much longer and Valery would be hurt if he didn't bring home a full report on his activities. How times change. Yesterday, total dependence. Today, Mr. Independence. Or was there another reason his son was not anxious to spend time with him? Henry quickly forced the thought out of his mind.

He strolled across the courtyard to the jail section of

the administration of justice complex and asked to talk with Jeremy Bruce. But because he was not Bruce's designated lawyer his request was refused.

Crossing the courtyard again Henry had to briefly make way for a group of uniformed officers apparently returning from their time of duty patrolling the city streets and now on their way to their lockers. As they passed, one officer was entertaining the others with an off-color joke and in the good old American tradition he accentuated his punch line with a profanity. This sent the other officers into howling laughter. But it sent Henry into a walking prayer.

"I haven't thought of you but once today, Lord. It's so easy not to. Our whole modern world seems to be geared toward self-reliance and human interaction and I need to hear someone misusing your name just to bring you to mind. I guess I'm not in the habit of looking to you on a daily basis yet. Help me in that, will you?"

Chapter Nine

Henry was in the process of looking up the phone number for Geiger Realty office when Blanchard's piercing whistle got his attention and the attention of everyone else on that floor of the building. He motioned Henry into his office and introduced him to Dr. Barry Beauchamp who turned out to be a surprisingly young man. He was slight of build with light sandy hair and freckles that betrayed his long exposure to the sun. Dressed in a white polo shirt, safari shorts, and sandals, it appeared he'd been untimely plucked off the beach. He looked very much out of place among the three somberly dressed men. Blanchard made the introductions to Henry and Scottie then asked everyone to sit.

"What's this all about, captain?" Beauchamp asked.

Blanchard smiled and motioned to Henry to take over.

Before Henry could start, Beauchamp went on, "You know I was in the Disneyland Hotel last night. My wife and I and our two boys checked in at 7:30. I wasn't in San Diego at all last night."

"I see. Thank you," Henry got in. "You know then that

Dr. Pangbourne was killed?"

"Of course, I know. That picture was on the front page of the afternoon Los Angeles paper. I saw it," he said, pushing up his round horn-rimmed glasses. This gesture, which he repeated several times during the interview, seemed to imply nervousness. At no time did the glasses slip down the bridge of his nose so that they, in fact, needed adjusting.

"So you were seeing the sights at the amusement park last night—"

"Our boys were, yes. I was a little tired and my wife and I . . . We hadn't seen each other you know. We stayed at the hotel."

"Yes, of course. You were on the *Inquisitor* for the whole trip?"

"Yes. I think the only people that didn't make the whole trip were a couple of our equipment operators that left the ship when we tied up in Mexico."

"Yes," Henry said, then cleared his throat and went on. "I wanted to ask you about the little submarine."

"What about it?"

"I was wondering if you could tell me how it got its name?"

"Its name? You mean 'Old Score'?"

"Yes."

Beauchamp looked from one face to the other with an unbelieving smile. "Wait a minute now. You mean to say you got me here . . . you send the state police after me so you can find out about the sub's name? I got two hot and sweaty kids outside in the car hopping mad at me cuz I took 'em away from Donald Duck. And all you wanted to know was how we named the stupid submarine? I don't believe this."

"Simmer down there, mister," Blanchard boomed. "We got a murder investigation underway here and you're

110

gonna tell us whatever we wanna know. We got a very good reason for wanting to know about that submarine." Then to Henry, "Haven't we?"

Henry cleared his throat again and proceeded quietly, almost sheepishly, "Dr. Pangbourne seemed to take or . . . feel a great significance for the name. The first time I saw him he was sitting on the front of the sub almost fondling the name. It was scrawled on the top of the boat with a yellow chalk or—"

"Yellow bottom paint," Beauchamp corrected.

"Did you name the boat?"

"Yes. Yes, I did," he admitted quietly. "How'd you know?"

"I'm from the Midwest myself, Iowa," Henry said. "And I've heard the story about the time they were putting up a statue of a wheat sower on the top of the capitol building in Lincoln, Nebraska. The workmen left the statue standing unattended for a time and when they came back someone had scratched the words 'Old Score' on the headpiece of the sower. And rather than having it filed down and repaired they went ahead and put the statue in place. So it became known as 'Old Score.' I didn't think anyone but someone from Nebraska or the vicinity would know about the story or think of that particular title for a submarine. Am I right?"

"Yeah, . . . on the nose."

"Would you tell us about it?"

"Well, we didn't have a name for the boat really, and we were all joking about it on our way home. Someone should come up with a good name. When we left Mexico things were pretty loose. Somebody had brought some tequila aboard and I blame it for the accident really. I don't think it would have happened otherwise. We never would have put the sub down again if—"

"What accident is that?" Blanchard asked.

"Oh, we almost lost Dr. Pangbourne. The experienced divers were taking turns going down in the sub in the clear Mexican coastal waters just to look around. They'd dive out of the bottom of the sub when they found interesting fish and bottom specimens. They had plenty of oxygen left and we weren't due in San Diego for a week so they were taking their sweet time. The rest of us with families were pretty anxious to get home. Fresh water was running low.

"Anyway, on the last dive something happened to Pangbourne's line. It's still pretty confusing as to what happened. Conflicting stories and so on."

"Who was he diving with?" Henry asked.

"Oh, one of the graduate students aboard. Jeremy Bruce."

Scottie let out a low whistle. Blanchard said, "I think you better tell us about it. In detail."

"I'll tell you what I know, which isn't much."

"Why was he diving with Bruce?"

"No specific reason. I think it was just their turn to go down. Everything was going along fine. We have no communication with the divers when they're outside the sub so we didn't know what was happening. Then near the end of their dive time, we got a Mayday call from the Bruce boy in the sub. We brought it up as fast as we could without endangering them. When we got the hatch off and looked in, Bruce was giving Pangbourne CPR."

"He was unconscious?"

"Not just unconscious. We couldn't find a pulse for what seemed like an eternity. We got him out and worked on him a good twenty minutes before he came around. It was a very sobering time."

"Did Bruce give an explanation?"

"He said he found him unconscious, and his line was fouled."

"So the Bruce boy saved his life then?" Henry said.

112

"On the surface it did appear that way . . . divers are responsible for each other."

"But you have doubts?"

"Yes, I guess I do."

"Can you tell us why?"

"We couldn't find anything wrong with Pangbourne's oxygen supply. The valves were all working and there was ample air left in his tank."

"I'm not a diver," Henry said, "but I've heard that divers sometimes develop a sense of euphoria after they've been down for awhile. That they might even forget to breathe. And if Pangbourne had been drinking . . . "

"Yes, something like that could have happened, I guess," Beauchamp agreed. "I certainly don't have any proof of foul play. It's just . . . well, maybe I better not say. It's so much speculation on my part."

"Would you be surprised to hear Jeremy Bruce is a suspect in Pangbourne's murder?" Blanchard asked.

Beauchamp sat very still studying the floor. Then, "You know when I saw that picture of Pangbourne in the paper, Bruce was the first person I thought of."

"Why is that?" Blanchard asked.

"It's because of the things that went on before the dive. And because of the way Pangbourne acted afterwards. I suppose every cruise like ours develops its patsy—its one person who is the butt of jokes and pranks. Well, Bruce was ours. And he was ideal. A big gullible paluka that would believe just about anything anyone told him. To top it off, he started spouting his creationism propaganda and arguing against the well-accepted theories in our geological time scale. Well, you can imagine what a shipload of scientists thought of all that. The kid brought most of the hazing on himself actually."

"You mean he was a closet creationist?" Henry asked.

Beauchamp laughed, "That's about the size of it. I'm

113

sure if Pangbourne had known of his religious bent the boy would never have been chosen for the trip."

"Why not?"

"What do you mean why not?" he scowled at Henry. "Creationism is a system based on a literal interpretation of the Bible. It's not scientific. You've got to go with hard evidence, and the geological evidence supports the evolutionary time scale."

"But Jeremy insists the evidence supports creationism. Maybe it's a matter of interpretation of the evidence. Is that possible?"

Beauchamp smiled a superior little smile, very reminiscent of Dr. Hazard over his soup. "No, my friend. No, no, no. There's a basic difference in approach here. Let me refer to an allegory you'll understand. Do you remember what the serpent promised Eve if she ate of the forbidden fruit? She was promised knowledge. And knowledge she got. And ever since, thinking people have been struggling to keep its quest for knowledge alive while the religious fanatics have been trying to force us into a world of blind obedience to their little world of the Bible, as if we could return to a former state of innocence—"

"Wait a minute. Wait a minute now," Henry protested. "Eve was offered a specific knowledge. She was offered the knowledge of good and evil. And that certainly separates us from the lower forms—"

"There are a few extra chromosomes in there, too," Beauchamp smiled. "But I still think you've proved my point. Religion is not a friend to the free quest for knowledge."

"Oh? Who was it that preserved secular knowledge during the Dark Ages? It was the Christian church. And the educational system we have in this country has its roots in Christianity. Why, Harvard University was founded by—"

114

"I noticed you used the word *preserve*. That's quite appropriate. They don't mind preserving what is old and safe. And, sure we teach our kids the three *R*s. But when it comes to the cutting edge of knowledge the church is there wagging its finger—"

Scottie jarred everyone with a sudden burst of profanity. Their talk had been so ponderously quiet the others all jumped at his sudden outburst. "What's this have to do with anything? This isn't getting shoes for the kids. Let's get on with it."

"Let's get back to Jeremy Bruce," Blanchard said. "What actually happened? You say he was at odds with Dr. Pangbourne . . . "

"Yes, Pangbourne seemed to be the instigator of a lot of the practical jokes. Maybe he felt a special need to harrass the kid because he came from his own institution, I don't know. But he sure leaned on the kid, and everyone else seemed to pick up on it. It got pretty bad. You know, we were all confined on board that little ship for long periods of time."

"Can you give us an example, doctor?" Henry asked.

"Okay. There was the time Bruce was arguing with some of the other graduate students on deck about the diluvian flood—you know, Noah's ark and the whole legend. Pangbourne heard them and started gathering some of his cohorts around, encouraging Bruce to go on. Bruce took the bait and enthusiastically started giving the usual examples of catastrophic evidences that support the idea of the great flood—the Grand Canyon trenches, the miles of sedimentary rock, the quick frozen mammoths in Russia, the canopied moisture layers on the other planets. And Pangbourne sat there as if he were drinking it all in. Finally, when Bruce ran out of steam there was a long silence, I remember. Pangbourne sat there nodding his head in agreement. Then he said something like, 'So you

115

feel the flood covered the entire earth, mountains and everything.' Bruce stood there nodding his head in that funny way of his and grinning like a ninny. Then Pangbourne said, 'I just have one question. What did you do with all that water? Oh, here it comes now.' Right then on cue some of Pangbourne's pals up on the bridge deluged Bruce with two barrels of water. Totally drenched the poor dunce and everything around him.

"That part of it was pretty funny," Beauchamp continued. "Bruce even laughed at it himself. But then things got out of hand. For the next thirty days I don't think one day went by when Bruce's clothes didn't get wet in one way or another. Everybody seemed to be in on the act. Then one day, we were near the equator in shark-infested waters, I remember, and Bruce had reached the end of his patience. The squirrely little guy from Stanford with the high-pitched voice shot Bruce with his makeshift water squirter once too often. Bruce picked him up like he was a rag doll and heaved him overboard with one quick gesture just like this." Beauchamp demonstrated with an easy overhand move as though serving a tennis ball.

"The razzing didn't stop, but at least his tormentors became much more judicious and worked only in groups."

"You mentioned something about the way Pangbourne acted after the diving incident," Henry said.

"Yes. That's what really has me worried. I think Pangbourne knew he needed to fear Bruce. He stayed in his bunk the whole day, the day after the dive. Recuperating, I guess. And then when he was up and around he just wasn't his old self. Very quiet and withdrawn. I heard one of the seamen make a joking remark at Bruce's expense. Pangbourne told him to pipe down and, at the same time, he looked around for Bruce almost as if he were afraid of the kid. Afraid he might hear and knock a few heads together."

"You have anything else to base your suspicions on?" Henry asked.

"No, I guess not. Pangbourne was very anxious to get home and get off the ship, I know. Some of the divers wanted to go down again but he said no. We headed right for home at top speed. So we got the sub named just in time for the last dive, then never used it again. It's a funny thing about you mentioning his strange reaction to that name. I got that same feeling. After the accident, Pangbourne called me in and asked about my naming the boat. I thought he was going to chew me out about the sloppy paint or not getting his permission or something. But all he wanted to know was when I had named it."

"*When* you had named it?" Henry asked.

"Yes. I told him it was after we had sealed them in for that last dive and were waiting for the crane operator to lower them into the water. There was a lot of clowning around going on about then. Some of the guys were making like swashbucklers from old Errol Flynn movies and stuff. I know it doesn't make much sense now in the cold light of day. But you gotta remember we'd been couped up quite a while. Anyway, I hopped on the sub with the paint-brush and can and slapped on the name and said, 'I dub thee "Old Score" ' or something equally silly.

"Pangbourne kept insisting I had done it on one of the dives before. But I hadn't. I still don't understand what all the fuss was about. If he didn't like the name he could paint it out."

"The paint didn't wash off in the water?"

"No. It was ship-bottom paint designed to dry in salt water. He kept insisting he'd seen the name before. I told him he probably saw it during his dive but he insisted he'd not been swimming above the boat."

"Sounds like a tempest in a teapot," Blanchard put in.

Beauchamp laughed. "Of course, he was just ticked off

117

because he wasn't in on naming the boat."

"I get the feeling you didn't get on too well with Pangbourne," Henry said.

"Who did? But what does one do? He had the only game in town."

"You sorry you went on the trip?" Henry asked.

"Oh, no, it was worthwhile. I guess I really can't complain. We knew when we started that we biologists would be getting the short end of the stick with the geologists. We were promised a stop at the Galapagos Islands which never materialized. He said there wasn't time but we ended up clowning around on the Mexican coast so we wouldn't get home too soon. Another thing that irked me, three weeks before we got home most of our bottom specimens were taken away from us—actually taken out of our lab without our permission—just so the press releases could be controlled by Pangbourne. That really irked me."

"He never returned them?"

"He promised to ship everything to its rightful owners after his big press announcement. Who knows what's going to happen to them now. A lot of the deep water specimens disintegrate at sea level. They have to be kept pressurized." He shrugged, then went on, "But I'm still glad I went. It'll look good on my resume to have been with Ralph Pangbourne on his last trip. Very prestigious."

"What did you think of the way he died?" Blanchard asked.

"Weird. But I don't know . . . Considering the man, his personality and all, I think it's rather an appropriate way to go. I mean we all have to go some way, don't we? For him it was—fitting. His own death is probably some kind of practical joke."

"You have any guess as to why the 'liar' sign was posted at the stock?" Scottie asked.

118

"Well, it is rather necessary for a practical joker, isn't it? Lying, I mean, in order to make the joke work. Poor guy."

"Why do you say that?" Henry asked.

"I mean, he spent his whole life building a reputation—his niche in the world of scholarship—and now when people think of him, the first thing that will come to mind will be the way he died."

Henry and Scottie watched from the window in Blanchard's office as Dr. Beauchamp and a woman in a fashionable sunsuit corralled two carrot-topped boys from the police station parking lot where they had been tossing their Frisbee, packed the youngsters and themselves into their small station wagon with Nebraska plates, and headed out into the northbound traffic.

"I suppose you're going to tell me he could have driven down from Disneyland last night," Scottie smirked.

"Well, it is possible—" Henry said.

"I knew it. I knew it," Scottie slapped his thigh. "Hey, listen, we got a cleaning lady that comes in and cleans the offices at night. You wanna grill her, too? Maybe she can't account for her activities last night between 9:00 and 12:00. Course that would be a waste o' time, wouldn't it? We should all know she couldn'ta done it because she wears a cross on a chain around her neck." He laughed a laugh of recognition. "That's it, isn't it? I can see it on your face. Jeremy Bruce couldn'ta done it because he's a born-again Christian and you are too. It finally dawns on me. Boy, you people really stick together, don't you? You got your own little club. You help me and I'll help you.

"But let me ask you this," Scottie got serious. "Has it occurred to you that Bruce just may be guilty? Maybe just a momentary slip from grace. You know, nothing serious. Eight, ten years ago the punks that ran dope across the

119

border here used to plaster their cars with Jesus stickers thinking that somehow that made them immune to suspicion. Well, it didn't. That's one lesson you better learn in a hurry in police work, mister. You don't look into the human heart when you read a guy's bumper sticker."

"Okay, Scottie, that's enough. You made your point," Blanchard said. "Let's see what we've got now."

Henry moved back to the wooden-backed chair and sat. "I've got a list of loose ends here I think we ought to look into." Pulling out his list, he went on, "Hazard's alibi; he was looking at the local news at ten and he talked long-distance to his wife sometime around ten-fifteen—"

"I already called the station," Scottie said. "The first news story was about the rest home food poisoning just like he said. And the phone company said there was a long-distance call from Phoenix to his house at 10:14 and it ran for five minutes and thirty seconds. Again, just like the man said." Scottie closed his book with a confident snap.

"I'd like to confirm Mrs. Pangbourne's story, too," Henry went on, "about their house being sold. She said—"

Scottie interrupted with, "I already called the Geiger Realty Company. Pangbourne did take the house off the market yesterday when he got home. The realtor seems to think Pangbourne found a buyer for the house himself and was trying to cheat them out of a commission. Apparently he tried a couple fast moves on them in the past so they're keeping an eye on the county recorder's list of sales."

"You've been busy, haven't you?" Henry said.

"That's my job," Scottie smiled. "All the doors seem to be closing, don't they?"

"Oh, we still have the missing briefcase problem. Why is that still missing if the Bruce boy killed him?"

Blanchard grunted agreement. "He's got a point there,

Scottie. I think we're still a long way from home. Steckman is the guy that's looking for something, remember. And if the briefcase had a lock on it he'd probably take the whole thing with him and bust it open at a later time."

"But he's still looking."

"Sure. What he's looking for wasn't in the case," Blanchard said. "That reminds me, you better wear this." He reached in a side drawer and shoved a small metal object across his desk toward Henry.

"What is this?"

"Put it on your belt. If it beeps, call my number. If and when we find Steckman we want you on hand for a positive identification."

"Yeah, we want you along," Scottie smiled. "Maybe Steckman can tell us some more fascinating stories about 'Old Score' in Lincoln, Nebraska."

"Does this mean you're still releasing Bruce?" Henry asked, trying to ignore Scottie's jibes.

Blanchard drummed his desk top with his thick stubbly fingers as he thought it over. Henry could sense Scottie standing slightly behind him shaking his head no for his boss's benefit. Henry pressed on: "Doesn't look too good arresting one suspect when we have a call out for another."

Blanchard still had not agreed so Henry pretended his silence was a yes.

"Could I ask you to release him now? I'm headed for the school anyway. And I'd like to talk with him." He stood up and waited.

"Swing your car around to the north side," Blanchard finally said. "We'll send him out through the patrolmen's locker room door so the press don't see him."

Henry didn't wait to ask the why or wherefore of this maneuver but picked up the beeper and headed for his Volvo.

121

The car was hot from sitting in the parking lot all day, but that was not without its benefits. The faint familiar aroma of Valery's bath oil struck him and triggered a host of memories. Two years ago in Amsterdam when the car was new, half a bottle of the oil had spilled on the floor pads in the backseat. The details of how it got spilled or who had left the lid loose or why it was in the car in the first place totally escaped him. But the pleasant thoughts associated with countless intimacies he had shared with his wife flooded his mind and he wished he were home.

He rolled down the window and drove around to the north side of the building as per Blanchard's instructions and turned off the engine and waited.

Scottie was right, of course. He did feel a special sympathy for Jeremy Bruce because of his Christian convictions. The youngster may be guilty, but emotionally Henry would hate to see it turn out that way. And he had been anxiously looking for other possible suspects because, if Bruce were innocent, the prime suspect suddenly became . . . He quickly slammed his open hand against the padded dash to keep from thinking about it. He got out of the car and leaned against the front fender and waited.

Chapter Ten

Jeremy didn't look much like a secret sharer as he emerged from his daylong confinement. He was scowling heavily and reeked of cigar smoke. He plopped his grumpy self into the front seat of the car without much talk and waited. Once they were underway Henry asked how he was.

"Who's side are you on, anyway?" Jeremy demanded.

"Remember I told you to call your folks."

"They got a lot of nerve treating a citizen like that," he went on, describing some rather unsavory details of two of his cellmates, one on withdrawal from drugs and the other harassing the first by flicking imaginary caterpillars off of his shivering body. The stark desperation of Jeremy's voice forced a smile on Henry's face.

"What's so funny?"

"I'm sorry, I'm sure it wasn't funny," Henry said, trying to straighten out his face. "Believe me I'm on your side, but you do seem to lend yourself to practical jokes."

Jeremy didn't take well to the remark so they drove in silence for several blocks. Then Henry said, "You mentioned Dr. Pangbourne had asked you to prepare an outline of a paper you were asked to present—"

"What about it?"

"I was wondering if you'd let me read a copy of it. You did make a carbon I presume."

Jeremy looked meaner than ever, "No, I didn't make a copy."

"Wasn't that rather foolish?"

"Of course, it was. But I didn't have time. I thought he was just going to look it over and give it back to me."

"I see . . . " Henry mused. "You know, of course, the problem the police are having with that. They feel since you were already the butt of some of Pangbourne's jokes there was little or no chance he would have turned to you for such an important presentation."

"I know, I know."

"Can you explain why he would do a thing like that?"

"I thought maybe it was a reward for saving his life. I did, you know."

"Yes, I heard. We talked to Dr. Beauchamp and he told us about your dive. He also said he wasn't surprised when he heard you were a suspect."

"Oh, yeah?"

"Yes. Do you know why he'd think that?"

"No," Jeremy said quickly. His eyes were darting about, scanning the dash in front of him.

"Son, listen to me. I get the feeling you're not leveling with me. Beauchamp also said you'd practiced a little deception in order to get included on the trip. If Pangbourne had known beforehand of your creationism bent you'd never have been included."

"Okay, that's true. I wouldn't have. But I didn't lie. I just kept my mouth shut on the subject—"

"But you can see how that looked, can't you?"

"And did Beauchamp tell you about the little shoving

match he had with Dr. Pang?"

"No, he didn't mention that."

"No, I guess he wouldn't," Jeremy snorted. "He was trying to hang onto some of the sea floor specimens for himself. He knew it was against the rules of the trip but that didn't seem to phase him."

"So there was no love lost between Beauchamp and Pangbourne. But it would be rather difficult to place Beauchamp at the murder scene. Don't you see? Others had motives too, there's no doubt. Pangbourne had plenty of enemies it seems. But you had opportunity and your reason for being on the scene doesn't seem to set well with anyone else. The only explanation I can come up with is that he was planning one more practical joke at your expense."

Jeremy shook his head in frustration, then started slamming his large hands against the padded dash so violently the dust started flying.

"Easy, easy. That isn't going to solve anything," Henry said, half expecting to see two big dents on his poor car. He made a mental comparison between the raps Jeremy had just extended on the dash and his own rap to the dash earlier and realized the enormity of the potential violence pent up in Jeremy.

After another stretch of silence, Henry asked, "Do you want to pray about this?"

"I've been praying. I've been praying 'til I'm blue in the face."

"Well, the Lord said to pray without ceasing."

"I thought—I thought this whole thing was going to be an answer to prayer. We've been working so hard on it for so long."

"Working on what?"

"The acceptance of scientific evidences for creationism. And then with our finds on this trip and the chance to

125

present a paper on it—it was too much to hope for."

"Can you tell me what the paper was going to be about? I mean, in a way I'd understand."

"Sure. It was on the finds I made—or we made on the trip. I was hoping we'd get a chance during the trip to examine the continental shelf off the coast of Siberia. That's the land area under the shallow waters along the coast. It's quite an unusual area because we feel it has been spared much of the violent upheavals that have taken place elsewhere on the earth's crust."

"Violent upheavals? What—"

"I'm talking in geological terms, of course, where the earth's crust might move but a few inches a year."

"That's not too violent, I'd say," Henry said.

"It is if those few inches are the result of an earthquake. Anyway, this shelf off Siberia offers us an excellent time record because we think it is free of the turbulence other places have experienced where new sediment gets buried underneath some older material. It's been very stable and the sedimentary material has been building up slowly over the eons. It was beyond my wildest dreams that we'd get a chance to stop there and drill some test cores. But we did. We stayed in the area much longer than I expected—"

"Always near Russian ports?" Henry asked.

"Yes, the mouth of ports afforded the best sedimentary layers, Dr. Pang said. I could argue that point, but you know, he was the boss."

Jeremy had undergone a remarkable change once again. The frustrated enraged bull had disappeared and in its place was the erudite truth-seeker back on track, talking about the subject he loved. Henry didn't understand everything he was being told, but he encouraged Jeremy with appropriate questions.

"So what did your core samples show?"

Jeremy smiled with anticipation. "I can't say categorically yet; we have some stones that have to be age-dated with additional tests, but we think we have a significant find. We found, at very deep levels, remnants of organisms that normally appear very late on the biologist's phylogenetic tree. And yet on top of that, by as much as thirty feet, we found formations that read out as dating in the billions of years. Now, according to the evolution model, this can't happen. Either their age-dating system is cockeyed or these advanced organisms appeared much earlier than the biologists say they could have appeared.

"Don't you see?" Jeremy was excited. "Either way it contradicts their theory. They say the earth is extremely old. And they need an extremely old earth in order for their theory of evolution to work; although I can also argue that point, but let it go for now. So if it is extremely old, what are advanced organisms doing underneath those old rocks?"

Henry mulled this over in his mind for a mile or so. Then, "I don't know. When I talk to you it sounds so convincing. And then to question someone like Dr. Hazard or Pangbourne, they have an answer for everything, and anyone foolish enough to embrace creationism comes off looking like a Bible-thumping fanatic who checked his brains at the door."

"Has it occurred to you that they have a vested interest in perpetuating the evolution model?"

"Now wait a minute—"

"Think about it. The whole study of biology is structured on categorizing and departmentalizing organisms into branches of their sources. 'This little bug is related to this little bug over here because the chromosome count is the same or their intestinal tracts produce the same enzymes. See how important I am. Stick with me and I'll show you the natural source of life.'

127

"And the sociologists and anthropologists hop on the same bandwagon. 'Let's experiment on monkeys. If we can make monkeys hop to our tune then we'll know human beings will behave too, because after all, he's only a little ways over on the evolutionary tree. See how important I am. Stick with me and I'll show you how to make man behave.' You see the symbiotic relationship among the disciplines?

"And the supporting cast to this house-of-cards charade include the paleontologists digging for the missing links, and now even the physicists and engineers promising to unlock the secrets to the source of the universe with the next billion-dollar rocket to the stars."

"There aren't too many people you approve of, are there?"

"Listen. To deny evolution is to admit a miracle and this they cannot do."

"Jeremy, listen. Vested interest or not, I just can't believe that many people can be wrong. Why, you're attacking our entire system of higher education. These reputable scientists aren't that stupid. I think you've painted yourself into a corner."

Jeremy grimaced, and for a moment Henry feared again for his dashboard. Then he seemed to relax. "Okay. I know, I sound paranoid. Maybe I am a little. But why then did Dr. Pang give me the note?"

"Note? What note are you talking about?"

"The note that told me to be in his office at nine-thirty."

"Note? What the sam hill? You told us he *told* you to meet him there."

"He did, in the note—"

"But didn't it occur to you that the note could be forged?" Henry berated him. "Why didn't you tell me about this before? This changes everything. Let me see it."

"I—I don't have it. I'd have given it to the police but I guess I lost it in all the moving."

"All right, all right now. Let's be nice and calm about all this," Henry said, calming himself down. "How did you get the note?"

"I found it on my bunk the day before we docked."

"You mean it just suddenly appeared?"

"Sure. Dr. Pang often did things that way. We were pretty crowded on shipboard and you never knew who was overhearing what, so he wrote a lot of notes."

"He'd written notes to you before?"

"Well, no. But I knew what his handwriting looked like."

"Never mind that. What did the note say?"

"It said something like,

'Jeremy,

I'm interested in your Siberia findings. Would you like to do a short paper for our summer conference? If so, meet me in my office at school at 9:30 p.m. tomorrow with outline in hand.

Dr. Pang' "

"I see . . . but knowing Pangbourne's attitude, didn't it occur to you to question him about it?"

"No. He was busy and—"

"Why ever not? You'd already been the butt of several jokes. Didn't you smell a rat?"

"Mr. Garrett, I've been a Christian nearly all my life. And this wouldn't be the first miracle I've seen happen. I just knew it was an answer to prayer."

"But apparently it was not."

"What do you mean?" Jeremy asked.

"I mean somebody was setting you up. Somebody on board knew you had a grudge against Pangbourne—now be quiet and let me finish—and that you had a one-track mind on this creation business, so they maneuvered you into being at Pangbourne's office at the crucial time so you'd have no decent alibi, and they planted your book in his office and your pen on the body."

"I don't know . . . "

"What do you mean, you don't know? You enjoy being the prime suspect in a murder case?"

"No, of course not. But why did they take my outline."

"Because they didn't want to leave you with even a shred of an alibi. And the same person probably took back the note you say you lost. When did you say you lost track of it? Were you still on board ship when you realized it was missing?"

"Yes, I was."

"You see, you see? It all fits."

But Jeremy was having trouble with it. He shook his head and thought. "You remember when I came rushing down below deck to find you?"

"Yes?"

"Well, Dr. Pang had just come on deck with his stuff ready to go ashore. Most of our people were piling into the university van and we couldn't all fit in very well so Dr. Pang asked if I'd mind riding with you since you were going there anyway."

"Yes, yes. What's your point?"

"Well, when he said good-bye he said, 'I'll see you later at the school.' Sort of like a question and I said, 'Sure, you bet.' But if he hadn't written the note, why would he say that?"

"Hmm. I think he meant it like 'I'll see you later' as in 'good-bye.' He used the same expression with me. When I told him I was Philip's father he said he would be seeing Philip later at the school. He didn't mean sometime specific in the immediate future necessarily."

Or did he? Now that he seemed to convince Jeremy, Henry had some new doubts of his own and he tried to

130

remember just how Pangbourne had said it. *Was Philip going to see . . . was Philip . . . did Philip . . . ?* There had to be another explanation. After all, Philip had not been on board. He couldn't have forged the note or stolen the pen . . .

But the girl, Tracy, had been on board. And Steckman. And how many more who may have hated Pangbourne enough? No doubt tempers were short, but the murderer would keep a short rein on his feelings until after the boat had docked. Kill him someplace away from the boat.

Back at the university Henry pulled up in front of Jeremy's apartment.

"Thanks again for the ride."

"What are you going to do now?" Henry asked.

"Oh, I'll be hanging around until summer school starts. I was hoping to get a job—"

"I meant like the next few hours."

"The police asked me not to leave the area."

"Philip and I are having dinner together around 6:30. You're welcome to join us."

"Oh, no. Thanks anyway. I think I'll hang around here. I've had all the social contacts I care to have for awhile," Jeremy said, airing out his smelly shirt by flopping the front of it away from his chest. Henry was glad to see he still had the remnants of a sense of humor.

He was about to drive away when he heard Philip calling him. Dressed in a terry cloth robe, the young man bounded down the apartment stairs and over to the car. Apparently he had just stepped out of the shower for beads of water still stood on his dark hair and dripped from his beard with every jerk of the jaw.

"Dad, I'm going to have to cancel out on the dinner invitation."

"Oh, why so?"

"Tracy has been released from the hospital and I want to spend time with her. She's partly immobilized and needs help—"

"She's welcome to come along with us."

"I don't think she'll feel up to it."

"Well, we needn't be long. I'm sure she can find a roommate or someone to sit with her while we eat. She has to eat too, doesn't she?"

"Sure, but—"

"I'm not going to be around long. I think you can spare the time."

Philip hung his wet head and looked at the ground, deep in thought. Rather than wait for another excuse from him, Henry slipped the car into reverse.

"I'll see you a little after six, son."

Philip reluctantly let the car door slip out of his grasp. Henry swung the car around and watched through the rearview mirror as his son went slowly back up the steps.

Chapter Eleven

Henry went by his motel office and checked for messages. Nothing from Chapin yet. He wished he had gotten a firm time commitment out of his old boss about the replacement. Then on foot he retraced his early morning steps across the campus leading to the student fair area and the now infamous humiliation stocks. It was still roped off with the police's yellow line, and several curiosity seekers were standing about gesturing and making guesses about how the event must have happened. Apparently all the fair activities had been cancelled for the day, because the booths that hadn't been taken down stood by forlornly like the last remnants of an Elizabethan ghost town. But the stocks which held everyone's attention cast a different kind of spell; its connection with violent and mysterious death had somehow imbued its boards with a chilling fascination. Henry found himself being mesmerized by the place himself and had to shake his mind free in order to continue his real purpose on campus.

Referring to the handy little map of the campus he found on the back of the faculty address book he was still carrying, he made his way toward the science buildings.

The offices for the geology professors all seemed to face onto one common hallway on the first floor of the Foster building. Except for two professors working away at their desks, all the offices including Pangbourne's were closed up. One small room with a computer terminal in it seemed to be the only room that would remain open when the instructors weren't there. Henry continued on out of the building, passing some rather small hedges on his way toward the biology building. He noticed there were well-placed campus-walk lights all along the way.

He found the lecture room in the biology building he was looking for. A four o'clock class was just letting out and Henry waited until the students and their professor left, then he stepped in and surveyed the sterile looking windowless room. Although it was large he could see at a glance there was not another person there. Rows of plastic arm chairs on terraced levels looked down on a smudged blackboard and a long demonstration table. On the teacher's side of the table were several small compartments, all locked. But in the middle of the table there was a kneehole for the speaker, should he or she decide to address the class while sitting at the counter. The kneehole was large enough to hide a person.

Henry was rationalizing these possibilities as he studied the small map. The conference room adjacent to the lecture hall where the three professors had their meeting was on the north side of the hall. Since Pangbourne's office was south of the hall he probably cut through the lecture hall on his way back to his office. Conversely, Hazard and Mumford probably went out a door on the north side of the building since the faculty parking lot was in that direction.

Someone could have been in the lecture hall during the meeting, perhaps listening at the door then hiding when the meeting was about to break up. The lights were probably off. Henry played with the switches trying to simulate what might have occurred. He found he had a great latitude in light level for the room. By controlling a dimmer switch he was able to put a series of faint overhead lights on the tiered chairs, probably designed for note-taking during films, but the front of the room remained in near total darkness. For someone coming from a well-lit room the change would leave the person virtually helpless for several seconds. The murderer would wait until Pangbourne had groped his way past the counter, then step out and strike him. This seemed much more plausible than someone waiting for him in bushes along the sidewalk. At 9:20, classes were just beginning to get out.

But if this was the way it happened it would mean the murderer not only knew Pangbourne's schedule, but he probably knew his own way around campus. While he was pondering this, Henry walked over to the conference room door and pushed it open. It was dark inside, but rather than walk back across the lecture hall to the light switch to give himself more light he decided to feel about for the switch. This was a mistake. It wasn't on the wall panel next to the door as he expected and as he stepped into the room his right shin came in sharp contact with a metal object. Whatever it was, it created a pleasant metallic twang followed by the jingle of glassware. Henry stood still and tried to hum softly a few bars of "The Stars and Stripes Forever." Finally the slip of light from the doorsill on the north side of the room spread about enough for him to spot the switch, about three inches from his reaching fingers.

Hazard had described the room correctly; it measured approximately twelve by twenty-four feet with one corner devoted to meeting space with a long table and chairs, and the necessary coffeeepot in the corner. But most of the room was reserved for storage of biology materials. One

135

entire wall was dedicated to jars of preserved marine organisms, many of them still emitting chilling lifelike appearances. The object that caught the attention of Henry's shin was a metal four-wheel cart with several small bottles all neatly lined up with labels and measuring markings on the side. If his memories of beginning college biology served correctly, these bottles were part of the supplies for lab tests on small animals. He stood up the three bottles that he'd upset, then gently pushed the large, cumbersome cart over to a part of the room that would leave the traffic area clear.

Someone whistling in a happy, off-key manner was approaching from outside on the north side of the building. A key sounded in the lock and the door swung open in a jerky motion. A college-age girl in a white smock, struggling with a large tray of bottles, came backing into the room.

"Hello," Henry said.

"Oh, my gosh," the girl cried, almost losing control of her tray. "You scared the life out of me. There usually isn't anyone around this time of day." She slid the tray onto a nearby counter top.

"Sorry about that. I'm Mr. Garrett."

"Oh, hi. I'm the lab technician, Bonny. Can I help you?"

"I was wondering if Dr. Mumford's office is around here."

"Yeah, it's right next door here," she said, pointing a thumb toward the door on the west side of the room. "You from the hospital or something?"

"Hospital? No, I'm not. I don't suppose Dr. Mumford is still about, is he?"

She gave a slight chuckle. "No, he certainly isn't. I take it you haven't heard what happened to him."

"Has there been an accident?"

"I don't think you could say accident," she said, unlocking a glass supply cabinet. As they talked she proceeded to put all the bottles from the tray and the large cart back in their proper places, under lock and key. "I think it was a stroke or something. That's why I was wondering if you were from the hospital to pick up some of his stuff."

"Would you mind telling me what happened?"

"You a friend of his?"

"We met at the cafeteria today. I was hoping to talk to him again. I'm investigating Dr. Pangbourne's death."

"Oh, yeah. Man, weird things have been happening around this place," she said, shaking her head.

"Dr. Mumford—did he pass out or . . . "

"No, oh, no. He was wide awake through it all, if you can call it that. He had a one o'clock lecture in the hall right next door here. I got him going and I was waiting here— waiting for him to buzz for me. I'm his lab tech. He was reviewing for finals and I was to bring out a dissected frog for review when he buzzed for it. But about ten minutes into the class a coupla students came busting in here yelling and calling for help. I went in the hall and saw Dr. Mumford standing at the lecture table. It was scarey, man. His hair was sort of on end and he had knocked off his own glasses, the students said. And he kept shouting over and over, 'This can't go on. This can't go on.' And he had a wearied look on his face. Some of the girls in the class were crying and all.

"I dismissed the class and some of the guys and I steered Mumford in here and got him quieted down a little before the school nurse and the dean of students got over here."

"Once he quieted down, did he seem all right to you?"

"Oh, I don't think so. He could follow us around with his eyes, you know, but I never did hear him say anything but, 'This can't go on.' I heard that people with strokes sometimes latch onto one word or phrase and can't say anything else. I bet he had a stroke."

Henry thought of the browbeating Mumford had endured at the hands of Dr. Hazard that noon. "Did he seem upset before the lecture?"

"Not that I could notice. He just stuck his head in the door there to make sure I had the cart ready to wheel in, then he started lecturing."

"So you don't know of anything that could have caused it?"

"No, he seemed pretty normal. He forgot his keys this morning. I even had to let him in his own office. That's about the only thing out of the ordinary."

"You suppose the students were acting up or anything?"

"Oh, not that group," Bonny smiled. "That was his pet class. You had to be a sharp biology major just to get in there. He picked his teaching aids and everything from that group."

"I see," Henry said, then ambled over to the cart and played with one of the small corked bottles. "Any possibility he could have exposed himself to some chemical that would—"

"No, he was just talking, without anything on the counter. O' course, there's always the possibility he's got a PCP lab hidden in the basement somewheres. I'm joking, of course. Dr. Mumford is a fine man. Very straight arrow."

"I see. And do you know what hospital they took him to?"

"Why, University Hospital, of course."

"Oh, of course."

Chapter Twelve

The clerk at the lost-and-found window in the administration building had suggested to Henry that he check back with her later in the day. She had promised to do some looking around for the missing briefcase. But when he got there the window was already closed for the day. A few feet away were the mail slots where the faculty picked up their campus mail. Henry went to the front of the boxes and tried to look through them to see if the clerk was still in the room behind the closed window. He couldn't see any signs of life.

But the mail slots did give him an idea. What had become of Pangbourne's campus mail? M . . . O . . . P . . . He ran his fingers over the cubicles, then came to rest at "Pangbourne." It was jam-packed with letters and circulars but on the front of the whole pack was a brief note, "Dr. P., please see me. Harriet."

As he was pushing the mail back into its place Henry became aware of someone watching him. That someone let out a whistle, then called "Peterson." Henry quickly looked hehind him and realized that two campus policemen were closing in on him from both ends of the hallway. The one that seemed to be in charge stopped a few feet from Henry, rested his hand on his nightstick and asked, "Sir, could I ask you what your business is here at these mail-boxes?"

"What? I, ah, was just checking to see if anyone had picked up Dr. Pangbourne's mail."

"Have you been authorized to pick up Dr. Pangbourne's mail?"

"Well, no, I haven't . . . "

"Would you mind stepping in here a minute, sir?" the officer said, pointing toward a secretarial office opposite the mailboxes. When Henry hesitated, the officer named Peterson took a half-step back which made it appear any false move would elicit a physical confrontation. Henry gingerly walked into the office and stood next to the desk so that he would be facing both officers rather than being sandwiched between them.

For a minute or so he verbally sparred with them, returning their questions with questions of his own, not wishing to expose his unique connection with the police unless it became necessary. Verifying such a thing could take hours. And the campus police were not about to explain their interest in questioning him either.

Then he saw his way out. In the corner of his eye Henry spotted the familiar well-tailored figure of Dr. Hazard in the hall, busily stuffing mimeographed notices in some of the mailboxes. The police were finally persuaded to open the door and let Dr. Hazard vouch for their suspect.

"Yes, Burt, he's clean," Hazard said with a smile. "As a matter of fact, he is with the city police investigating Dr. Pangbourne's death."

"Oh, okay then," Burt backed off. "We didn't know.

140

We were told to challenge everyone, you understand. Anyone we didn't recognize."

"What is the trouble, Dr. Hazard?" Henry asked.

"Oh, I think some of the students got a bit too anxious about their grades. There've been some papers taken from the mail slot of the dean of instruction."

"Oh? When was this?"

"Yesterday I believe . . . "

"It was reported this morning, sir," Burt corrected him.

"But the box may have been robbed yesterday, is my point," Hazard said.

"You mean everything was taken or just a packet or whatever with the grades?" Henry asked.

Hazard looked to the officer for the answer. Burt said, "Everything was taken. It was picked clean. And our clerk remembers there was quite a bundle there when she sorted the mail yesterday afternoon.

"Peterson, maybe you better get back out and keep an eye on the boxes," Burt said, and the other officer returned to his watching post.

"I admire your thoroughness, Burt, but aren't you carrying this a bit too far?"

"I'm just following orders, doctor. We're to watch until we close up the building. Dean's orders."

Hazard shrugged and started back to his distribution task. "Oh, by the way," he turned again to Henry, "I believe I've solved the riddle regarding Dr. Pangbourne's third version of the summer geology program."

"Oh, have you?"

"Yes, I started calling people on our second list and it appears our friend T.T. Halverson from Florida State has had to cancel out due to his wife's illness. That no doubt was the change Ralph was making on the schedule."

"I see. And you know who was to substitute—"

141

"It's a bit late for that now. We'll just keep his name in. Halverson agreed to send his paper on anyway and we'll simply have someone read it for him. Not very good for the question-and-answer session but it's the best we can do under the circumstances. I'm looking into the possibility of a telephone hookup for that. Oh, here, you might be interested in one of these," Hazard said, handing Henry one of the flyers he was putting in the mail slots. It was an announcement for a memorial service for Dr. Pangbourne to be held in the university chapel Monday at 10:30.

"Thank you. I suppose you heard about Dr. Mumford's problems."

Hazard stuffed for a bit without answering. Then, "Yes, poor old John. I hope it wasn't brought on by our lunch."

"Do you know if it was a stroke?"

"Stroke? No, no. Doctors say fatigue, but of course, they're still running tests. No sign of stroke."

"I suppose seeing him is out of the question."

"No doubt. I talked to his wife a few moments ago. Even she is only seeing him in brief intervals. Poor old John. I'm afraid his teaching days are about over."

Henry stopped in front of Pangbourne's mail again. "I see there's a note here from someone named Harriet. Have any idea who that might be?"

Hazard glanced at the note quickly, then, "Oh, that's our clerk. No doubt she put that on there merely to let Ralph know there was more mail for him than she could get in the slot. You can buzz her if you like," he said, pointing at a button above the mail slots. "She doubles on the switchboard from 4:30 to 5:30."

Henry pushed the button.

Hazard smiled. "You folks aren't leaving a stone unturned, are you?"

"Not if we can help it. Why?"

142

"Oh, nothing. I admire you for it. Wish I could help in some way."

"But you think we're wasting our time. Is that it?"

"No, it's not that. I'm sure you find a lot of dead ends in looking for clues. I'm sure it's all necessary. My smile is one of nervousness. I've never been involved in anything like this before."

"Do you think Dr. Mumford's problem might somehow be connected to Dr. Pangbourne's death?"

This erased the smile from Hazard's face as he started to contemplate this possibility. But before he could answer, a woman's voice called from behind the mail slots, "Can I help you, Dr. Hazard?"

"Oh, not me, Harriet, but this gentleman would like to ask you some questions about Dr. Pangbourne's mail."

The top part of the Dutch door opened up and a plump, older woman wearing a phone operator's headset looked out. "What do you need? I still have to listen for the board."

"I was wondering who would be looking after Dr. Pangbourne's mail. I'm sure the police would be interested in looking through it."

"Well, I don't know. This problem has never come up before. I suppose the police could have it. The wife has already looked through everything."

"She has? When was this?"

"Oh, sometime this afternoon. I really don't remember what time."

"Did she take anything?"

"Just a cablegram."

"Cablegram? Did you notice what country it was from?"

"Yes. Israel."

Henry noticed Hazard's attention quicken and the stuffing stop.

143

"And that's all she took?"

"Yes. She asked us to keep any new mail separate and she would be back later to look through it."

"I see . . . " Henry said, deep in thought. Then he noticed Hazard looking at him again, wearing the same knowing smile. Harriet started to swing the Dutch door shut again.

"Oh, one more question. The mail that's missing— what time yesterday did you finish sorting?"

"Oh, golly, we start around 1:00. I'm pretty sure it was still there around 2:30. A lot of our books come United Parcel and we don't put out the U.P. notices until around 2:30."

"And there were United Parcel notices in the dean of instructor's box?"

"Oh, yes. He gets samples of textbooks from publishers almost every day. Oh, there's the board ring. Gotta go."

"Thank you," Henry said to the closing door.

Hazard had finished with his circulars and he came over. "Interesting about that cable, isn't it?"

"Yes."

"I didn't know his wife was back in town. That cable could be rubbing salt in an old wound, couldn't it?"

"Yes, I suppose it could."

"Regarding your earlier question," Hazard went on. "I do hope you didn't misunderstand my little joke this noon about old John being involved somehow in Ralph's death. The man is sixty-nine years old, you know, and when he gets excited he loses all control of that right arm of his. Motive I could grant you, but wherewithal, no."

"Yes, I see your point."

"And one more matter for you to consider, as if you don't have enough on your mind. Do you know the name of our dean of instruction?"

144

"No. I don't think I've heard it."

"Hallard," Hazard said and motioned for Henry to follow him. He stopped and pointed at the mail slots reserved for deans and department heads. These were larger and separated from the other faculty boxes. His finger was on a small nameplate that read, "Dean G. Hallard."

"The similarity leads to a lot of confusion. Mine is right beneath his—W. Hazard."

"So you're thinking someone else may have been confused too? They may have been after your mail and—"

"Exactly. A stranger wouldn't expect there to be a Hallard and a Hazard and both deans."

"Have you been expecting anything unusual?"

"I've been trying to think of what it might be. All I can come up with that would be out of the ordinary would be correspondence regarding our summer geology program."

"But you'll let us know if anything unusual turns up."

"Oh, by all means," Hazard said. "Well, I must be off. If you think it is safe for you to walk the halls of our institution without further attacks on your person I will leave you, or could I drop you someplace?"

"No thanks. I think I need the walk."

It was a short stretch back to the motel from there but it afforded enough time for Henry to run these latest events through his mind and to separate the wheat from the chaff. The Mumford breakdown could have been caused by so many different things it was virtually useless to try to speculate on the matter. But the pilfering of the mailbox—if it's involved with Pangbourne's murder it could turn the murder into a federal case, whether Chapin liked it or not. But what of the two deans and—it could mean someone like Steckman ripped off the mail. He no doubt wouldn't know about the names. But why would he be into either box? If he was shadowing Pangbourne he

145

must have known he had been in physical contact with Hazard. Why the mailbox then? And then again it may have nothing to do with the case.

Henry groaned aloud and rubbed his forehead as he walked; what kind of a puzzle was this anyway? The whole thing turning on fits and starts. Nothing coming clear. Each time he felt he had ahold of a piece of the puzzle it seemed to break apart in his hand and become the new pieces that didn't fit together, much less fit into a master view. What was missing? What was the key? He got called into the matter because of Chapin. Supposedly, the scientists were trying to take the government's property, but then once on the scene the head man changed his mind. As though it were some joke. Why bother making a joke out of that? Then Pangbourne implies there is something fishy going on on board, but what?

And Henry's attempts to get back together with his son seemed to be backfiring as well, and was he helping to clear Jeremy Bruce's name only to see his son take his place as the prime suspect? Maybe he should have stayed at home tending his garden.

Henry closed his eyes and for a moment saw Wendel Hazard's face smiling at him. Smiling that superior, half-smirk of a smile. Was he secretly laughing at their floundering, or was he really smiling out of nervousness? What was it Abe Lincoln had said? After the age of forty a man is responsible for his own appearance. He wondered if Abe would extend his axiom to cover a smirk-smile. In that moment he was tempted to agree with Scottie; he'd like to pin the rap on Hazard just to see that know-it-all smirk get wiped off his face. But that was fatigue talking. He had to keep cool, he told himself. Keep cool and keep working.

146

Chapter Thirteen

Still nothing from Chapin at the motel desk. He went to his room, washed up, pulled out a clean shirt and tie, then checked his watch. Just five-thirty. He looked longingly at the bed. There was time and it would feel so good on the back. But then he thought of the Frankfurt Hotel and the similar back spasms two years ago when, after relaxing in bed for a couple of hours, he had to call a maid and porter to help him get into an upright position again, and the unbelievable pain that nearly made him black out. Vertical was bearable, horizontal was a bit better, but getting from one position to the other without bellering was the trick. It wasn't worth the risk.

He eased down onto the desk chair and opened his dog-eared Bible at the concordance. What would it have listed under family? In just the short period of time he had been doing this he'd gained a new respect for and almost a fear from reading this surprising book, like an amateur electrician climbing around in a dusty old attic and being jarred to life by gripping two live wires he thought were long since dead. He had been surprised and startled through the Psalms. The contemporary significance of those old passages as seen through his newborn eyes had sent him reeling more than once. And now in Paul's letter to the Colossians he was hit with more personal bombletts:

Children, obey your parents in all things: for this is
well-pleasing unto the Lord.

That was enough to warm the cockles of any father's heart. Unfortunately, it was quickly followed with the admonition:

Fathers, provoke not your children to anger, lest
they be discouraged.

That hit close to home. He had provoked the boy's anger. But now that it was done, how could he make amends? He wished he could flip the pages and miraculously pick a verse at random that would solve all his problems. After all, wasn't he willing and waiting for God to use him? He read on for a bit until he found his mind wandering, then went into the bathroom and hung by his arms from the shower stall overhang, trying to get a few moments of relief.

As Henry was hanging and swaying there, the last verse he had read began disturbing him:

And whatsoever ye do, do it heartily, as to the Lord,
and not to men.

Whatever you do—do it heartily—and do it for the Lord, not Philip. Was it possible he was being too concerned with Philip's thoughts toward him? And like it or not, he had taken on the assignment for Chapin. Was it possible he was not doing everything he could on the investigation?

The image of Mrs. Pangbourne popped into his mind. Why did she suddenly appear at the school going through the mail? He expected her to be spending her afternoon in church. Perhaps if her "period of mourning" was over he should give her a call. He got the number out of his trusty little faculty address book and dialed the Pangbourne house. The line was busy. Henry checked his watch again and estimated he could get over to the house to see her and still get back in time for the dinner with Philip. He slipped on his shirt, hung his coat and tie over his shoulder, and hit the door, all without a second thought for his back.

On the way over he formulated in his mind a diplomatic way he might ask the necessary questions, but when he arrived he cancelled all the canned rhetoric. The hi-fi was blaring a lively old Glen Miller number which came across nicely through the porch woodwork. He rang the chimes a second time before the door finally swung open. Sylvia Pangbourne greeted him with a loud friendly, "Hi there," and raised skyward the highball glass in her hand. She was done up in a black party outfit with a low-cut sequined blouse and silk pajama slacks.

"Mr. Gar-Gar, isn't it? You're just in time to verify my story."

She grabbed Henry by the hand and pulled him into the living room where a man and two ladies with concerned faces sat.

"Listen, everyone, this is the policeman that saw me do it. Go on, tell 'em how I shot down that crummy old chandelier. Didn't I?"

"Yes, you did," Henry said.

One of the ladies rose from the couch and tried to talk Mrs. Pangbourne into sitting down. "Sylvia, honey, let's eat something. Fran brought a nice salad—"

"Those are my neighbors, Mr. Garrett. They think they're gonna sober me up. You see, they don't understand about Irish wakes."

"What's that? I can't hear you," Henry said. The other man in the room got up and turned off the stereo.

149

"Oh, don't stop the music, Bernie," Sylvia scolded. "You gotta have music at an Irish wake. I think I'm entitled to an Irish wake if I want one, don't you, Mr. Garrett? After all I am Irish."

"How're you going to do that?" Bernie asked, kiddingly, "You don't have a body. You've got to have a body before you can have a wake."

"Oh," Sylvia said, momentarily stumped. "Well then, we'll have half a wake. That's it. That's what we'll do. And it's just right too, because I'm only half Irish." This she found terribly funny and had to seat herself for fear of falling down in her hysterics.

Henry was about to excuse himself when her laughter started tailing off and she studied him.

"Don't go, Mr. Garrett, you just got here. Join the party."

"I think I'll come back when you're—later."

"When I'm sober? You may have a long wait, my friend the policeman. What is it you want?"

"I heard you were over to the university today.

"You betcha I was."

"Were you looking for something special in your husband's mail?"

"Yeah, that's right. A letter. He wrote me a letter."

"Did he send you a letter?"

"He said he did. Remember that note he left me on the hall table? Well, he said he wrote me a letter."

"Why didn't you tell us about that when we were here before?"

"Because I figured it was none of your damn business."

"Sylvia . . . " her neighbor admonished her. Sylvia went on.

"I went over every inch of this crummy ol' house. Said it was important. I looked in his office. I looked everywhere. Then I looked in his mailbox. He used to leave his paycheck in the mailbox for me to come by and pick it up. And sometimes he'd leave a mushy love note, too. Sometimes they were so bad I'd have to tear 'em up on the spot for fear of having an accident and having 'em found on my body. But there was no little love note for ol' Sylvia this time. Oh no. He musta been drunk, too. He sent the letter to the wrong woman. No more mash notes for Sylvia."

"So he wrote to the Israeli girl?"

"Oh, you know about that, do you? Of course, you would. It's always the wife who's the last to know. Well, here, let's let the whole world know." She rose and staggered over to the piano and pulled the cablegram from her purse. "This is what I found in the mailbox instead of a letter to me. It's a reply to a letter from Ralph. Ol' Ralphy boy playing his last little joke on ol' Sylvia. Ain't it a beaut? Just listen, 'Darling, darling.' One darling's not enough. She's gotta use two. 'I forgave you before you even asked.' Isn't that touching now? He musta been naughty to her. Oh, Ralphy, Ralphy. But now listen, ol' Ralphy, the letter writer is slipping. She says, 'Your letter confusing. Do you want me come USA? Can be free to travel July one. On pins and needles. Love, Veronica.' "

She crumpled the cable in her hand and stared at it. "Well, little Jezebel Veronica, there'll be no USA for you, little girl. There'll be no Victorian mansion for you to mess about in, you, you . . . It'll be over my dead body. My dead body and Ralph's dead body. Oh, Ralph . . . "

The two neighbor ladies were at her side as the heavy sobs started rolling out. But she had one more outburst before the crying and the numbing of the liquor took over, "Well, hotshot Ralphy, what do you think? You made me so mad I went back to church and blew out your candle. What do you think of that? No candle for you, Ralphy."

The women finally got her seated and went into the

time-honored holding and patting tradition of the species. The two men stood around not knowing what to do with their eyes or hands. Finally, Henry excused himself and backed out of the house.

Chapter Fourteen

The trafffic was heavier than he expected and he didn't get back to the university and his son's apartment until 6:45. Philip and the girl were standing at the foot of the stairs waiting for him. The wait hadn't done much for Philip's temperament. But while he didn't mind showing his rudeness to his father he was very considerate and helpful with Tracy. He helped her get into the front seat, then climbed into the back and directed his father toward a small Italian restaurant. Tracy was locked into a cumbersome looking arm cast and she wore a cosmetic dressing over the upper corner of her left eye. Except for being a little groggy from medication she claimed she was feeling fine and glad to be out for a little while.

The restaurant seemed to cater exclusively to university students. Henry observed the important things of college life haven't really changed; he recalled eating in a place very much like this in his own college days.

After they ordered their meal there was an awkward pause in the conversation flow. The silence was broken when Tracy said, "Philip tells me you recently moved to

California. How do you like it?"

"We like it. We like the casualness of the life-style out here as compared to back east. I guess the word is 'laid back,' isn't it?"

She gave him a courtesy smile and played with her water glass. Philip, it seemed, was checking to see if all the wallpaper in the room was hung straight.

Henry said, "You a native Californian, are you?"

"Mm-hmm. Born and bred right here in La Jolla."

"Mmm. And now you're in the university graduate program?"

"Yes, in geology. Same as Philip."

"How did an attractive girl like you happen to get into geology?"

"Now there's a chauvinistic question if I've ever heard one," she kidded him. "My father's in research for some oil companies and I always enjoyed tagging along with him."

"You must be doing quite well. I understand it was quite an accomplishment to be included on the *Inquisitor* expedition."

"Yes, well, that's what I used to think," Tracy said, between quick side-glances at Philip. "I thought it rather curious that I would make the list since Philip's grade point average was higher than mine, but then I guess I had some other attributes that didn't show up on the charts . . . " She swirled her water glass with a surprising vigor, then said, "I shoulda listened to my mother."

Philip readjusted his chair but didn't speak.

"That reminds me," she continued. "Philip tells me you've recently had quite a religious experience."

"Yes, I ah, yes, I have."

"Or isn't that something I should be talking about?"

"Oh, no, I'm happy to talk about it. As a matter of fact, part of the reason I came down to San Diego was to tell

Philip about it. But now that I get down to it I don't know if I can explain to someone else what has happened to me."

She leaned forward with interest, "You mean you've been born again, like, like Nixon's old aide, what's his name? Colson?"

"Yes, I think that's a good description."

"Is it?" Philip asked.

Henry was surprised to hear from him. "Is it what?"

"I think it's the wrong term to use—*born again.*"

"What would you call it then?" Tracy asked.

"I'd call it just the opposite. I'd call it dying."

"Dying?" Henry asked.

"Of course. Anyone who believes in God is already intellectually dead. He's already given his whole brain process to someone else. If that isn't dying, I don't know what you call it."

Philip was talking to his father but he was addressing everything he said to Tracy as though she were a necessary interpreter. He went on at some length explaining the importance of original thinking and how educated man was the master of his own destiny.

"But is it really so easy to psychoanalyze anyone—" she started, but Philip interrupted.

"Oh, I don't think it's too difficult in this case. After all, I've been an observer for quite a few years. Actually the whole scene is rather simple, almost predictable from where I sit. You see, my father found himself in an intolerable situation. He found himself working for an organization that was doing evil and sinister things to an unsuspecting world. He found himself in an anxiety crunch. So what does he do? Does he do the intellectually honest thing and write a book or a series of articles exposing the errant organization? Oh, no! He takes an easier way. He bails out. Stop the world, he wants to get off. Just give me a set of simple rules to go by and leave me alone. Let someone

155

else make the hard choices in life; just give me that old-time religion—"

"Philip!" Tracy cried. "That's a terrible way to talk to your father."

Philip turned his sorrowful dark eyes to hers, "You think it gives me pleasure to say it? But it's the truth."

"The truth? Who elected you dispenser of the truth? I think maybe you got an overdeveloped sense of self-righteousness."

He studied her and flexed the muscles in his jaw. Then: "Funny you never seemed to notice it before your ocean cruise."

"Yes, it is, isn't it? I suppose I should say 'touché.' "

"I didn't mean that. I'm sorry."

"Oh, are you now? Are you really?" she said with a steel edge on her manner.

The salad arrived but it did little to change the heavy atmosphere hanging about the table. The young people passed the bread sticks and ate politely but without appetite. Henry munched thoughtfully, then said, "There is a good deal of truth in what Philip says. Perhaps I would never have converted if I hadn't come to the end of my tether, as it were. I think Lincoln put it well when he said he turned to God because of an overwhelming conviction he had nowhere else to go. But I don't buy this idea that I'm somehow retreating from the world. I figure the smart thing to do when you are sick is go to the hospital; when you are thirsty you go to the well . . . "

Before he could get wound up, a group of Tracy's friends came over to the table to find out about her cast and to sympathize with her. She told them she had fallen down her steps.

Henry felt a sense of inner panic as he realized his moment was passing and he had not communicated. Perhaps if the girl had not been along, or perhaps if this murder business were not lurking in the back of everyone's mind, he might be able to get at what he wanted to say.

While the girls had changed the conversation to some light campus gossip about a basketball player and cribbing, Henry looked across the table at his son and remembered his strained relations with his own father. There had been time in Henry's sophomore year in college when he was home for a fall weekend and his father had asked him to go duck hunting with him. But Henry had an interest in a blonde, blue-eyed neighbor girl and he rebelled at the prospect of spending the precious forty-eight hours sitting in a cold damp duck blind, flailing away with shotguns at birds he cared nothing about. When he had refused his father's repeated invitation they exchanged heated words; his father had gone storming out of the house leaving Henry free to while away his hours with the little blonde, who it turned out was destined to become the wife of one of Iowa's greatest pig breeders.

It wasn't until many years and three children later that Henry realized the significance of that moment from his father's point of view. He hadn't lacked for companionship on his duck hunting outings; there were always several business associates to go along with him if he wished. But it was his son's companionship he wanted. He wanted to be part of his future, to have a feeling of oneness, to share from his own experience what he'd learned from life, and to learn and laugh with his son about what is new and exciting in the outside world.

Henry knew all that to be true now as he looked across at his own son because that same scene was being played again, except this time he found himself in the role of the other character. Were the young always destined to be so self-centered? The sins of the children are revisited upon the same children, only now grown older.

Henry was finally shaken from his reverie to find the

157

table-hoppers gone and Tracy was asking him, apparently for the second time, what he knew about Dr. Mumford's breakdown. He shared what he had learned from the girl Bonny in the preparation room, which wasn't new to Tracy or Philip. Apparently the word had spread rapidly across campus.

Henry asked, "Do most people think there's a connection between his breakdown and Dr. Pangbourne's, ah, death?"

"Oh, yes, they were friends, you know," Tracy said.

"They were?" Henry said and looked to Philip for confirmation.

"As far as I know they were. I know they had lunch together frequently."

"That's curious . . . "

"Why do you say that?" Tracy asked.

"I got the distinct impression Dr. Mumford did not get on too well with the geology department people. Dr. Hazard and he were arguing about a new associate instructor position—"

Tracy interrupted. "Oh, that! Yes, well, Pangbourne wasn't above dangling that plum in front of a lot of people. I think he implied to Mumford it would go to biology. He also had all us graduate geology students falling all over each other doing little favors for him to stay in his good graces."

"Suppose Dr. Mumford got word the position was going to a geology applicant," Henry asked. "Do you think he would be angry enough to kill over it?"

Philip and Tracy exchanged looks and smiled, "Dad, Mumford's got to be close to seventy. How's he going to overpower a man like Pangbourne?"

"You agree?" he asked Tracy. "It's possible Pangbourne was taken completely by surprise."

"Well, I think he would do anything to protect his department. He is very dedicated to helping his students.

158

I'd say he's the most conscientious teacher I've ever had. But he's such a *nice* old man. No. I can't see him doing such a thing."

"And what about Hazard?"

"That guy's a cold fish," Philip began. "He's calculating enough but I can't see him as the violent type. I'd say if he were going to kill someone he'd do it with poison or a high-powered rifle. But why would he want Pangbourne dead? He owed his job to him. Pangbourne plucked him out of a dead-end job in a junior college."

"You don't think a little professional jealousy might have got to him? Maybe he wanted to be the real division chairman instead of just in name only?"

Philip and Tracy exchanged quizzical looks again. This time Tracy answered, "If he was jealous of Dr. Pangbourne he certainly never showed it. And I don't think he's ever written a professional paper. He just doesn't have the standing in the academic community to challenge a Pangbourne."

They each sat lost in their own thoughts until their main courses arrived and the conversation turned to lighter subjects. Yes, Becky was planning to return east in the fall for her senior year. No, Philip's mother did not seem to miss being away from the eastern seaboard as Henry had expected. And yes, the new house really had four upstairs bedrooms.

As father and son chatted on about family matters, Henry noticed a dark look of concern creep into Tracy's expression.

"Please excuse our family chatter, Tracy," Henry said.

"Oh, that's okay. I'm glad to know more about Philip's family."

"You aren't in pain, are you?"

"What? Oh, no," she laughed. "I was just thinking about something maybe the police should know."

159

Both father and son quickly gave her their undivided attention.

"Oh, it's no big deal. It probably doesn't mean a thing. Just a curious coincidence probably," she hesitated.

"Well, what is it?" Philip said. "Drop the other shoe. You mean something on board ship?"

"Not exactly. Dr. Pangbourne told us the story on board ship. But it apparently happened here in town at his house. He related this incident to a group of us on deck one evening when we were telling stories. I think the general topic was bothersome neighbors. Anyway, it seemed his house is in a nice older section of town and it backs up to the house owned by one of our city councilmen. And Ralph—Dr. Pangbourne—and this city councilman didn't get along too well. Politically there was no common ground between the two of them, and the councilman's dog, a big boxer bulldog, used to break through the hedge that divided their properties and use the Pangbourne yard for his privy. The councilman thought that was very funny.

"Then one Sunday when Dr. Pangbourne had a lot of work to do the councilman had a big fish-fry party in his backyard. The councilman prided himself on being a great deep-sea fisherman and he was hosting the fish fry of his own catches for all his city hall pals. I remember reading about the incident in the papers about a year ago, so I know it's factual."

"If it was in the papers," Philip put in, "don't you think the police would know about it already?"

"But they don't know what actually happened. I mean the whole story. Now let me finish. This dog was rather special. He did a lot of tricks and the councilman was showing him off to the people before their dinner. Each time Fido did a trick they would toss him a piece of shellfish they were cooking. Dr. Pangbourne was watching all this from his study window. Finally, the noise of the party

160

got so bad—apparently they had rock-and-roll records piped into the backyard—he called up the councilman to ask them to pipe down. The councilman read him chapter and verse from city ordinances justifying the loud music for that part of the day and told him to bug off.

"Well, that tore it for Pangbourne. He got a bit of hamburger from the refrigerator, went sneaking out into the backyard and coaxed the big bulldog through the hedge into his own yard."

She leaned forward and continued in a more confidential tone so they wouldn't be overheard. "He took the dog into his garage and killed it!"

"Killed it?" Philip asked, his eyes widening.

Tracy nodded, "He killed the dog. Then with some tubing and his tire pump he pumped air into its intestinal tract until the dog's carcass appeared bloated. Then he carried the dog over to the front door of the councilman's house and laid it on its back, spread-eagled on the threshold with its big belly showing."

Philip started laughing in anticipation. She went on, smiling to herself now, "It wasn't long before the dinner was over and the first dinner guests started to leave. When they saw the dog they screamed and the party turned into a panic."

"They figured the dog died from bad shellfish," Philip laughed.

"Of course," she said, "but just in case they didn't know what to do next, Pangbourne started calling ambulance services and emergency hospitals, using the councilman's name, and saying they all needed their stomachs pumped. I guess there were something like fifteen ambulances on the scene before the evening was over, people sprawled out on the lawn with induced vomiting, most of the guests hauled away—to hospitals—"

Philip was getting tears in his eyes from laughing so

161

hard. Tracy was being infected again just from watching him and she had to brace herself against her cast to keep the giggles from hurting her too much.

"That's Pangbourne," Philip cried. "Oh, yes. That's Pangbourne . . . We're really gonna miss that man . . . "

"But the coup de grace . . . ," she sputtered "the coup de grace, as he called it, was when he called the press, anonymously of course, and told them which hospital the councilman was in."

This brought on more laughter.

"Needless to say that was the councilman's last fish fry," she said and leaned on the flimsy Philip for support.

As they started to sober up Philip finally noticed his father was wearing only a slight smile. "You don't think that's funny, Dad?"

"Oh yes. Funny . . . Man's inhumanity to man I guess is always man's basic source of humor."

"But the style of the man, don't you see? You could have used him in your old company," Philip said and shook with laughter again. Perhaps it was because Philip was at the end of a tough sobering semester and the girl was freed from a confined shipboard life, whatever the reason, their laughter attack continued far beyond what the story warranted. Finally in a somewhat weakened condition they started quieting down.

"I can believe Pangbourne would do such a stunt," Henry said, "but why do you think the police should know about it?"

"What?" Tracy asked, drying her tears. "Oh, oh, I almost forgot. It was the way he killed the dog. I should have mentioned it."

"And how was that?"

"He didn't want to leave any telltale marks on it, you see, so he suffocated it by tying a plastic bag over its head."

"I see, yes . . . " Henry looked back and forth between the students. They were definitely through laughing now. "And you think someone who heard that story may have gotten an idea from it?"

"I don't know. It may be just coincidence."

"But it may have given the murderer his idea," Philip said. "So it must be someone on board who heard that story."

"Not necessarily," Henry said. "I get the feeling our Dr. Pangbourne was not only fond of practical jokes; he liked to brag about performing them, too. After all, isn't that half the fun in doing them in the first place? No. I'd guess he told that story more than once."

"But the stomach pumping thing," Tracy pondered. "He'd have to be careful who he told that to or he could find himself in a nice lawsuit, not only for the expensive dog and the hospital bills, but for the pain and mental anguish he caused all those dinner guests."

They were mulling all this over when a high-pitched intermittent tone was heard. Henry turned toward the kitchen.

"I think somebody needs to answer their microwave oven."

"That's you, Dad."

"What?"

"That beeping noise is coming from you."

"Me? Oh, yes . . . " He took the device off his belt loop and turned it off. "Excuse me while I make a phone call."

Chapter Fifteen

He reached the number Blanchard had given him and an operator put him through to the captain; the background sounds told Henry the captain was in a noisy squad car in hot pursuit of something.

"Where are you? I'll send somebody over to pick you up."

"I'm in a restaurant two blocks south of the university on Collins Road. What's up?"

"We think we've spotted your man."

"Steckman?"

"I'm on a pretty popular frequency here. I'll tell you about it when we see you. We have a car headed your way, anyway. Hang loose and we'll have somebody over there in no time." *Click*.

Henry returned to the table and gave Philip his car keys and his MasterCard for the dinner, explaining he would be picked up in a few minutes.

"Who's picking you up?" Philip wanted to know.

"The city police."

"Dad, what's going on? How are you involved? Is it

about Pangbourne's death? It is, isn't it?"

Henry looked into his son's eyes, trying to see what was behind his eager questions. "It's a long story, son. I'm only here to observe. This may be the break they've been looking for." Then to Tracy, "Do you remember a crewman that went by the name of Duffy?"

"Yes. What about him?"

"Any feelings about him?"

"He seemed to be all right. Tended to business. Hung around the radio rooms a lot."

"The radio room number two?"

"Yes, part of the time."

"I thought that was off limits to the regular crews."

"Oh, the two operators didn't mind if we came in when their secret gear wasn't in operation."

"What was in the radio rooms, other than the usual radio equipment?"

"I don't know. In room one was our special depth-sounding gear. Sometimes we could pull in TV signals from satellites on the horizon. Baseball fans would sometimes pester the operators to try to pull in one of the west coast games."

Shortly a horn sounded in front of the restaurant and Henry said hurried good-byes. On the street his heart sank as he saw who was behind the wheel; Scottie pushed open the passenger door on his unmarked police car. Why did it have to be him again?

"Shake a leg. Get in."

He did so and Scottie raced away from the curb. The police radio in the car was turned up high in order to monitor the pursuit progress of the other cars and Henry had to shout in order to be heard.

"Is it Steckman we're after?"

"We think so. He fits your description."

"How'd you happen to find him?"

"We didn't. He found us. Captain had a stakeout at Pangbourne's house and we spotted him trying to jimmy the back door."

"How long had the stakeout been on?" Henry asked.

"Most of the afternoon. Enjoyed your little performance over there around five o'clock," Scottie smiled.

"Where is Steckman now?"

"Shh," Scottie said, and leaned toward the blaring radio as it sent out traveling commands to different police cars. Henry had not been in the states long enough in the last twenty years to pick up any of the code jargon used by the local law enforcement people so it all sounded Greek to him. Finally, Scottie heard the command he was waiting for, gave a brief affirmative response into his mike, then performed a tire squealing 180 in the middle of the busy boulevard they were on and raced in the opposite direction.

"The guy doesn't know the town very well. We think we've got him cornered in a cul-de-sac."

"How'd he get away if you say you had him at the Pangbourne house?"

Scottie had time to shoot him a disgusted look before he shouted, "Part of the new police fair-play policy. We believe in giving a suspect a sporting chance to get away."

During the next ten minutes of racing up and down everything from stretches of freeway to back alleys and listening to the strange intercom commands, Henry deduced what was happening. San Diego is a city divided between the flatland near the ocean and several bluffs east of town. There aren't a lot of access roads between the two areas and it appeared Steckman had gotten himself into one of the lower valleys with nothing but bluffs ahead of him and a host of police cars behind. Since Scottie had been approaching the area from the east, where the university was located, he was ordered to cruise the fingers

166

of the bluff from up above.

This whole chase began to remind Henry of one of his father's protracted hunting expeditions as he and Scottie varied between short fits of activity in which they raced from street to street—all the while listening to hurried undecipherable bursts on the radio, and then several minutes of patient, silent hunting when Steckman's car would be lost from view.

Scottie drove out into a vacant lot and followed what looked like a bike path. There were intermittent areas where weeds blocked their view but Scottie plunged on, the weeds scraping hard on their undercarriage.

"Easy does it, man," Henry counseled. "We can't see where the edge of the bluff is."

"Whatsa matter, no guts?"

"Now that's a dumb thing to say."

"I can see bike tracks. The kids know what they're doing."

But he finally pulled the car to a stop and the two men got out and moved toward the edge on foot. There was no shrubbery near the edge. Just loose dirt on sedimentary brown rock and lots of heavy tracks left by dirt motorcycles where they had plowed up the hill. The cliff was not steep at this point, angling down approximately a forty-five degree angle to the suburb below. They were standing near the tip of the V made by the bluffs, and Scottie pointed down at the streets.

"At least we got the right cul-de-sac."

Through the trees far below they could make out the black-and-whites on many of the streets leading toward them. They all were slowly edging forward, probably checking each alley and parked car as they moved. They could still hear the radio buzz back in the car but there hadn't been a voice on it for several minutes.

Henry checked the horizon. It was going to be a beautiful sunset. A gross of sailboats were playing around near the north end of the bay. By squinting his eyes and using his imagination he could make out the silhouette of the big aircraft carrier at the Navy yards. He thought about the *Inquisitor* and wondered how he had gotten from there to where he now stood. Scottie was shielding his eyes against the sun trying to get a glimpse of the late model T-bird Steckman was supposed to be driving.

"You see anything? It's a light tan car."

"Too many trees."

"C'mon. I'm gonna pull the car over to that point so we can see better."

"I'll stay over on this side," Henry said. "That'll give us two perspectives." He wasn't anxious to get back in the car with Scottie.

"Good idea. Sing out if you spot anything."

Scottie trotted back to the car and swung it around to the other side of the bluff, the car bouncing and pitching as it careened across the uneven ground. He pulled it close to the edge of an outcropping of rock, pulled on his brake, turned down his radio and hopped out of the car, leaving the door open for quick access when the time came. With his hand shielding his eyes and standing on the dusty rock he reminded Henry of a Remington painting—the lone Indian brave gone bad in the city and looking for his way back to his reservation. Or perhaps just scouting a new location for more tepee condominiums.

There was an intensity to the silence there on the hill. The day had been so crammed with noises of human comings and goings that waiting quietly before the wonder of a Pacific sunset seemed strangely out of place. Henry strained for a break in the silence. Car tires whirred their eternal whispers on distant freeways, the cries of kids playing softball on an unseen playground drifted up toward them, a family of wrens in the scrub oak below were cheeping their way through a boundary dispute.

Henry thought of his father sitting pensively in his duck blind. What was he? Perhaps in his early fifties when Henry tagged along with him. With his old red hunting cap, his pale blue eyes and firm weatherbeaten jaw he had always impressed Henry as being very, very wise. In that day a man's true worth was judged by many different standards, but the final standard, the one all men in the community understood, was how a man did his hunting. Father was an expert. Men from all over the county would call or come by the house seeking his advice on the value of a used shotgun or the migratory pattern of the Canadian geese for that hunting season.

Henry was fifty-two himself now, but he didn't feel very wise. He had gained knowledge of many things and had many answers, but life seemed to be constantly changing the questions on him. About the only conclusive statement Henry could make from his experiences was, How very fragile humans are. They break so easily. They use words like *always* and *never* and *perfect* and *honor.* What right do they have to such words when their very bodies scream out to them that this is a very temporal existence, when everything they touch in this world is imperfect, when they know what is honorable but cannot embrace it with their whole heart? Those words are foreign to their very nature. How did they come by them? It must be they were in the breath that God first breathed into man for there had been no evidence they had been self-generated.

Henry blamed his philosophical retreat on the red ball in the west, just now flattening out on the horizon. Oh, it would be nice if they could latch on to Steckman down below. Then if he would confess they could be done with this cat-and-mouse game and Henry could go home and forget about the sinking feeling he had in the pit of his stomach. And the pain, the pain.

He looked over at Scottie and asked with gestures if he saw anything. Scottie only shrugged.

Then an excited voice on the radio announced to Captain Blanchard that car 16-B had just found the elusive T-bird abandoned in a clump of oleander bushes. Henry moved closer to the edge trying to think what oleander bushes look like from this height. The hillside brush to his right started shaking. The wrens' argument was turning violent. But the shaking was too much for wrens. A bare arm came into view, then a head of kinky blond hair. Steckman shrugged to free himself from the dry twigs and scampered up to the crest about twenty feet from Henry.

"Mr. Steckman . . . " Henry called.

Steckman turned toward him like a cornered wild animal. He was out of breath and had light cuts on his body and tears in his sport shirt from his frantic struggle up the hill.

"Garrett—what's the company—doing here?—This has—nothing—do with company—" he got out between gasps for air.

"Tell me about it."

"Just leave me—lone," Steckman dropped onto a small boulder nearby and held his heaving side. Henry started edging toward him.

"What is it you're looking for?"

Steckman smiled, "Long story—a very long story—you really wouldn't be—interested."

"Hey, hey, that's him," Scottie called from across the void and raced toward his car. As the Dodge ground into action Steckman hauled himself up and started running. Henry made a halfhearted attempt to tackle him around the waist while trying to reason with him, but Steckman turned and gave him a vicious elbow to the side of the head and sent him sprawling. By the time he got back to his feet

Steckman was running low trying to disappear into the tall weeds.

Scottie swung the car around in a large loop, a maneuver designed to force Steckman away from the streets in the distance and back toward the edge of the cliff from whence he came. Henry jogged along behind and watched as the car started closing in. Steckman was running away from him now along the edge of the cliff and it was only a matter of time before he was brought to earth. He made one last effort to get into a large clump of standing weeds. He made it but the car was only two seconds behind him.

Then the top of the car was lost from view and Henry heard a thump and a scream. At a run he followed the tire tracks into the brush but soon had to stop in a hurry, coming up on his toes. Part of the cliff had been washed away and a new rain gully, hidden in the bush, had surprised them all. Steckman lay at the bottom of a ten-foot drop still screaming in pain. He was lying facedown pounding and clawing at the loose dirt he had fallen into. His legs and feet looked like they belonged on a discarded puppet. For a moment it appeared the police car with Scottie in it had vanished into thin dusty air. Then Henry heard the soft clump, clump of a car rolling down the cliff to his left. There were pauses now between the noises from the car, indicating a steep embankment. He moved as close to the edge as he could but could neither see nor hear any sign of life from the lost car.

Going back to the new washout Henry watched helplessly as Steckman's screams turned into moans then to whimpers as he lapsed into unconsciousness. Apparently Steckman, running at top speed, had fallen into the gully, the car then had come crashing down onto his legs and flopped over and on down the hill.

Henry decided the best thing he could do would be to get help. He turned his suitcoat inside out and tossed it

171

onto the highest weed he could find near the washout so he could identify the spot on his return, then started back toward the road. Scottie must have had time to use the police radio because by the time he got to the curb Henry could hear police cars screeching toward him.

It took a good twenty minutes before a paramedic team could get to the scene and another fifteen to get Steckman strapped to a litter and hauled out of the sandy ravine. Henry asked to ride with him to the hospital. Blanchard didn't seem to mind. The rescue team hadn't arrived as yet and he was beside himself worrying about the car and his missing detective. Several times, as he paced the edge of the bluff, he scolded Henry, "You were working as partners; you should have looked after him. You should have covered him." Henry wondered what he could have done differently, but kept his mouth shut.

Chapter Sixteen

Steckman did not regain consciousness until they arrived at the hospital and the emergency team started working on his legs. Then it was another hour shuffling him to and from x-ray and the different examining rooms before Henry could approach him. The two uniformed policemen had not been given any special instructions except to guard the prisoner, so Henry acted as though he was in charge. Steckman's leg fractures required surgery and pin-setting which couldn't be done until the morning, so they had immobilized him and put him under sedation. Henry had to work fast before Steckman dropped off to sleep.

"Looks like you're going to be laid up for quite a spell here."

"What happened?"

"You remember falling in the hole?"

"What hole?"

"Never mind. You have compound fractures in the thigh bones of both your legs. They're going to set them in the morning. You want to tell me what you were looking for at Pangbourne's?"

Steckman smiled, "You asked me that before somewhere, didn't you? Compound fractures. That could be serious, couldn't it?"

"The doctor said he thought they would mend well. It'll take time though. You remember seeing me on board the *Inquisitor*?"

"Yeah, I remember. What's the company doing in this?"

"Mr. Chapin is afraid, concerned about the security of the Precursor."

"Chapin. Precursor," he laughed. "Oh, brother. This is getting funnier all the time."

"What do you mean?"

"Look, I've got interests to protect in this. I can't go blabbing my head off. But I'll tell you this—it had nothing to do with the Precursor. I just used that as a ploy to get on board."

"Can you prove that? The way it looks to me, Pangbourne had been persuaded by someone, maybe you, to claim ownership of the Precursor and not return it to the company. Then he changed his mind. The way I figure it he decided he couldn't get away with it so he decided to give it back. But that didn't set too well with someone else on board." Henry waited to let this sink in; Steckman was already looking ashen but gave no other sign of unease. He plunged on, "And perhaps that someone was planning to sell the Precursor to a foreign agent. You would certainly qualify on that score, wouldn't you, with your contacts in Europe? And where else have you served?"

"Just Europe," he said flatly.

"You certainly had opportunities to make contacts over there. I know couriers don't make that much money. Let's see, you were paid by the Canadian government, weren't you?"

174

"That's right."

"Pretty tough to make ends meet in Europe today on a Canadian courier's salary."

"I'm out of the service now, didn't you know?"

"Yes, I'd heard that," Henry stepped closer to the bed and leaned on the elaborate metal rigging encircling Steckman. In a soft voice he said, "But let's get back to this scenario I was discussing, hypothetical though it may be. When the other party who had his contacts with a foreign power—let's say, for the sake of argument, the Russians—when he found out Pangbourne was reneging he decided to kill him to prevent the return of the Precursor to the company."

Steckman smiled and shook his head. "I wasn't trying to get in his house to kill him. I can assure you of that."

"What?"

"You heard me. I had no weapon on me. The police saw that. How'm I supposed to kill Pangbourne? The man's a bull."

"Was a bull."

"What?" For the first time Steckman looked nervous. White showed above his green-brown eyeballs as he stared at Henry.

"He's dead. He was killed sometime last night. We think on campus."

"I don't believe you."

Henry went to the door and called to the uniformed officer standing guard in the hall, "Sergeant Archer, do you still have that evening paper handy?"

The paper was found; Henry folded it so the Pangbourne story was topmost, then went back in the room and lowered it in front of Steckman's face. Henry watched his eyes race down the article and back and forth across the picture of the body locked in the stocks. If he was acting, it was an academy award performance.

"And they think I did that?"

"You're number one on their list."

"But I didn't. I haven't seen Pangbourne since he left the ship yesterday."

"And you haven't seen a paper or—"

"No. No, nothing. I've been too busy."

"Too busy doing what?"

Steckman rolled his head away and clenched his dishwater blond curls.

"Are you in pain?" No response. "You want me to ring for the nurse?"

He rolled back and stared into Henry's eyes. "Listen. I could be in a spot. The people I'm . . . the people behind me that could clear me might not say anything."

"You better tell me what it's all about."

"You working shadow with the police?"

Henry nodded.

"You wouldn't have to tell them if I could clear myself off the record. Okay?"

Henry studied him. "All right. Off the record. But it better be good."

"You were right about one thing. My salary. I'd been looking for a way to, you know, augment my income." He smiled as he said it, then took a deep breath and went on. "But I wouldn't sell anything to the Ruskies. I'd never do that.

"I was called back to Ottawa last year because of my mother's illness. They gave me some easy assignments there and in the states for awhile. But that was running out soon and I'd have to make up my mind whether to leave the service or sign on for another hitch, probably in Austria this time. You know what Austria is like. I was knocking my head trying to decide what to do.

"Then this thing fell in my lap. Washington office, I don't think it was from Chapin though, asked me to ride shotgun on this Precursor equipment from Guantanamo out to San Diego. For some strange reason they wanted it transferred by train, and the long ride out gave me plenty of time to think about it." He let out with a big casual yawn.

"Time to think about what?" Henry asked in an excited manner. He wanted to get at the meat of this before Steckman dropped off.

"What I was gonna do. How I could cash in on my special position. I read up on the *Inquisitor* thing, just to pass the time. And then it hit me. The major expense of the *Inquisitor's* trip was being underwritten by an Ace-Hemming Industrial Electronics firm. They're just a small firm up in San Jose valley. What would they be doing underwriting the cost of an expensive expedition like that? What was their business, I wondered.

"So after I delivered the equipment I went to a local stockbroker's office and acted as if I wanted to invest in the company. I looked over their perspectus and found out they're making a major effort in alternative energy development. Specifically OTEC."

"OPEC?"

Steckman laughed. "No not OPEC. O-T-E-C . . . " He spelled it out. "It stands for Ocean Thermal Energy Conversion. You know what that is?"

"Something about using the ocean's temperature differences to generate energy."

"You got it. Electrical energy." He was rambling on now in an easygoing manner, waving his hand about as he explained. "You take the warm ocean water to heat some chemicals, mostly ammonia, stuff that boils at a low temperature. That drives your electrical turbine. Then you cool the chemical gases back down to liquid with cold ocean water and you start all over again. Like a closed system. All you need to generate electricity is warm

177

water and cold water. Only the trick is to find a place where you have cold water close to warm water currents. Get me?"

Henry nodded.

" 'Long with the older stuff the expedition was doing, they were gathering this water temperature info for Hemming Electronics." Steckman rolled his eyes and smiled a satisfied smile.

"I don't get it. What does this have to do—"

"You don't get it? Don't you see? Finding the right place in the big Pacific Ocean was very important to Hemming. It's worth thousands. Millions. Pangbourne guarded those findings like crazy. He even got the company to require security clearances on all the personnel on board that handled his electronics and sounding gear."

"That's standard procedure. I think the company would have made those requirements anyway," Henry said, then leaned close to Steckman's head. "Go on."

"Well, whatever. Anyway, I had access to the clearance papers for the crew. So I pulled out one of the cleared crewmen's papers, threw it away, made some phonies for myself under the name Bernard Duffy and got myself on the crew. Then I hightailed it back to Canada and found myself some companies that would be willing to pay for that kind of information."

"Industrial espionage."

"You got it."

"Did it pay well?"

"Oh, you bet. I had four companies, two Canadian and two American, ready to do business. They didn't care how I got the info, you know. No questions asked. They gave me twenty thousand just walkin' around money for goin' on the expedition. An' a sliding scale from 50 to 200 thousand depending on how good my info was."

"And how good was it?"

178

Steckman laughed lazily, "Zero, man. Zero on any scale. Why d'ya think I was still lookin'? An' Pangbourne, that devil Pangbourne, he musta found out about me. I musta stayed too close to the radio rooms or somethin'. When we got close to home in Mexican waters I kept waiting for him to shortwave the location coordinate back to Hemming Industrial. But he never did. Maybe I scared him off. I dunno. Then I started going through his stuff when I could. He had to have a log or sump'n somewhere with all the longitude and latitude readings. Then finally at the enda the trip I thought I struck gold. You remember yesterday when you saw me comin' outta his quarters? Pangbourne's quarters?"

"Yes, I remember."

"Well, I had his logbook unner my shirt." He slapped his hand against the bed guardrail and laughed. "I thought I had it, man. I found it jammed up under his mattress an' I had it." More giggling laughter. "He had marked the best places where the hot spots and the cold spots were close together an' I telegrammed my findings to Canada. He had it down to latitude and longitude in degrees—minutes, seconds, microseconds, everything. I was home free, I thought." More giggles, but this time he started to slip away.

Henry shook him, "But what? What went wrong?"

Steckman opened his eyes and slapped a heavy hand on Henry's shoulder, "You know where the hot spot was? It figured out to be in the cooking stove department in the big Sears store in Honolulu, Hawaii. You get it?" he laughed. "An' the 'cold spot' turned out to be exactly in a big Hotpoint refrigerator store in Hilo."

Henry was frowning at him as he laughed uncontrollably.

"Don't you get it, man? The whole logbook was a dummy. He planted it there for me or anybody who

179

wanted it. Who wanted to make a fool of hisself. The folks in Ottawa thought I was crazy. Dontcha see? They thought I was the joker—"

"Okay, so you went by his house looking for the real log. Right?"

He got something like a nod out of Steckman, but his eyeballs were rolling.

"Did you go by the university, too? Did you go in Pangbourne's office?" Henry yelled to him while he slapped his hand. "Did you take the briefcase? The big black briefcase?"

But it was obvious Steckman wasn't coming back. Henry laid his arms down, pulled the sheet up to his neck and watched him drift away.

Part of it did make sense, though. Pangbourne said that strange things had been going on on the cruise so he didn't know whom to trust.

And then Henry thought of the way Pangbourne had orchestrated their movement yesterday morning; Pangbourne led the two of them into his own quarters, then left Henry there alone. Could be he suspected Henry of wanting to do a little searching of his own. And no doubt the phony logbook was there under the mattress at that time.

Chapter Seventeen

Henry was still leaning over Steckman and mulling this over in his mind when Blanchard came charging in. Staring red-eyed daggers at Henry, he marched to the opposite side of the bed but paid no attention to the prisoner-patient.

"He's asleep under medication," Henry said. "You should have been a bit earlier."

"He's dead," Blanchard barked. "Scottie is dead."

"What? Scottie's dead?"

"I want to know why you weren't in that car."

"I thought I told you, captain. We were watching from two different sides of the cliff. He had the car on his side when Steckman here appeared, climbing up the hill—"

"You were working as partners. You're older than him. You should have been wiser. You should never have let him drive like that so close to the cliff edge. He was the best detective I ever had. It should never've happened," Blanchard said, his words virtually identical to what he had said at the bluff.

Henry watched Blanchard's big meat-hook hands flex

and release on the bed railing, and he could imagine what he would like to be doing with them on Henry's face. A myriad of defensive arguments raced through Henry's mind but he decided against using them. Blanchard was not interested in logic or truth. His anger would only be satisfied with his beloved Scottie being restored to life.

"Captain Blanchard, I'm very sorry to hear about Scottie. I'm sure it's quite a personal loss, too—"

"Oh shut up," he said and started pacing, which looked strange because his body was too broad for the space allowed for pacing.

"You think perhaps you should turn the investigation over to someone else?" Henry asked.

"No, I don't think perhaps I should turn the investigation over to someone else," he mimicked. He continued pacing and doing nervous things with his hands. He looked empty without his cigar. The silence hung heavily in the room; someone dropped what sounded like a bedpan out in the corridor but it changed nothing for the two somber men in the room.

So Scottie was dead. The great girl-watcher and condominium builder. Dead by his own foolish hand while trying to make a boring, tedious job interesting. Perhaps if he had been killed more dramatically, perhaps in a hail of gunfire, his captain could accept it more gracefully. But to be brought down so ignominiously no doubt preyed on Blanchard's mind.

Blanchard finally tired of his mourning and concentrated his attention on Steckman. "You're sure this is him?"

"Oh, yes. I talked with him. He recognized me all right."

"Officer Archer said they didn't have a chance to question him."

"Well, no. I thought if I talked to him alone, without a

police uniform in the room we'd get further."

"Still conducting your own investigation, eh? You're a real sweetheart, aren't you?"

"We're all looking for the same thing."

"Are we? I'm beginning to wonder," the captain snorted. "What were you doing over at Pangbourne's this afternoon? That woman could be suing us, you know."

"I was doing a bit of Scottie's work for him," Henry began, looking into Blanchard's hard glare. He went on to tell him of the stolen mail, the two deans, Hallard and Hazard, the cablegram and the missing letter Mrs. Pangbourne said her husband had written. "And I suppose you've heard about Dr. Mumford's collapse?"

"Mumford. Now who's he?"

"Who is he?" Henry enunciated with exaggeration, "In my book he's one of the prime suspects. He's the dean of the life science division—"

"Oh, the old geezer with the tremor in his hand. He's one of your prime suspects?" Blanchard asked in a condescending manner. "My, my another seventy-year-old prof wiping out his contemporary. Happens every day. I shoulda seen it."

"It's possible."

"Really now. Can you see him carrying the 200-pound body across campus?"

"There are big demonstration carts in his department that would support that weight very nicely."

"And motive?"

"Pangbourne leaned on him once too often. And maybe a bit of professional jealousy. Pangbourne was taking an associate professor position Mumford thought belonged to his division."

"Nonsense. Old people don't kill for things like that. Hotheaded twenty-three-year-olds kill over things like that. Not old men."

183

Henry wondered at himself for pursuing that line. Remembering the time frame there was no opportunity for Mumford to have done any such thing. Unless it was Mumford and Hazard working together, and that possibility seemed quite remote. There was no love lost between those two. Henry decided he was getting punchy.

Blanchard had started pacing again but now moved slowly to the head of the bed and peered down at Steckman. "And thirty-year-old men. Wouldn't you say he's about thirty?"

"Our records say thirty-two."

"Thirty-two. And what can you tell us about him?"

Henry told him of Steckman's courier past and that he was aboard the *Inquisitor* as a working seaman, but he held his tongue about his specific purpose for being aboard. "He's been searching for something that Pangbourne had somewhere in his possession," was all he would let out.

"Which was?"

"Captain, you'll have to ask him yourself."

"I see. The old game of keeping your own secrets again. That can get pretty old, you know. We've leveled with you all the way."

"Captain, all I can say is this chap was playing his own game which had nothing to do with the Precursor security. He may have been ready to kill to get what he wanted but the fact he was still looking after Pangbourne's death leads me to believe he had nothing to do with his death."

"Oh, it does, eh?" Blanchard sneered, but Henry had a point to make and ignored the policeman's attitude.

"Yes, you see we're dealing here with a murderer with a point to make. He or she did not simply want to kill the victim. They wanted to humiliate him. To rub his nose in it, as it were. To play one last practical joke on the great practical joker. And a thief, such as we have here, does

184

not hang around to play games."

"You are assuming, of course, Steckman is nothing more than a thief. I do hope you remember that tracking him down was your idea."

"Well, there's always the possibility that he's lying," Henry granted.

"And there's the possibility this guy knocked Pangbourne on the head and somebody else came along, found him unconscious and tied a bag over his head."

"Yes. That sounds like something a seventy-year-old man could do quite easily, doesn't it?" Henry fenced. "Or a woman."

"And it also means the person that struck the first blow is also culpable and could be convicted in a court of law."

"Oh, does it? I guess I don't know the law that well."

"Don't you think it's about time you let us professionals handle matters? What was it he was looking for?"

"Captain, the man's not going anyplace. You can ask him yourself." Henry was having difficulty justifying his stance. It was so easy to promise Steckman he would keep his secret. But now looking into the tired grey eyes of the law he had second thoughts. "I wouldn't let him get away with this crime. If you don't have a break in the case in a week, ask me again."

Blanchard nodded. This seemed to satisfy him and his expression softened. "It's the principle of the thing, you understand. Just between you and me, my money is still on the religious kid. Come on, let's go," he said moving toward the door. He swung it open and looked back at Henry. "The guy's asleep. What are you waiting for?"

Henry was still leaning over Steckman's head and wearing a pained expression on his face. "Captain, I wonder if you'd mind coming over to this side of the bed. I don't seem to be able to get myself upright."

Chapter Eighteen

As the captain drove Henry over to the university to pick up his Volvo, the silence in the car was in stark contrast to all the jabbering they had done in the hospital room. For Henry's part, he was more than a little embarrassed by his condition. He had cried out in pain when the captain had jerked him into a vertical position and his walk to the car had been a good imitation of John Wayne in a drunken stupor. The car rolled discreetly to a stop in front of Philip's apartment complex and for the fifth time the captain gave Henry his fish-eye look as though he expected him to turn into a butterfly and float out the window any moment.

"You gonna be all right?"

"Yes, I think so. There's my car."

"You staying here?"

"No. The motel across campus," Henry pointed.

"I'm putting Mickey on this case full time. The full autopsy is scheduled for the a.m. and we're gonna start going over the entire list of passengers and crew on the *Inquisitor.* You be in in the morning?"

"Better start without me."

Blanchard nodded, started to say something more, then thought better of it and drove away.

Henry turned his torso slightly askew and walked up the stairs to Philip's door.

"Oh, hi, Mr. Garrett. How's it going?" Jeremy asked. "Gosh, but you look beat. C'mon in." He had a half-eaten apple and a large book in his hands, and reading glasses propped up in his tossled hair.

"Thanks. Is Philip in?"

"Yeah. He's in the john. Just got back from his date with Tracy. I'll let him know you're here."

"No, that's okay. I can wait," Henry said and sat down near the desk where Jeremy had been studying. "Well, what did you think of your visit with the police now that you've had some breathing time?"

"Kind of frightening, you know? I mean it's one thing to hear about it happening to somebody else, but when it happens to you, man, it's frightening." He sat and rubbed his eyes.

Henry looked around the room as he had done earlier that day. Its appearance had taken a turn for the better since Jeremy's return. And there was now a small Polaroid shot of Tracy and Philip he did not remember seeing tacked to their makeshift bulletin board. He rose to look at it more closely.

"You think you would like to have her for a daughter-in-law?" Jeremy asked.

Henry smiled. "They do make a handsome couple, don't they?"

"Yeah. They were practically inseparable last year. Then just before the expedition they broke up. I never expected them to get back together, you know. Otherwise I'd have never said anything about her and Dr. Pang. Love is crazy, isn't it?"

187

"Do you know why they broke up?"

"I think Philip was upset because she got to go on the expedition and he didn't."

"Are you sure he wanted to?"

"Are you kidding? We were all ready to give an arm and a leg to get on board. We figured the new associate professor was going to be chosen from that lucky group, too."

"And how did you qualify for the trip, Jeremy?"

"Grade point average," he said, then added simply, "I'm very smart, you know. And I'm an experienced scuba diver. I think that helped."

"Do you still consider yourself in the running for the associate professorship?"

Jeremy laughed, "No, no. I blew whatever chances I had on the trip. That's a closed little club I guess I'll never crack, not being an evolutionist, you know."

Henry smiled, but decided against pursuing that line of conversation again. Then he looked over their record collection for lack of something better to do. It appeared Jeremy had gone back to his reading but he broke the silence with a soft question.

"You think I killed him, don't you?"

"No, son, I do not."

"Oh, really? I'd like to know why you say that."

"Primarily because of Dr. Pangbourne's personality traits."

Jeremy scowled a question mark back at Henry who then went on, "Let me explain. One of the police investigators suggested that Pangbourne was playing one more of his little pranks on you. His theory was that you were to work hard at preparing your outline and then Pangbourne would tell you it was all a joke. You supposedly got mad at that point and lowered the boom on him. But it doesn't jell with the other Pangbourne pranks. There's no style to it.

188

It lacks the Pangbourne panache, if you will. There's nothing he could regale his audience with later. That's why I feel that note you got on board telling you to be in his office at 9:30 must have been a forgery."

This bit of reasoning delighted Jeremy and he started talking happily about a great load being lifted, et cetera. But something troubled Henry as he carried this scenario one step further in his mind. Why was Pangbourne's office door open for Jeremy? He expected it to be open and it was. But Henry remembered when he had gone through the office building earlier in the day that all the empty cubicles were locked. Why, at 9:30 at night, was Pangbourne's office open if he didn't open it? He waited for Jeremy's enthusiasm to run down, then asked,

"Tell me, who has access to the master key of the buildings?"

"Oh, golly. The department heads do, of course. The maintenance people seem to get into everything—"

"How about lab techs, or teaching assistants?"

Jeremy was still thinking about this when the bedroom door, which had been ajar, swung open and Philip came out frowning.

"It's not too difficult for lab techs and teaching assistants to get hold of master keys if they have their minds set on getting hold of them," he said. "If you have any more questions, Dad, why don't you ask me? Speaking of keys, your Volvo keys and the credit card are on the end table there by the door."

"Oh, yes, thanks."

"Thank you for dinner. Tracy said she enjoyed meeting you."

"Good. I hope we didn't tire her too much."

"No. She was a little groggy but okay."

"Good," Henry said, then filled in an awkward pause by pocketing his keys and card. "We always seem to be

189

getting off on the wrong foot. Don't we, son?"

"I wonder whose fault that is."

Henry smiled. "Here we go again with whose fault things are."

"Yeah, well. It's there, isn't it?"

"Not in my book, it isn't." Henry put his hand on the door. "Should I tell your mother you send your love?"

"Yeah, I guess. You going home now?"

"I plan to."

"Oh, well, yes. Tell her and Becky hello."

"We love you, son."

"Yeah, well. Good to see you. 'Night, Dad."

"Good-bye, son. Good-bye, Jeremy."

"Good-bye, sir."

Chapter Nineteen

Henry had thought of asking Philip to come with him to the motel to help him pack and carry his suitcase to the car, but it somehow seemed inappropriate. Once at the motel room he started his call procedure to Chapin, and while he waited he carried articles out to the backseat of the car piecemeal to spare his back any heavy duty. When Chapin finally connected he read the riot act to Henry about the hour of his call. It seems Chapin was afraid to take the call at his house so he was standing in a public phone booth a half mile from his house in his bathrobe and slippers.

" . . . And do you realize what time it is back here? You're getting mixed up with Europe. When you're in Europe it's okay to call Washington in the late evening. But not when you're in California."

"I apologize about the time thing. But I wanted to tell you I'm going home."

"Home? What do you mean home?"

"I mean I'm going home. There's nothing more I can do on the matter now. We located Steckman. He's laid up in the hospital with two broken legs and a pretty good alibi. I personally don't think he had anything to do with trying to make off with your equipment. What happened to my replacement? I thought you were going to get back to me."

"Wait a minute. Wait a minute. Let's get back to Steckman. What happened?"

Henry went on at some length explaining how Steckman had been captured and about his story of industrial espionage.

"How do you know he's telling the truth?" Chapin wanted to know.

"For one thing his story was too elaborate to make up on the spur of the moment. His mind was already groggy from sedatives when I started questioning him. People just don't think that fast. Plus it ties in with the other information we have on his activities."

"Maybe he had that story all planned in case he got caught. Tell you what. Why don't you check up on him? Talk to one or two of the companies he said he was working for."

"What's the point in that?" Henry wanted to know, a good bit of testiness showing in his voice. "They're certainly not going to admit they hired him. The laws against stealing company secrets, I understand, can be pretty severe."

"There's no need to use that tone of voice with me, Henry," Chapin remonstrated.

"Again, I apologize. I've had a very bad day and my back is acting up again."

"I am your superior, you know. That's a very unprofessional manner you're slipping into."

"Yes, well, I'm not feeling very professional tonight. I'm not a field man. I'm a rapidly aging accountant and I've reached the end of my tether. The Precursor is safely under naval guard and your wandering courier is in the prison section of the county hospital. I don't see that we have any more concern with—"

"There's been a prominent man murdered, Henry," he interrupted. "A general in the reserves I might point out."

"And I'm convinced it's a local matter."

"But you can't say that with a certainty, can you?"

"I've found nothing that would indicate it's a company matter. Frankly, I think you are imagining things. Pangbourne apparently was a very abrasive personality and he generated a good many enemies. His run-in with us was simply the last in a long series of incidents—"

"Henry, what's wrong? This isn't like you at all. You've never left an assignment unfinished before. If what you say is true, that's fine. But the least you can do is wait and see this through."

"You don't have a replacement on the way, do you?"

"Henry, we're really strapped for people. Put on your back brace and tough it out now, okay?"

"Are you privy to any information about this case I don't have?" This was a technique Henry liked to employ. He would get a rapid exchange going on one subject, then switch quickly to a new subject with a penetrating question. If the subject hesitates with his answer it usually implied a lie. Chapin paused, then said,

"Not that I'm prepared to share at this time."

It wasn't a long pause but then such a nondescript answer hardly needed much preparation. It was too long. Henry got the distinct feeling Chapin was bluffing simply to keep his pawn Henry on the job.

"Okay, let's just say my reluctance to continue is a personal matter. If you come up with any hard evidence you'd like to share with me you can reach me at home. After all, I'm not all that far from San Diego. Good-bye, Mr. Chapin."

The blunt talk with Chapin did nothing to ease the knot

193

in Henry's chest. If anything it only served to aggravate it. But he was doing what he had to do. He had never been a quitter before. But all the doors were closing. All but one. All but Philip's. It was time for Henry to get out. Good ol' plod-along Henry was not the brightest of the company agents, but at least he could always be counted on to finish his work. He wondered what was going on in Chapin's mind right now as he drove back to his home in the wee Virginia hours.

Henry got his old piano moving strap out of the trunk of the car and fashioned a halter between the Volvo's cumbersome headrest and his own armpits and then started his lonely trek home. The halter arrangement worked well at relieving his back pain but he found he had to stop every thirty miles or so and disengage himself to keep the circulation flowing in his arms.

On one of these stops on the south side of Los Angeles he called home and asked his wife to get the old Army surplus hospital bed ready for him. They bought the bed for Henry the last time this had happened in Washington so they could put him in traction at home and he wouldn't need to be hospitalized. In their move west, Valery had set the bed up in one of their spare bedrooms, just in case.

It was well after one o'clock in the morning when he pulled the Volvo into the driveway. When Becky and Valery, both in their bathrobes and slippers, came bounding out of the house their worried expressions told Henry he had alarmed them too much with his phone call. In spite of his protestations they insisted upon helping him into the house and up the stairs. They meant well, of course, but the lifting and pulling at his elbows only worked to aggravate his problem. Since they had no direct personal access to the inflamed nerve causing the problem, their good intentions didn't help. So similar, Henry thought, to his own attempts to help his son despite his own ignorance of

194

the boy's inner turmoil.

He finally got the ladies out of the bathroom so he could get in the shower and enjoy the moist pulsating heat pounding on just the right spots. A half hour later he was in his old traction harness between the clean white sheets, and the gentle stretching pressure from the ankle straps and the headgear began to assert its relaxing effect.

His doctor had told him his problem was primarily psychosomatic, a matter of a nervous mind sending distress signals to muscles at a weak spot on the spine; the muscles then tightened on a nerve until its outer casing became inflamed. This in turn made the muscles respond again until the cycle became progressively worse. And the only way to break the cycle was to relax the muscles until the nerve could settle down. Hence, the traction.

Valery was staying close, keeping a critical eye on his facial expressions and asking the usual questions a concerned wife asks. When she got around to asking about Philip, Henry found the semi-restricting headgear made it convenient for him to respond in monosyllables. Philip was fine. Working hard and he sends his love.

"And did you accomplish what you set out to do?" she asked.

"I don't know. He knows how I feel at least."

"Fine. Then I think we should leave it at that," she said, patting his hand. Then again, as an afterthought, "He knows where we live."

Becky arrived with some hot cocoa and a straw and a comic production ensued as she tried giving her father sips of his favorite nighttime brew while lying flat on his back.

"Look out now," Valery said, "you're going to spill all over my clean sheets."

"I've got a tissue there, Mom."

"Oh, those skimpy tissues of yours won't sop up anything."

195

Henry smiled and found he was enjoying all the attention, however indirect. The banter kept up until Valery started insisting everyone go to sleep. If they knew about the Pangbourne thing neither of them let on. Perhaps just as well.

But as he lay in the darkness listening to the house quiet down, a new restlessness overcame Henry. When the last gurgle of water had run its course through the bathroom pipes, Becky stuck her head back into his room. " 'Night, Daddy."

"Is that you, Becky?"

"Yes."

"Come in a minute, will you?"

Her shadow moved across the darkened room and she picked up his hand.

"I was wondering if you'd like to pray with me."

"Sure, Daddy. About your back?"

"No. That's not what's on my mind. I think maybe it's a blessing in disguise."

"What do you mean?"

"Have you seen any news today?"

"About Dr. Pangbourne?"

"Yes."

"I saw it in the paper tonight. I did't say anything to Mother about it. That was your man on the expedition?"

"Yes," Henry whispered. He gave a long quiet sigh, then, "I think Philip may have killed him."

"Oh, no! Oh, Daddy, no."

He felt an overwhelming need to weep for his boy, but he gripped his daughter's hand and steeled himself against it.

"Are you sure?" Becky asked.

"There's so much that points to it. I think the guilty party was someone who knew his way around the campus. And someone who knew Dr. Pangbourne's schedule.

196

Philip knew both."

"But surely he wasn't the only one."

"He had the motive," Henry said, then blurted out the sordid details of Pangbourne's affair with Tracy, the continuing light of Philip's eye. "And when I saw him the night Pangbourne was killed he was wearing a suit and tie."

"I don't see what that has to do with it."

"Don't you?" Henry asked. "What would inspire Philip to get so dressed up in the middle of the school week? Certainly not to meet the returning Tracy. That's not the style of today's college student. The standard dress down there is jeans and a soft shirt—that's the way he dresses to meet his classes as teacher assistant. And I've been racking my brain to figure out what would motivate Philip to put on a suit on a school night like that. And the only thing I can come up with is that he wore it to impress a scholastic superior.

"Pangbourne said he had many appointments going on into the evening. One of them I feel must have been with Philip. He was already mad at Tracy, mad enough to punch her out quite seriously. Then he meets with her lover who may also have promised him an associate professorship but then changed his mind and withdrew the offer. Either way, Philip was in a fighting mood. And I'm sure you remember the temper he can generate."

"Yes, I remember," Becky said quietly.

"And there I was, supposedly working with the police, supposedly trying to help them discover who did this. Now you see why I say my back problem may have been a blessing in disguise."

"What did Philip say when you asked him about meeting with Dr. Pangbourne?"

"I couldn't bring myself to ask him."

Becky started to say something but then held up. Neither of them spoke for several seconds. Henry's little detour into self-pity was complete as he felt a cool tear escape from his left eye and roll down into his ear. He was glad it was dark. *Tomorrow will be better,* he told himself. He would get his emotions in shape and think more clearly now that he had some distance from his problem, now that he could stop thinking about his back.

Becky was more experienced in oral prayer and did most of the talking. She covered the bases of most of their concerns, then closed by committing all of their troubles to the Lord's care and infinite wisdom. Henry, who normally did not sleep well the first night he was "in harness" had prepared himself for a night of fitfulness, but he didn't even hear the door close behind his retreating daughter.

In fact, he didn't stir until around four in the morning when he found himself acting as a suspension bridge across a deep chasm somewhere in the Pyrenees Mountains. At least, it looked like what he knew of the Pyrenees from pictures in the *National Geographic* magazine. And then in keeping with the logic found only in dreams, he not only found groups of people walking to and fro across his swaying body but also found himself to be one of a group waiting his turn to cross. At the edge of the bridge stood Scottie, the young detective he thought had died. But now he was busily handing out small bumper stickers which all the bridge walkers were expected to attach to their clothing or the bundles they were carrying. There were some slight arguments as people grabbed for bumper stickers that suited them.

It was an odd assortment of travelers. One girl Henry recognized form his school days in Iowa. But most were characters from his recent troubles in San Diego. Dean Mumford had recovered nicely and had his tremor under control. Dean Hazard was there too and was insisting upon taking his new granddaughter across the treacherous divide. Ralph Pangbourne, still wearing the plastic bag over his head, appeared on the scene just as it was Henry's turn to start crossing with his group. He was in a jovial mood and was acting as a pied piper for a group of junior-high-age students that included Philip, Tracy in pigtails, and Jeremy in a basketball costume. The fact that they had all retreated in age and size didn't seem to disturb anyone.

There were many complaints aimed at Pangbourne for bringing so many young people with him. It would make their crossing more difficult, they grumbled. But he made light of their concerns and started lecturing the group with equations and physics formulas with large words all intended to prove the bridge's stability increased in proportion to the number of its passengers.

Someone called from the distant cliff announcing it was the group's turn to cross. Henry couldn't make out the caller but his voice sounded suspiciously like Steckman's. Why they had to cross en masse was unclear but that is what they did. The bridge version of Henry kept calling out instructions for people to keep their hands on the rope railings as they inched forward.

When everyone was finally on the body bridge, Henry found his torso was stretching very thin so it made it difficult for people to keep their footing on him. This made it necessary for him to start yelling for everyone to "walk lighter, walk lighter." This helped a little, but by the time they reached the middle of their crossing, around Henry's elongated belt buckle, the wind came up and they started swaying serpentine fashion. Several started screaming. Pangbourne, though, was making a joke of it all and started swaying the bridge intentionally as if he were on a swing. Henry-the-bridge was screaming for him to behave himself. He was endangering the lives of everyone on board. Just as he tired of his game the wind whipped Pangbourne's plastic bag from his head and all eyes watched in silence as the air currents slipped the bag to

199

and fro down the seemingly endless crevice below.

Then finally the wind turned manageable again so the party started inching forward once more. But the hemp of one of their guide railings had become badly frayed and started unraveling now at a rapid pace, despite Henry's frantic attempts to keep it together. When it snapped the entire party screamed and started leaning heavily upon the one remaining guide rope. Henry-the-passenger was calling for everyone to stop leaning on the rope, but no one was paying any attention to him. Baskets and articles of clothing started falling from the panic-stricken people. Scottie's service revolver went, then the pink baby blanket Hazard had his granddaughter wrapped in. Henry's stretched body was being jerked violently back and forth as the travelers each performed their own balancing act. Then the inevitable happened. Henry heard a death rattling cry as someone behind him began to lose balance. As the person fell, Henry-the-passenger's footing was jerked from under him and at the same time he lost his grip on the rope and started to fall.

When he awoke back in his old Army bed the room was quiet but there seemed to be traces of a receding noise or presence still lingering in the darkness. Had he screamed aloud as he "fell"? He tried to shift his thinking to something more pleasant so he wouldn't end up back on that ridiculous bridge again. But then he remembered Becky's penchant for interpreting dreams. She no doubt would say that his subconscious knew who had killed Pangbourne and was trying to tell him something through his dream. Henry spent the next several minutes trying to embed the events of his dream into his memory so it wouldn't all be lost to him in the cold light of day. He must have fallen asleep again in the process because the next thing he knew it was morning and Valery was smiling down at him.

Chapter Twenty

Morning, Val."

"I'd almost forgotten you snore in this contraption."

"Oh, sorry, hope I didn't wake you."

"Oh, it wasn't that bad. Sort of like a big old pussycat purring. Rather enjoyable, actually. How's the back?"

"Feels fine in this."

"Sure you don't want to see the doctor?"

"No need to."

"But don't you want to know what's causing this?"

"We already know what's causing it."

"And what is that?"

"Not enough sex."

She rapped him on the top of his great toe. "Becky is still upstairs. She'll hear you," Valery whispered.

"Well, she's a biology major going into her senior year. It's high time we let the cat out of the bag."

"You know what I mean. Don't get cute or I won't let you up."

"Okay. Bring me the bedpan."

"On second thought," she said and released the foot weights. "You want to come down for breakfast?"

Henry gingerly pulled himself to a sitting position, then eased his feet over the side of the bed. "Yeah, I'll come down."

While Valery was in the process of helping him get disengaged from his head strap, Henry grabbed her with some serious ravishment in mind.

"Honestly, you were only gone two days."

"Each moment away from you, darling, is like—"

"Oh, honestly, Henry. Where are your highbrow Christian principles?"

"I'm practicing them."

"Like fun you are. An old married man."

"I certainly am. The Bible has special instructions for us married men."

"And what might that be?"

Henry snuggled especially close to her left ear and whispered, "To drink deeply from our own well."

"It does not say that."

"I beg to differ with you."

"Where? Where does it say that?"

"I forget. Somewhere in the Old Testament."

"Yeah, like fun it does," she laughed. "Look out now. You'll hurt your back."

"Oh, Val . . . let's lock the door and look for spiritual insights in the Song of Solomon."

He could feel her resistance start to soften. She kissed him in her unique way on the mouth, then whispered, "Becky leaves for work at 9:15. And you need a shave."

"Is that a date?" he tease-whispered. "What specifically does that comment mean?"

She slipped away, "It means if you want to see your daughter at breakfast you should come now."

"Ah, Val . . . "

She rewrapped her robe, smiled back at him at the door and was gone.

Breakfast consisted of eggs Benedict and cinnamon rolls. A good omen. Becky wanted to know all about Pangbourne's death, and with the *Times* article about the affair spread before her she fired questions at her father. He gave her a cursory review of his activities in San Diego, but instead of pursuing the topic she suddenly changed.

"What kind of dream did you have last night?"

"How do you know I did dream?"

"I heard you cry out. It sounded like you stepped in front of a London bus or something."

Henry smiled. "Something like that."

"Don't pay any attention to his dreams," Valery said. "He's always had them. They used to scare the daylights out of me, but I sleep right through them now."

"But don't you see, Mother? It's his subconscious trying to tell him something. Only it's in like a code."

"Oh, puff."

"Let her have her fun, honey," Henry said. "It's not hurting anything."

"Oh, all right. But let's not let them out of the family. They can be dreadfully embarrassing."

He laughed and assured her this one was quite tame. He did a rerun of his dream, announcing again all the characters and tying each of them into what little he knew of them in reality, then concluded with the fall from the bridge.

"Did everybody fall?"

"No, just the person behind me and myself. Why?"

"It might be quite significant. But it was only you and the other person . . . "

"Yes. Of course, I don't know what happened to the

203

others after I woke up."

"Honestly, Henry," Valery scolded, "you'd think your dreams had a life of their own the way you talk."

Henry gave a sheepish chuckle but Becky was thoughtfully staring at her last bite of eggs.

"You know what that scene reminds me of with the suspension bridge and all? The old chestnut we all had to read in high school, what was it called? A long short story?"

"You mean Thornton Wilder's *The Bridge at San Luis Rey*?"

"Yes. That's it. There was a group of people crossing on a suspension bridge in that story too, and it broke and they fell to their death."

"Yes, I remember. Very sad story," Henry said. "Why do you call it a chestnut?"

"Oh, I always found it rather hokey. I mean, all the people on the bridge had just come through some cataclysmic experience that changed their lives, and now they were on their way to live better lives when they all just happened to meet at the bridge. I always found it kind of hokey that they would all meet at the bridge at once."

"Yes, I see," Henry said. "I'd forgotten about that part. I'm afraid our parallel is incomplete. Only two of us fell from my bridge. Maybe I only thought of the bridge because I was already sort of suspended like a bridge in my traction. Funny how part of the time I was the bridge and part of the time I was one of the pedestrians."

"Oh, that's not so hard to figure. You had been playing two roles down in San Diego. First as an investigator and then as a father. Your subconscious picked up on that and gave you two characters in your dream."

"And the three graduate students? Why did I see them as being the junior high school age?"

"Wishful thinking. You'd like to see your son at an earlier age again where he'd be more manageable. Maybe more dependent on you."

"Now really," her mother interrupted with a note of incredulity. "How can you say such things as though you really knew?"

"But it's true, Mom. I mean I may not have all the interpretations right but your dreams do relate to your life. They just have sort of a left-handed way of telling you. Don't you see?"

"No. I certainly don't. Things can be made up afterwards to fit the facts."

"Look, I'll explain," Becky pontificated. "Let's take that bridge crossing thing. Normally when you cross a bridge you're going from one *place* to another. But in a dream that might symbolize a different kind of change. Maybe, instead of changing places, you're changing attitudes or friends or jobs or . . . " She looked softly into her father's eyes, " . . . age. That could be it. Maybe the father's role in relation to his children is changing and the change is a bit rocky and dangerous at times."

Henry patted her hand. "You're quite the little psychiatrist, aren't you?"

"Thanks," Becky said seriously. "That bumper sticker thing is quite interesting too, isn't it?"

"What do you mean?"

"I mean they can be so symbolic. Do you remember reading any that the bridge crossers had pasted on themselves?"

"No, the only thing I can relate to bumper stickers was a comment the young police officer made. He said, 'You can never tell what's in someone's heart by reading their bumper sticker.' Or words to that effect."

"That's it!" Becky exclaimed. "Somebody had on the wrong bumper sticker to go with their real feelings. You sure you can't recall any of the slogans?"

"No. Nothing. I didn't read any of them."

"Too bad," Becky said. "It would be so simple if you had."

"Well, of course it would," Henry laughed. "I mean the whole secret to getting away with murder is deception."

"Now, let's think about that," Becky said, pressing her hands prayerfully on her mouth. "Could it be possible that someone is deceiving himself? I mean maybe mentally unbalanced or maybe somebody is so different from what we think he is that we don't even see it."

"Honey," her dad advised, "people just don't change all that much. We had a psychiatrist at the agency lecturing us on the topic. About the only things that will truly produce personality changes over the long haul are frontal lobotomies or some chemical manipulations on the brain, extensive psychoanalysis or a profound religious experience."

Becky smiled softly, "And that happened to you, didn't it? The religious experience."

"Yes. But your mother insists it didn't change my personality," he joked.

"Now let's think over the dream again."

Valery let out with more complaints explaining that they had suffered through many years of meaningless stories with Henry's nightmares. But Becky would not be denied. She justified her stand with the news that she had taken a college course on dreams, then put her argument beyond challenge by announcing, "And after all, it was an upper division class."

"Well, I can't argue with logic like that," Valery said, then quickly changed the subject, "Do you have any more dirty clothes? I've got to do a load this morning."

"No, I brought everything down last night," Becky said.

"Watch your time now, dear. You don't want to be late for work." Valery stacked her dishes, then headed toward the garage and the washer-dryer.

"I'm on my way, Mom. I just want to say something to Daddy."

"Oh," Valery said and hesitated at the door to look back at her husband and daughter. No one could put more meaning into a simple "oh" than Valery. This time it was a blend of nuances somewhere between surprise and disappointment. So there were to be secrets between the born-again Christians, were there, it seemed to say. And she was to be left out in the cold. In the cold garage.

"You know I've been thinking about what you said last night," Becky said in a confidential tone after the door to the garage had clicked shut. "About Philip. I don't think he did it."

"Becky, you hardly know the situation," Henry said.

"No, but I know Philip. It isn't like him. I know about his temper and all, but I think he's too much of an organization man to do anything like that on his own."

"Philip, an organization man? You've got to be kidding. Have you ever heard him take off on the federal government?"

"That's the wrong organization. He belongs to a special university clique, remember. The beard and the sloppy clothes are all part of the uniform. We've got 'em at our school too. Only they're a little passé now."

"I don't quite see how that tells you he's innocent."

"I remember once in grade school—I must have been in the fourth grade and Philip was starting the seventh—we were in that American school at the West German air station. And Philip wanted so much to be a crosswalk monitor. He lost out to another boy and it really crushed him for awhile. You remember?"

"No, it all escapes me," Henry frowned. "I guess I was too busy with other things."

"Anyway, a day came not long after that when Philip
207

got in a fight with the boy who got the monitor job he wanted. Philip used a lot of words against the boy, but when it came to actually exchanging blows he didn't do very well. He ended up just standing there letting this other boy punch him in the face and I was screaming and hitting the other boy on the back trying to make him stop.

"When he finally did stop, Philip didn't wipe the blood off or anything. But he turned with kind of a half smile on his lips and went in to the principal's office. Before the week was out Philip had the monitor job away from the boy that beat him up."

"So you think he had the whole thing planned, you mean?" Henry asked. "I don't know—"

"I think it demonstrates a very sophisticated mind that wouldn't have to kill in order to get his own way."

"If what you suspect is true, it also demonstrates a very devious mind," Henry pointed out. "Almost a necessary trait for a murderer. I'm afraid I can't go along with you on that; although the Lord knows I'd like to."

"I guess I'm not explaining it very well," Becky said. She rose and slipped on her backpack. "I gotta go. This'll be my first day at the rehabilitation house. I'll be assigned my own patients to work with, so it's getting kind of exciting."

"Okay. Good luck."

"Thanks, Daddy. You need any help getting back in your harness?"

"No, your mother and I can handle it."

"Okay. See you this evening."

Henry stood at the front window and watched Becky disappear down the street, riding the new moped she insisted on buying for herself. Philip's black eye in the seventh grade was only a pale blur in his mind. Had he asked the boy about it? Or was he on assignment then and had only heard about it from Val's letters. Henry felt another dull ache pass over him as he thought of the family moments he had lost.

Chapter Twenty-One

Valery was still in the garage with the washing when the San Diego call came in. A woman's voice asked for verification that he was Henry Garrett, then connected him to a very distressed Philip.

"Dad?"

"Philip? Hello."

"You know that old story about the police giving their suspects one phone call? Well, it really is true. This is it," Philip said and laughed nervously.

"You mean they've arrested you?"

"Yes, I think so. I'm a little hazy. They were waiting for me after my eight o'clock class. Handcuffs and the whole bit," he laughed again.

"Now think. Have they charged you with Pangbourne's death?"

"I think just about questioning. I don't know, Dad."

"Have you told them anything?"

"Told them anything? What anything?"

"Okay, fine. When they ask you anything—anything I mean—just keep telling them politely you can't talk until you've conferred with your lawyer, and your father is in the process of getting one, okay?"

"Yeah, okay."

"It might get a bit sticky, but just hang in there. I'll be down as soon as I can. Good-bye, son."

"Bye."

When he turned to hang up the phone Henry saw Valery standing silently in the doorway with a basket of unfolded laundry. She opened her mouth to say something, but turned and went back into the kitchen. Henry followed slowly and pulled a chair up to the opposite side of her work area where she was already folding clothes. He recognized the beginnings of a silent routine she had used on rare occasions of family disputes. After three tea towels and two bath towels were folded without a word being exchanged, Henry said, "Can I help?"

"I've done this for twenty-six years without your help. I don't see why I shouldn't be able to do it now."

"Ah, Val, please don't be like that."

"So this was the big secret you confided in your daughter now, is that it?"

"I told her my suspicions. I didn't want to worry you."

Two more towels got folded in silence, then Valery picked up one of Henry's T-shirts, shook it out and buried her eyes in it. She had always been the stoic member of the family and her sudden turn to tears surprised Henry. He walked around the table and started rubbing her rounded back.

"Honey, I think he's just been brought in for questioning. That doesn't mean he's going to be arrested—"

"What's happening to us?" Valery demanded. "What's happening? We spend our life working and caring for them and for what?"

Henry turned her around and took her in his arms. She clutched at his back with a desperation and cried, "Don't

211

shut me out, Henry. Don't shut me out."

This comment had a piercing effect on Henry as though he had been wounded somewhere near the heart. He had been so wrapped up in his own little world of struggling with his Christian philosophy and trying to reconcile himself with his son that he had not realized what Valery must be going through. When each of their recent discussions about his faith had ended without agreement he had felt silence was the better course. But now he realized that silence was taking its toll. Without meaning to he was dropping the ball on the second rule of his new creed: to love one another. They stood quietly, locked in each other's strong embrace, each knowing the other's thoughts without the words; twenty-six years had done that for them. When Valery recovered her composure she asked, "Are you sure Philip did it?"

"No, of course not."

"But you think he did."

"Honey, I don't know. Come help me pack and I'll tell you everything I know. Where's my old back brace?"

"You're not driving back down there."

"No. I was thinking of taking a plane. They no doubt have shuttle flights that run all day between LAX and San Diego."

"Oh, I don't want you to go."

"You want to come with me?"

"You know I'd be of no use to you down there."

"I'll be all right. I'll rent the biggest most comfortable car I can find," Henry said, steering Valery upstairs toward the bedroom. "I'll just take my briefcase. I don't want to carry any more than I have to. Will you call the airport while I shave?"

The busy work of packing and dressing was soon over with and Valery had gathered the flight information. There were frequent San Diego flights during commuter hours.

212

The last one back in the evening left at 11:00 p.m. Reservations really weren't necessary. Seating seemed to be no problem and Henry could pay at the gate at the last minute.

"This flying is really getting to be quite a casual thing, isn't it?" she said. "Almost like hopping on the local bus."

"Yes, it seems it is," Henry said absently as he caught the thread of a new thought line. Is it possible Mrs. Pangbourne made two trips to San Diego? She could have hopped a commuter flight in Santa Barbara after her afternoon class. But that's a relatively small airport. Too great a chance of being recognized. But suppose she drove to L.A. and got a shuttle flight at the big impersonal terminal. She would have ample time to get down to the university and confront her husband, perform the act, then get back to LAX and pick up her car and drive on down late that night. That would certainly explain her sleeping late the next morning. But what about the nonsense with getting the body into the stocks? Did she have an accomplice? Or did she hide the body and then come back for it later? An awful lot of work for a woman in the middle of the night. And why the humiliation stocks and the "liar" sign? The theory started to crumble. Becky certainly would not hear of it because the woman made no appearance in the bridge dream. Ah, to be a junior in college again and have an answer for everything.

Valery was still sitting on the bed with no indication of moving.

"You going to drive me into L.A.?" he asked.

"I was wondering if you wanted to say a prayer with me first."

Henry was not strong on foxhole religion—prayer to him was a daily occurrence, not a desperation rite. But this was the first positive sign Valery had made about faith and he was not about to pass up the opportunity. He sat

213

next to her and took her hand.

"I'd like that," he said. "Would you like me to start?"

"Yes, I guess so," she said nervously.

"Lord, we pray you will be with Philip and Valery and me in a special way in this time of trouble. We don't know what the future holds, but we ask that your will might be done in us and through us. I especially pray for Philip that he might grow close to you and learn to rely on you from this experience. Amen."

Valery looked up at him with a startled expression on her face. "That's it? You mean that's it?"

"I don't . . . What do you mean?"

"You mean that's all you're going to pray?"

"Why, you can add something. What do you want us to pray?"

"I want you to pray that Philip will be innocent."

"I see," Henry mulled. "But the man has already been murdered. And if Philip did it how can—"

"We can pray Philip did not do it," she insisted. "You say God is omnipotent. That He is in charge of everything. Heaven and earth and all. Then pray that God will make him innocent."

"Val, that's beyond my understanding. That time thing. And God has granted people free will. Some people do choose to do evil. He doesn't seem to prevent that from happening and—God forbid—but if it is Philip, then it *is* Philip."

"I know, I know," she said and rested her head on his shoulder. "I guess I'm not making sense. I'm just thinking what this will do to the family name."

Here we go again, Henry thought. He couldn't imagine the Lord getting too overwrought about their family's good name. He bit his tongue and held her close again, telling himself she didn't mean it the way it came out.

On the way to the airport, for Val's benefit, he ran over

again all he knew about the events of the case, keeping it positive and making sure he related all the other possibilities that could have led to Pangbourne's demise; the man had been a liar, a trickster, an adulterer, and a professional tyrant, and any one of these traits could have led to his death. Valery assumed that Philip's connection had to be something to do with his schooling and Henry did nothing to set her straight on the matter of Tracy. If it became necessary there would be time enough for that later. In a way he was still shutting her out by shielding her from all the truth. An old habit he had slipped into years ago. He told himself he did it because he loved her, but was it really the best thing to do? With Valery's composure restored, she bade him good-bye with her Old-English stiff upper lip.

Once on the plane, he leaned back for a few minutes' rest and tried to form a plan of action. If a lawyer became necessary there were plenty of old Navy staff judge advocates he knew from his Washington years that were now retired in the San Diego area. Tapping a first-class man should be no problem. But first he would go to Blanchard's office and find out just how much the police knew. When he left there was no indication they had made a connection about Tracy and the love triangle. What had put them onto it?

Henry gripped the armrests of the second-class seat as the image of Chapin standing in the phone booth in his pajamas suddenly popped into his mind. He had told Chapin that the reason for his sudden departure from the case was a "personal matter." But what must have gone through Chapin's mind as he drove home after that phone call? That "personal matter" comment would have gotten Chapin thinking, then he would have punched into his private computer terminal to scan Henry's background for anything that would cause this strange reaction in his normally docile agent, and what would he find there but that son Philip was now an earth science graduate student at the university in question. That would be enough to put Chapin into action. The man had a vindictive streak in him a yard wide; Henry had seen it demonstrated more than once when foolhardy company people had tried to cross him, and there was no doubt Chapin would be cruel enough to call the local district attorney with an "important tip."

The more he thought of it the more convinced he became that Chapin had put a three-thousand-mile finger on Philip because father Henry was getting out of line. The agency was still playing hardball. What did they want of him? Hadn't he paid his dues?

Henry allowed himself the pleasure of slipping into his own little vindictive daydream as the jet engines droned on. He imagined a set of circumstances in which he confronted Chapin. Chapin with his aristocratic forehead and aquiline nose. Chapin with the elegant drawing-room manners and Phi Beta Kappa key. He was younger than Henry, but shorter and lighter. Henry estimated he would have no trouble handling him in a physical confrontation. And this was quickly proved correct in his mind's eye, as the arrogant troublemaker started pestering Henry, first with abusive jibes, then physical prodding with a long stick until the longsuffering and noble Henry was completely justified in retaliating. With one deft yet vicious blow from the edge of his right hand Henry karate-chopped into the delicate bone structure of Chapin's right eye, sending him writhing and screaming into the far corner. The blow was carefully measured. Not enough to blind him permanently but just strong enough to send bone chips from the skull into the eyeball causing retinal damage which could only be mended by extensive, time-consuming, and painful surgery. Take that, Mr. Phi Beta Kappa.

For the first time that day Henry's back started throbbing. Back to reality. He tried to clear his mind by counting the diamonds in the pattern of the headrest ahead of him. He had been down that road before and knew it was no good. The road of retribution, retaliation, pride, justification, honor, and rationalization. Even at best it produced no victories, only stalwart enemies and a sore back. But at times like these that narrow road of love and mercy and grace seemed too difficult. Even the words seemed strangely out of place. *Oh, Lord, I don't understand this turning the other cheek and I can only marvel at the idea of loving my enemy. But I can trust in you. Help me to trust in you. And you know I can't keep those back muscles relaxed. If I'm going to make it through the day it will have to be with your help. Amen.*

It seemed the plane had just reached altitude and cruising speed when it started to descend. It bumped its way through the mid-morning haze that still clung to the coastline like wisps of grey cotton candy, and touched down on the asphalt runway with sudden jerks as if to say it's time to come back to the real world.

To satisfy his curiosity about Mrs. Pangbourne's possible flight from L.A., Henry was conducting a little test to see how many people would look at him enough to recognize him at a later date. He was surprised at how people avoided his eyes. Except for a quick glance at the exit by the stewardess and a confrontation in the terminal with a young boy in a Hare Krishna outfit soliciting funds, Henry felt his anonymity had escaped intact.

He was able to rent an old Dodge station wagon from a car rental stand and after persuading them to lower the pressure in the tires to a dangerously low level to baby his back he floated down into San Diego's business district and the central division station.

217

Chapter Twenty-Two

Captain Blanchard welcomed him into his office with a broad smirk on his face. "I was beginning to wonder when you'd show up."

"Good morning, captain," Henry said, soberly.

"I was wondering why you took off the way you did without saying good-bye. You know it's a funny thing about this job. All you need is a little patience and lo and behold, most of your questions get answered for you," he laughed. "Strange how you didn't happen to mention your son's involvement in the case. That was quite a smoke screen you put up for us, wasn't it? I gotta hand it to you."

"Have you filed murder charges against him?"

"All in good time, friend. All in good time."

"May I see him?"

"We're not through questioning him yet."

"Just how do you figure he's involved?"

"I don't think I want to discuss that with you, Mr. Garrett."

Henry decided to test the waters. "A word of advice, captain. If I were you I wouldn't put too much credence in the district attorney's hot tip."

It worked. Without his moving a muscle the captain's smirk became a grimace and a bit of his confidence seemed to ebb.

Henry went on, "You mind if I take a look at the articles found on Pangbourne's body?"

"What for?"

"I have a theory I'd like to check out."

"Sorry. No more fancy theories. In case you haven't noticed, the ground rules around here have changed."

"The least you could do is tell me if there was another pen found on his body."

"Why?"

"Because if there wasn't another pen I'd say Mumford's theory was probably right: Dr. Pangbourne 'borrowed' the pen from Bruce on board ship and it happened to slip out of his pocket when his body was being moved."

"What has that got to do with your son's case?"

"I'm assuming you're trying to show Philip had access to the Bruce pen. But remember, Bruce said he'd lost track of it on shipboard."

Blanchard smiled. "Pangbourne had an expensive Swiss-made pen in his shirt pocket. And as for your son having access, we figure Bruce may be lying to cover for your boy. Or maybe he had it in his duffel bag and didn't realize it. Then when your Philip decided to kill his ol' prof he picks up the pen intending to leave it as a clue, as you indicated."

"Really now, captain, don't you think that's rather heavy-handed? You know of some reason why he would want his roommate implicated? Or even why he'd want his professor killed?"

Blanchard scowled at his desk blotter. Henry went on, "And the religious book under Pangbourne's desk—was that a plant too? Remember Bruce said it was supposed to

219

be with his other books from the ship's library. Philip would certainly not have access to those."

"I thought you were supposed to bring a lawyer with you."

"I'm not sure we need one." Henry put his hands in his pockets in an attempt to appear as unthreatening as possible. "C'mon, captain, let me see my son. I could be saving you a lot of grief. What precisely do you have on him, anyway?"

Blanchard drummed his desk top with his thick fingers. "The D.A. wouldn't have him brought in without sufficient reason, you know." More drumming. "Okay. I let you see him. Are we gonna get a statement out of him then?"

"That sounds reasonable. Although I can't guarantee anything," Henry said. "I'll try."

"All right," the captain said gruffly. "I gotta wait here for the coroner's report. He's in the same room we had the other student in." The captain retrieved his keys again and showed Henry down the high security corridor. "Tell Mickey I said it was okay."

Henry looked through the wired glass peekhole into the small interrogation room and saw Philip sitting where Jeremy Bruce had sat, his head cradled on his arms on the table. Mickey was leaning back in his chair practicing his smoke-ring blowing. They both came alert as Henry entered.

"Mr. Garrett, what—" Mickey began.

"The captain said it was okay," Henry said, moving to his son's side. He put his arms about Philip and gave him a rather one-sided hug. Philip was more surprised and embarrassed than anything else.

"You okay, son?"

"Yeah, I guess so," Philip said. "Getting kinda tired of not saying anything."

Henry went back to the door and opened it. "I'll talk

220

with him alone, if you don't mind, Mickey."

He had found from years of experience that if he acted with dispatch and confidence, other people, even those supposedly in charge of a situation, would fall in line. He had no idea if Mickey was supposed to leave the room or not. Mickey's chair clicked forward and he rose.

"Oh yeah—did the captain—"

"He's waiting for the coroner's report. You can check with him."

"Yeah," Mickey said, not too sure of the situation. But he picked up his cigarettes and notebook and ambled out.

Henry slid into the chair next to Philip. "We probably don't have a lot of time. I've got to know what kind of a fix you're in. Do we need a criminal lawyer?"

"What are you talking about? Criminal lawyer? What are you talking—"

"Will you stop with the cool talk and give me straight answers now? Did you kill Dr. Pangbourne?"

"No, I didn't kill him," Philip sneered as though the question was ridiculous.

"Did you see him the evening he got back?"

"No, I didn't see him."

"What were you wearing the suit and tie for then?"

This seemed to rattle Philip. "Well, I wanted to meet with him. He'd more or less promised me the associate professorship and I wanted, you know, to find out where I stood. I couldn't do anything about my summer schedule until—"

"So you went to his office?"

"No. I went to Dean Hazard's office. That's where the profs usually congregate."

"What time was this?"

"In the afternoon. Four, I expect."

"Before you talked with Jeremy?"

"Oh, yeah."

221

"Okay," Henry said, making a conscious effort to keep the events straight in his mind. "So he wasn't there. Why didn't you keep on looking for him?"

"He was there. He told me we'd have to get together the next day."

"Son, not two minutes ago you said you didn't see him."

"I didn't see him to speak to. That's what I mean."

"But don't you see what a prosecuting attorney would do with testimony like that? You have to be specific."

"Look, I didn't kill him. What's the story here, anyway?"

"The story is we're trying to determine what it is they've got against you. Has anyone mentioned anything about Tracy?"

"Tracy! No, nothing."

"That no doubt means they know nothing about the love triangle thing," Henry said impersonally. "So let's leave it that way."

"You're quite the conniver, aren't you, Dad?"

"What do you mean?"

"I mean I thought Christians were supposed to be open and aboveboard in all their dealings."

"I'm just following the rules of the judicial game. You did say you were innocent, didn't you?"

"Yeah, sure I'm innocent."

"So why hand them a possible motive? You want me to hand them your body on a silver platter?"

"No. I just think it's funny. You sound inconsistent, that's all."

Henry marveled at the seemingly universal thought his son had slipped into, the thought that declares there is an unwritten standard to which all Christians must adhere. His own freedom was in jeopardy but Philip digressed to point out his father's "sin." Runners may stumble, cooks' soufflés may fail, angels may fall from grace, but Christians may not waver from the understood straight and narrow. And invariably it was the non-Christian who had not grasped the concept of grace that put up the most indignant cry.

It appeared his new faith and his lack of perfection was going to be a continuing stumbling block between him and his son. Too bad. He wished it could be otherwise. Henry had harbored the hope that somehow his superior knowledge would save his son from the unjust clutches of the police—Henry Garrett, free-lance detective to the rescue—and somehow Philip would be appreciative of his father's efforts and they would be reconciled. But apparently it was not to be.

Henry began discussing the possibility of bringing in one of the Navy lawyers he knew when a uniformed policeman put his head in the door.

"The captain wants the two of you in his office."

"But we're not through yet," Henry said.

"Better come. He sounded mad." The jailer shook his keys. "C'mon, I got to let you out."

The captain was still on the phone bawling out someone as they came into the office. Mickey, standing at the captain's side, motioned them into chairs. More sparks flew over the phone before he slammed the receiver down.

"They win an election and they think it makes 'em geniuses," the captain barked for his own benefit, then contemplated the open folder on his desk. Turning to Mickey, he added, "You know what really makes me sick about this whole thing?"

"What's that, captain?"

"It means Scottie died for nothing."

Everyone waited on Blanchard's anger as though it were a fifth presence in the room. Finally Henry cleared

223

his throat. Blanchard looked up.

"Get out of here. Both of you. Go."

"What's happened, captain?" Henry asked.

Blanchard closed the folder and rose. "You tell 'em, Mickey. I don't have the stomach for it." Then he took his broad menacing body out of the room.

"What's this all about?" Henry asked Mickey.

"Coroner's report. It appears Pangbourne suffered a massive heart attack. The murder investigation is being dropped."

"Sooo," Henry let out, exchanging surprised looks with Philip. "You figure the whole suffocation thing was staged. There never was a murder," he said to Mickey.

"Yup. That's what it looks like."

"But there's also the possibility the heart attack was brought on when Pangbourne was struggling for air."

"That's what the captain figured," Mickey said, "but the D.A. won't buy it. He said he'd never get a conviction because there's no way of proving which came first, the struggle or the heart attack. We're dead in the water."

"You're dead in the water," Henry repeated, "unless, unless we find some hard evidence to the contrary. Or a confession—"

"Confession? You're living in a dreamworld. Whoever's behind this is a cool customer. No. About the only thing we could hope for would be enforcing an old ordinance about mistreating a cadaver. I think it's a misdemeanor anyway. It's out of the homocide department," he said, jamming the offending folder into Blanchard's out box. "We didn't have anything on Philip anyway except a phony tip the D.A. seemed to think was something."

"But isn't it a bit premature to stop the investigation? There's been a giant deception pulled on the police department. Aren't you curious?"

"Budget, my friend. Budget. Plus I guess we've been

drawing some static from the university's governing board."

"Oh. What about?"

"They're mad about the way the case has been handled. Apparently they blame us for that picture of Pangbourne in the stocks that hit the wire services. They carry a lot of weight in this town."

"I see," Henry said. His eyes had narrowed and he'd started blinking more frequently. Something was beginning to click in the back of his mind.

"You ready to go, son?"

"I've got some books around here someplace."

"Come with me," Mickey said. "We'll get your gear."

"Meet me in the parking lot," Henry called after Philip. "I'll drive you back to the university."

"Okay."

Before Mickey and Philip were out of sight Henry was on his way to the phone in the hall. He looked up the number and dialed.

Chapter Twenty-Three

H ello," an elderly woman asked in a musical voice. "Hello, is this Mrs. Mumford?"

"Yes, it is."

"I'm Henry Garrett, an acquaintance of your husband. I was wondering how he was getting on today?"

"Oh, he's much better, thank you," she purred. "I just knew he'd be his old self again with a good night's sleep."

"Has he been released from the hospital?"

"As a matter of fact, I'm going over to check him out right now. I have some fresh clothes for him. The doctor said he might just as well rest quietly out of the hospital as in."

"I see. That's certainly good news, isn't it?" Henry said.

"Oh my, it certainly is," Mrs. Mumford bubbled.

"Then I don't suppose it would be possible for me to have a brief word with him today."

"Oh, I'm afraid not. You see we're going right up to the cabin in Idyllwild to get away for awhile. You know, the telephone and everything."

"Yes, I see. That'll be very nice and restful."

"Won't it though. Wendel Hazard, one of John's colleagues at the university, was kind enough to let us borrow his place in Idyllwild. Wasn't that thoughtful of him though?"

"Yes. Very thoughtful. I hope you'll have a very restful trip."

"Oh, thank you. So kind of you, Mr . . . . "

"Garrett."

"Mr. Garrett. Good-bye."

Henry only had a few minutes alone in the car before Philip appeared, but by then most of the pieces had fallen into place. He knew who had fallen off the bridge in the dream with him. He knew who had been wearing the wrong bumper sticker and giving off all the wrong vibrations. Henry had been racking his brain to come up with the deceptive murder suspect. But it wasn't the suspect that had been doing all the deceiving. Of course not. He should have seen it before. He, Henry Garrett of all people, should have seen it before. It wasn't a phony suspect. It was the misunderstood victim, the victim, the victim.

Philip heaved a sigh of relief once the car door slammed and he leaned back heavily in the passenger seat. Neither of them spoke for several minutes. Henry was busy with his own new theory for the Pangbourne "problem." He ran the solution over and over again in his mind looking for flaws. But there were no flaws. Only more and more answers.

Now the problem was how to expose it. What should be his plan of action? He was so engrossed in this problem he nearly sideswiped another car as they pulled into the eastbound traffic on Interstate 8.

"Watch it, Dad."

"Oh, sorry about that." Henry looked down to see the speedometer of the station wagon bouncing at seventy-six. He slowed down and looked over at Philip.

"Feeling better, son?"

"Yeah, I guess so. Kind of a frightening experience. Thanks for your help."

"That's okay. That's what a father's for."

Philip gave the closest indication of a thaw in their relationship by smiling back at his dad. Not a broad smile but there seemed to be something in it.

"I still can't figure out, if they never knew about Tracy and me, why did they bring me in like that?"

Henry didn't respond. Maybe sometime in the future he'd tell Philip about his company friend Chapin, but not now.

"Son, what's your feeling about your roommate?"

"Jeremy? He's okay. Why?"

"You think he's straight arrow about his religious convictions?"

"Yeah, I'd say so. I know he trots off to church every Sunday, if that means anything."

"Has he ever bent your ear regarding his creation theories?"

"Oh, yes," Philip groaned. "Oh, has he ever. Till I couldn't take it anymore. I finally had to tell him to can it or I was moving out."

"Was he getting anyplace with his crusade?"

"At the university? Of course not. This is a reputable institution."

"So you don't think there's a chance that someone on staff could have taken him seriously?"

"Of course not."

"I see," Henry mused. "Very adamant, aren't you?"

"What are you thinking, Dad?"

"How well do you know the teaching assistants in the biology division?"

"Fairly well, I guess."

"Well enough to get hold of a master key for their building?"

"Old habits die hard, don't they? You wouldn't be thinking of doing a little breaking and entering, would you, Dad?" When Henry didn't answer right away he went on, "Come on. I've been answering your questions."

"If someone from the university should open a door for me it would hardly be called breaking and entering."

"What are you looking for?"

"A stolen article. And if it should be found it would be our civic duty to turn it over to the police."

Philip studied the road ahead. "I don't know—I don't know. I don't think I want to get mixed up in anything like that."

"Okay, son. It was just an idea. I don't want you to do anything you don't want to do."

"What is it you're looking for? What do you think happened?"

"I'd rather not discuss it until we're sure. It could hurt some people unduly," Henry said as he turned onto University Drive. "You want me to drop you at your apartment?"

"No, let me off in front of the administration building. I have to post some grades," Philip said, shifting his schoolbooks in his arms in anticipation of getting out of the car.

Henry swung into the graceful loop in front of the administration building and pulled to a halt. "Philip, before you do anything else, call your mother. She's worried about you."

"Aren't you going home now?"

"Pretty soon. Bye, son. I'm glad you're okay. Please give Tracy my regards. It was very nice meeting her. In fact, I'm sure your mother would be interested in meeting her too. Maybe the two of you could drive up next Saturday."

"Yeah, well, we'll see. Our schedules are pretty full."

"Well, try. We'll be phoning you."

"Bye, Dad."

Henry cruised past the life science building, eyeing the large formidable structure and searching his mind for an idea. A bit further north of the faculty parking lot was a coin-operated lot for students. He swung in, parked and waited. It was eleven-thirty. The eleven o'clock biology classes would be letting out before long. He spent the time running several scenarios through in his mind as to what may have happened. He had the basic outline, but some of the details were still unclear. His main problem was going to be getting anyone to believe him. The thing was too fantastic, too bizarre to be taken at face value. He needed proof, some tangible evidence to tie his theory together.

But was any of this any of his business anymore? He had certainly been "invited out" by the police. Why not simply tell them the theory, then just walk away. Henry never pictured himself as much of a catalyst for change, but on the other hand, things were seemingly dependent on him now. And he wondered at the strange set of circumstances that had led him this far: first the business of Pangbourne threatening to confiscate equipment belonging to the company, then son Philip being threatened with arrest only to have that trouble suddenly cleared up too. And now the police suddenly dropping the case. Each event apparently designed to thrust Henry to the forefront as though it had been planned from above.

His Christian mentor, the congressman, told him he could expect to see the Lord's hand evident in his life once he committed himself to Him. Could it be happening in such a manner? His own manifest destiny? Whether it was true or not he certainly was not about to turn his back on the possibility. He'd have to play the hand out.

Chapter Twenty-Four

When the sidewalks started filling up with students, Henry walked back toward the large lecture hall he had visited the day before. Apparently, a rather disastrous final exam had just been administered because the departing students all seemed to be grumbling and comparing notes with foreboding groans. When the crowd thinned, Henry made his way through the lecture hall into the preparation room on the north side. No one there. The counter tops and carts had been swept clear of bottles and devices, lab work for the semester apparently at an end. The door leading into the faculty offices was ajar. At the end of the corridor a handful of students was clustered around a teacher's open door and, judging from their conversation, Henry decided they were complaining to the unseen professor about the unfairness of his exam. There were no other professors to be seen.

He approached the office with Mumford's name on the door and looked through the glass. It was a surprisingly small office for a division chairperson, or perhaps it only appeared small because of the condition of the room: floor to ceiling bookshelves with stacks of books and disorganized papers seemed to be everywhere. The only objects that hid their contents were the small desk, a two-drawer filing cabinet, and a small locker, with no lock on the simple chrome handles.

Henry checked the lock on the door to the room. It was the old-fashioned latch lock system that would respond to almost any skeleton key or an educated wire. The students at the end of the lecture hall were still engrossed in their own problems. He was virtually alone. Philip was right, old habits do die hard. What would be the real harm? Just a little bending of the rules, but it could lead to a much greater good. A little indiscretion could certainly be overlooked.

As he pressed his face against the window like a little boy at the candy counter, adrenalin started flowing and he could feel his pulse rate quicken. Back into the prep room, Henry started searching for a bit of wire that would do the trick. But in the process of opening and closing drawers he received a sharp twisting pain in the tender area of his back. He had to back against the counter and brace himself with his arms for a moment to get ahead of the pain. Surely God doesn't work like that. A jab in the back for every sin. An extra inch of nose for every Pinocchio-lie. Whatever the reason, it gave him a chance to rethink his line of action. He wasn't going to get carried away, he decided. Whatever the handicap he would play it straight.

"Oh, Lord, forgive me for looking to myself again. Help me to have faith in your rules. Help me to enjoy the liberty of your confines. I lift up mine eyes to the hills from whence comes my strength. My strength comes from you."

As he finished his combination prayer/relaxation moment, he opened his eyes and found he was calmly staring at the ceiling. It was a suspended ceiling with two-by-

232

four-foot sections of acoustical panels and inset florescent lights. But the one panel in the area above the sink where his eyes came to rest seemed to have a slight bulge to it, as though something heavy had been placed above it.

While Henry was still contemplating the unusual panel, a key clicked in the lock of the north door and Bonny entered once more. This time she was carrying an armful of freshly laundered lab coats which she proceeded to put in one of the built-in cabinets.

"Hello, Bonny."

She jumped and gave out a yell. "Mister, you gotta stop doing that. You scared the pants off me again."

"I'm sorry."

"Dr. Mumford still isn't here. Fact he's gone for the semester. The rest of the staff is finishing up his classes . . . " She stopped and looked at the ceiling where Henry was looking. "Something wrong up there?"

"I wonder what makes that one panel bulge down like that."

"You know, I was wondering about that myself the other day," Bonny said. She pulled out a drawer by the sink and used it for a step on her way up onto the counter. She then pushed up the panel next to the one in question and peered into the unfinished area above.

"Well, what do you know." She reached in and retrieved the object with both hands. "Here, catch."

Like manna from heaven, Henry, without moving from the spot, had dropped into his arms the large elusive black briefcase.

"Is that what I think it is?" Bonny whispered as she climbed down.

"Looks like it, doesn't it?" Henry said.

He placed it on the counter and snapped the unlocked latches. On top of everything was a thick sealed letter-size envelope addressed simply "Sylvia."

He took it out and showed it to Bonny. "Sylvia is Pangbourne's wife's name. It's got to be his missing case."

"You're kidding. How'd it get up there?"

"I'm sure the police will be interested in knowing that too."

"Police?" I thought you were with the police."

"Yes . . . " Henry said absently. He was already flipping through the contents of the case. The legal-size heavy envelope he was looking for wasn't hard to find; it bore the same two-tone brown colors he'd seen in the printer's office.

Henry flipped it open and looked through the contents. And there, among the list of report presenters for the summer geology meeting, was the name *Jeremiah Bruce.* Granted it was in longhand but it bore a striking resemblance to the other longhand notes throughout the case. Pangbourne had intended to use Jeremy's paper. The boy was right all along.

"Are you sure you should be going through that?" Bonny wanted to know.

But before Henry could answer, Wendel Hazard pushed open the door from the lecture hall. He came to a stop in the middle of the room and, hands on hips, he silently surveyed the briefcase, the open ceiling and the two people in the room. Henry put things back in the case and snapped it shut.

To Bonny, Hazard said, "Let's see, you're the lab tech, aren't you?"

"Yes, sir. Bonny Shaw, Dean Hazard."

"Bonny, I'll have to ask you to step out of the room a moment," Hazard said. "We shouldn't be long."

"Oh. Okay," Bonny said. She shut the cabinet where the lab coats were kept and quickly left by the north door.

Nothing moved in the room except for the slight heaving of the dean's vest. Apparently he had been running.

234

Henry decided to let Hazard play it the way he wanted to and he would only react. Hazard took a handkerchief from his back pocket and touched his forehead as he said, "I'm sure you realize that's college property."

"Is it?" Henry asked. "Looks like Dr. Pangbourne's property to me."

"It was found on college property."

"There's a phone on the wall behind you," Henry said softly. "Why don't we call the police and let them decide."

Hazard touched his forehead some more and returned his handkerchief to his back pocket. Henry didn't move.

"Now look, we've got the best interests of the university to consider. That briefcase isn't leaving this room."

"Oh, isn't it?" Henry asked.

Hazard tried to laugh, "What is it you think happened here, anyway?"

"I think a man was murdered in this room."

"No. No one was murdered. Don't be ridiculous—"

They both jumped as the lecture room door swung open. It was Philip. He too was short of breath.

"Dad. What's going on?"

"That's a good question."

Philip took a step toward his father and pointed toward Hazard, "I met the dean in the administration building and told him you were onto something. And he took off like a scared rabbit."

"It's okay," Henry said. "The dean was just about to explain how no one was murdered in this room."

"Let's not be childish now, gentlemen," Hazard said as casually as he could manage. Henry thought the facade was beginning to crack so he went out on a limb.

"Perhaps you can begin by explaining away the dried blood spot on the floor in Dr. Mumford's office." Henry didn't in fact see any blood spot, but he figured this would be a good way to get things going.

"Now look, this is getting out of hand," Hazard said. "I don't know about dried blood. Mumford's a biologist. It's not too unreasonable to assume in the normal course of his instructional duties some animal blood may have gotten spilled on his floor."

"Whether or not it is animal blood will be easy to determine, won't it?" Henry said.

"All right," Hazard said, leaning casually against the counter top. "You're the one making all the accusations; what do you think happened?"

"I think you and Mumford did meet with Pangbourne the night he got back. That much is true," Henry began. "But the meeting didn't go quite the way you described it. That business about you and Mumford fighting over an associate professorship was pretty much a smoke screen. Several of the geology graduate students knew they were being considered for the spot, so it's rather hard to imagine Mumford didn't know the new teaching slot was going to geology and not life sciences. The meeting may have started out being about the fossil class and a discussion of which discipline it belonged under, but I have a feeling the discussion soon got around to the summer geological conference and the paper young Bruce was going to present."

"Ridiculous," Hazard scoffed. "Why would Pangbourne be introducing such a topic in a meeting with Mumford? He's not concerned with the geological association."

"Ah, but Jeremy Bruce's paper was about some of the discoveries made on the expedition. Discoveries in which biological organisms were found out of place in the normal sequence of evolution. This no doubt would be a topic of interest to Dr. Mumford and I see no reason why Pangbourne wouldn't at least mention it. And once it was mentioned and the nature of the paper was made clear to Mumford—that nature being a strong contradiction to the

236

evolutionary theory—I can well imagine old Mumford getting his hackles up and then you joining in the argument against Pangbourne. The two of you were not about to sit idly by and see a wild-eyed Bible-thumping creationist get such an important platform to spout his theories—"

"You're forgetting one thing," Hazard interrupted. "Pangbourne had no more patience with Bruce than the rest of us. What makes you think he'd allow such a paper to be presented?"

"A good question, Dr. Hazard. That's what had us all stymied for a long time. Pangbourne had quite a reputation, didn't he? He was a hard taskmaster to his subordinates, a sophisticated practical joker to his peers, an adulterer to his wife, and a man commanding respect and awe to the general public that knew him. Quite a formidable personality. And anything we saw him do we'd relate to what we already knew about him in spite of what it was he might do."

"You're not making sense, my friend," Hazard sneered.

"To put it simply, I think Pangbourne had a change of heart. Some life-changing experience—maybe some religious experience to make him have a change—"

Hazard laughed. "Pangbourne? Religious experience? My dear friend, you don't understand the man."

"Maybe I'm wrong about that, but I've got the proof right here," Henry patted the black briefcase at his elbow. "Proof that Pangbourne was changing the summer conference a third time and he intended to have Bruce present his paper. The reason really doesn't matter at this point."

"Ridiculous," Hazard insisted for the third time, his ample vocabulary deserting him. "The idea that there was some sort of collusion between Mumford and myself . . . "

"Symbiosis was the word Jeremy used. It's a good word too. Two separate organisms banding together for a common cause. That's you and Mumford. And after Pangbourne died in this room with the two of you as witnesses you conspired to make it look like Jeremy Bruce did the killing. Let's see . . . " Henry pondered. "It probably went something like this. After Pangbourne was dead the two of you dragged his body into Mumford's office behind me here. You knew it would be undetected there because the clean-up crew had already been through here earlier in the evening and this would give you time to think. You went ahead and took Mumford home as if nothing had happened. Mumford gave you his key so you could dispose of the body. That's why Mumford showed up the next day and had to have the lab tech unlock his own office for him. You had his key.

"You went on home that night and tried to formulate a plan to get this Jeremy Bruce off your back. Why you were so adamant about Bruce not presenting his paper is still not clear to me. But anyway there it was. So you watched the TV news and took your call from your wife, and you thought and thought. Then in the wee hours of the morning you came back here, hid the briefcase so the investigating officers would think Pangbourne had left the area. Then you hoisted the body onto one of these demonstration carts." Henry pulled one of the carts over in front of him. "And you pushed it across the dark sleepy campus. If you had been discovered, you could always claim you were trying to get him to the university hospital since it was in that direction. The only risky part was putting him in the stocks and getting the bag over his head.

"Quite the little dramatic touch, that plastic bag and the stocks and the pen with Bruce's name on it," Henry continued. "It served two purposes for you. It pointed a guilty finger toward Bruce and it gave nationwide publicity to the university's natural science division. Any publicity was better than none, you no doubt reasoned, since the—

how did you put it—the 'diadem' of your science department was now dead. And there may have been just a tinge of resentment toward Pangbourne on your part—he always in the spotlight, you in the background. Him with his practical jokes, always getting the laughs. But the last embarrassment would he on him, the 'liar' sign you used to throw suspicion toward Bruce. But I think there may have been a bit of sadistic pleasure in that move too.

"But it was at the stocks you made your two mistakes. Number one, you found Bruce's pen in Pangbourne's pocket; no doubt he had 'borrowed' it from Jeremy just as Mumford said. But if it was going to be a clue there should be another pen in his pocket. So you took a pen from your own pocket and put it in Pangbourne's shirt. The only problem was there is no evidence Pangbourne ever wrote with that planted pen. Your planted pen releases a blue-violet ink that is quite uncommon; probably from the Swiss manufacturer Isensee, while Jeremy's pen released the most common dark blue ink, B-318, found in 80 percent of American ball-points. And that's the kind of ink Pangbourne used to write the note to his wife, and the kind of ink I've found throughout his briefcase. Now, I ask you, why would he carry a pen around with him that he never used? But if we look through your papers I'll bet we'll find that you used it."

Hazard rubbed his thumb and index finger along the corners of his mouth and studied his accuser in a scholarly, detached way. Philip took the occasion of the momentary lull in the conversation to close his mouth. Henry went on, "But it was the second mistake that finally put me onto you. The mistake with the plastic bag. On the morning when the body was discovered I remember seeing Dr. Mumford come racing across the grass and ripping open the plastic bag over Pangbourne's head. Why would he do a thing like that, I asked myself. It was obvious the man was dead. Surely he would know the police or someone had checked for a pulse before then. I figured it was just an emotional reaction on Mumford's part.

"That is until I learned Pangbourne had suffered a heart attack and did not die of asphyxiation, as you two were trying to establish. In asphyxiation both the lungs and the inside of the bag should be filled with carbon dioxide. But if the cause of death were a heart attack, only the lungs would contain carbon dioxide, and the air on the inside of the bag would hold normal air laced with oxygen.

"Mumford, the trained biologist, would think of that immediately. He knew the coroner would spot that in a moment. So when you called him that morning and told him what you had done he raced over here and ripped the bag open, so your slip-up wouldn't be detected.

"I wondered how he appeared on the scene so quickly and why he hadn't taken time to dress properly. And I wondered who called the press in so quickly. The police insisted they did not. It was our friendly little publicity seeker, wasn't it, Dr. Hazard?"

Hazard appeared to be very tired. His face had darkened and the belligerent look had faded. He pulled the stool out from under the sink and slowly lowered himself onto it. "He was going to give Bruce the associate professorship. Can you believe that?" Hazard asked with a wan smile. "Mumford and I couldn't believe our ears. He was notifying the dean of instruction, he said."

"Of course," Henry snapped his fingers in recognition. "That's why you took the mail belonging to the dean of instruction. You were trying to squelch the notice—"

Hazard went on as though he hadn't heard, "We couldn't let him do it. We tried reasoning with him, then threatening him. He was sitting right there in the corner, behind the table. When he got up to go, Mumford pushed him back down to argue some more. But Ralph grabbed at

240

his chest and slumped over on the floor. We thought it was a gag. We did everything we could. Honestly, we did. Both Mumford and I are trained in C.P.R. We worked on him a good forty-five minutes without response.

"Then we panicked, I guess. Mumford thought he would be blamed for his death since he had been physically confronting him. I was more concerned with getting Bruce out from under foot. I thought for sure Ralph had already reached the dean or had at least dropped a note to the dean about Bruce. I had to find a way to implicate Bruce in his death." Hazard smiled at Henry. "You almost had it right. But it was falling apart anyway. Mumford was falling apart. He couldn't stand to see the innocent student railroaded, but on the other hand he couldn't face the idea of Bruce on our staff. Between the rock and a hard place. He couldn't stand the pressure."

Henry shook his head. "You did all this just to keep Bruce off the staff?"

Hazard raised his steel-hard stare onto Henry. "You still don't understand, do you? You actually don't understand what's at stake. It's taken us 200 years to purge our places of learning of superstition and hocus-pocus. We scientists have been vilified, burned at the stake, humiliated—from Galileo on. But we prevailed. Religion was finally put in its proper place, in the humanities under religious studies, along with all the other inexact sciences.

"But there's a new wave moving across our land. A sinister wave which is trying its best to control pure science, to somehow demoralize it or submit it to a board of approval made up of TV preachers and opportunistic politicians."

Hazard rose to his feet as he warmed to his subject. "Well, let me tell you, we will not be compromised. We've come too far, paid too dear a price to submit to such nonsense. Empirical truth is not about to be compromised."

"So," Henry interrupted, "in order to preserve your big truth you're willing to tell little lies. Even when a person's life might be at stake."

Hazard smiled. "Touché. You use the tools that are available to you. It's a lesson we picked up from the medieval popes."

Henry picked up the briefcase from the counter. "Well, I'd love to stay and continue this conversation, but . . . "

Hazard spread his legs slightly and moved his weight forward. "That briefcase is not leaving this room."

The two middle-aged men eyed each other for a moment like a couple old gamecocks. Philip backed up a step and watched with saucer eyes. Henry, because of his background and training, had formulated a plan in his mind which he now decided was the time to implement. It worked a little better than he hoped.

"We'll see about that," Henry said, as he took two false steps toward the door to the lecture hall.

As he expected, Hazard raced to the door and spread-eagled himself there, back to the door. But instead of continuing in that direction, Henry had suddenly stopped and shoved the metal demonstration cart at the door. His intention was simply to block Hazard momentarily while he made his escape by the north door. But the cart and Hazard made it to the door at the same time and the corner of the heavy cart caught Hazard square in the groin, doubling him up in pain.

Clutching the briefcase like a fullback, Henry slammed against the fire bar on the north exit with his hip and the door flew open. He hit the sidewalk running and nearly had to hurdle over Bonny who was sunning herself on the lawn outside. Racing through the faculty parking lot he listened for the sound of footsteps behind him. But there were none.

Chapter Twenty-Five

O nce he made it to the station wagon, locked the doors and started the engine, he did a curious thing. Perhaps not so curious for Henry. He was thinking about how he was going to drop all the briefcase information onto Captain Blanchard's desk and have the contents used as evidence against Hazard and Mumford. All the contents? He got to wondering about the personal letter marked "Sylvia" and how Mrs. Pangbourne had told him of the highly intimate notes Pangbourne had sent her in the past. Was there any need for the police and the press to be privy to this last letter? He snapped open the case and put the "Sylvia" envelope into his breast pocket.

Then, just as he was making toward the exit, he heard Philip calling him. "Dad. Hey, Dad. Wait up."

Henry stopped for him and Philip climbed in the front seat next to his father. "Wow!" Philip let out and laughed.

"Hazard going to be all right?" Henry asked as they rolled out of the lot and toward the interstate.

"Yeah, he was on his feet trying to walk it off when I left." Philip looked over the case between them. "That's

Dr. Pang's case all right. Where did you find it?"

"Hazard had put it up above the acoustical ceiling panels in the preparation room. I imagined he planned to come back for it after everything had cooled down."

"Wow! I never suspected," Philip marveled. "You think there's enough evidence in there to do any good?"

"I think so. I think Hazard was probably right about the way Pangbourne died. But there's certainly enough to indicate they were faking evidence to implicate your roommate."

"Oh, wow!" Philip pondered in silence as they raced toward town. Then, "We're headed for the police station now?"

"That's right."

"Dad, how did you know about the ink in ball-point pens? Is that something you picked up in the company?"

Henry smiled. "No. I had the feeling Dr. Hazard was getting desperate and with a little more pushing on my part he'd implicate himself, so I made it all up about the pens. I wouldn't know one ball-point pen from another. All I had to go on was my hunch that Hazard was more the expensive pen type than Pangbourne."

"And the part about Dr. Pang having some sort of life-changing experience, you made that up too?"

"Quite the contrary. If you separate the legend that had built up around the man from the actual events I think you'll see what I mean. I was called into the case in the first place when our company operators left the ship while it was docked in Mexico. They reported Pangbourne was planning to keep some government equipment, and I was called in to try to get it back. And yet when I appeared on the scene two weeks later Pangbourne had changed his mind and said he was giving the equipment back. The question I should have asked was, What happened during those two weeks to make him change his mind? He even offered to tell me, as I recall, but I was too wrapped up in my own little world of problems to bother. His reputation told me not to get involved.

"I think the same malady affected the other people he was involved with. His wife was used to his devious ways, so when she heard he was taking their house off the market she jumped to the conclusion he was going to sell it privately to avoid paying a commission to the realtor. Then when she intercepted a cable from the Israeli woman, one of her husband's old loves, she assumed he really wanted to keep the house and bring the woman back to share it with him.

"And Madam Israeli, I think her name was Veronica something, probably jumped to an incorrect conclusion too: her cable to Pangbourne read, 'I forgive you anything,' et cetera. He had treated her very shabbily in order to break off their relationship a year ago. But now he was simply asking for her forgiveness and she took it to mean he wanted to rekindle the affair. But that wasn't his intention at all. He simply felt a need to ask her forgiveness.

"And Tracy . . . " Henry began, but didn't choose to complete his thought.

"Yes," Philip finished the idea in his mind.

"And the kind of language he used in the note to his wife—'wonderful news,' 'miracles never cease.' Hardly the language of a hard-nosed academic curmudgeon, would you say?" Henry asked. "More the language of a man of faith."

Philip smiled at his father. "You wouldn't be reading things into this whole business, would you, Dad? I mean, seeing things that aren't really there because of your own, uh, unusual outlook?"

"I don't think so, son. These things do happen, however hard it may be for you to believe them."

"Oh, yes, I'm sure they do." Philip fussed in his seat as

245

though to say the conversation was at an end, then watched the road ahead for several minutes.

"Dad, you mind if we pull off and stop at a restroom?"

"You're just nervous from all the excitement," Henry said. "We'll be there in no time."

"Okay," Philip said, grudgingly.

Henry had a pent-up singleness of purpose in his head and he wasn't about to be detoured until his delivery had been made. They raced on, through the downtown freeway exit and a series of yellow lights until they bounded into the police parking lot where Henry deposited the low-riding wagon in an "Emergency Only" slot.

The captain was not in his office but Mickey was in the process of passing out some duplicated notices to all the empty desks in the squad room area.

"Could you tell me where I might find the captain?" Henry asked.

He glanced at his watch. "Probably still downstairs having his coffee. Why?"

"Remember what we said about new evidence in the Pangbourne investigation? Well, I believe I have it."

"Sergeant Willard is wrapping up that case now. He's over across the hall there in general—"

"No. I think I want to share this with the captain if you don't mind."

"Well, good luck," Mickey said and pointed toward a stairwell. "I can't leave the area because of the phones."

"Dad," Philip said, taking the heavy black case from his father, "why don't I take the briefcase and wait for you in the captain's office while you track him down."

Henry went down the steps two at a time and found the captain among refreshment dispensers swapping laughs with another heavyset plainclothesman.

"Captain, may I have a word with you?"

"Well. Back again! What is it about us that keeps draw-

246

ing you back?"

"I've some information about Pangbourne's death."

"Let's hear it. We're among friends."

"It's evidence. I have it in your office."

"Something I can take to the D.A.?"

"I believe so. I think it proves Pangbourne's death was dressed up to look like the Bruce boy killed him."

"You mean planted evidence?"

"I mean arranged evidence. I found the missing briefcase."

Blanchard studied Henry's face for a moment, then drained his paper cup and threw it in the general direction of the wastebasket. "Let's see it."

Henry preceded him back up the stairs and found he had to wait for the lethargic officer of the law at the landing.

"You remember how Bruce insisted Pangbourne had asked him to prepare an outline of the paper he was to present?"

"I remember Bruce's story, if that's what you mean."

"Okay, well, I have proof, in Pangbourne's own handwriting, that he was going to have Bruce present his paper."

By then they had reached the captain's office. Philip was nowhere to be seen but the briefcase sat in the middle of Blanchard's desk.

"You're sure this is the missing briefcase?"

"No doubt about it. Pangbourne's notes in his handwriting are all over," Henry said, excitedly.

"I don't suppose you thought to protect it for a fingerprint check."

"No, I'm afraid I didn't. I had all I could do to get it here."

Blanchard snapped the case open and looked in. "There's supposed to be papers in here?"

247

Henry swung the case around so he could see in. It had been stripped of everything.

"What's the story here?" Blanchard demanded.

Henry stood gaping at the empty case for a moment, trying to put two and two together. Then without another word to the captain he raced from the room.

"Hey, Garrett. What's going on here?" Blanchard called.

Henry hurried out the side entrance he and Philip had used to enter the building moments before. There was no sign of Philip, either in the station wagon or on the quiet side street next to the parking lot. Henry ran around to the front of the building. Again, no sign of Philip—at least at first. But then Henry's attention was drawn to the east-bound city bus across the street. It had just picked up passengers at its stop and pulled out into the right-hand lane of the busy thoroughfare and was waiting for the light to change.

Henry thought he spotted Philip's familiar crown of black hair just settling in near the back of the bus. He raced down the station steps and jayran across the road and through the waiting traffic. But just as he approached the bus lane the light changed and Henry found he couldn't make it to the curb. He moved to the street side of the slowly moving bus and searched for Philip.

It was a new modern-looking vehicle with large low windows, but closed for air conditioning. Henry spotted Philip immediately and banged on the plexiglass window. Philip gave a surprised glance in his father's direction, then looked straight ahead again.

"Philip," Henry shouted, "think what you're doing. Think what you're doing."

As though in a dream, he couldn't make his presence felt. The roar of the engine increased as the bus picked up speed and rolled down the busy street. Henry made it to the curb and looked after the bus while he tried to determine his next move. But the memory of his son's profile as he turned his face away from his father kept burning its way into his thought process.

Chapter Twenty-Six

It was mid-afternoon when Henry once again pulled up in front of the old Victorian mansion. Sylvia Pangbourne, in a colorful summer dress, responded to the elaborate chime and graciously swung the large screen door open when she saw who it was.

"I was hoping to see you again in order to apologize to you for the way I acted the other day," she said. "I do hope you understand."

"No problem," Henry said as he stepped in. There was a cool ocean breeze drifting through the old house and it added to the pleasant sensation the place generated. The polished wood floors, the slight aroma of ferns and furniture polish and the opulent sparkles given off by the cut crystal and ornate plate glass mirrors and windows all seemed to insist that time had stood still for 100 years. But it had not. Henry took a deep breath and continued his distasteful mission.

"Mrs. Pangbourne, I have some news for you. Your husband's case has been found."

"Yes?"

"I found it. That is, we found it under rather sinister circumstances."

"What do you mean?"

"I mean we think it was hidden in order to deceive people—other people at the university—of your husband's true intentions."

"What intentions? What do you mean?"

"I mean there is reason to believe that people at the university were trying to make it appear that a student, Jeremiah Bruce, killed your husband."

"The student the police arrested. Yes, I read about him." She waited for Henry to continue.

"Yes. That's right. And we're looking for information to support that which will implicate the people at the university." Henry reached in his pocket. "A letter was found—addressed to you. And I was wondering if I might see the contents to see if there was anything incriminating . . ."

As soon as the letter appeared Mrs. Pangbourne's full attention was riveted on it. Henry could just as well stay silent. She took it in both hands and studied it as though she was weighing the contents. After a moment she looked up.

"I was on the veranda. Reading. I was going to have some lemonade. Would you like some?"

"Yes, that would be nice."

She gestured Henry toward the back of the house and then disappeared toward the kitchen with the letter. Henry felt like following her; he hated to see that nice fat envelope get out of his sight, but he finally decided against it.

There were new tufted pillows on the old-fashioned wicker lounges on the veranda, but Henry was in no mood for sitting. He thumbed through a textbook she apparently had been studying; it was on the history of the woman's movement, rather heavily slanted toward extremes, he thought—all the women seemed angelic and all the men villainous. The picture heading up the last chapter showed a large-breasted woman proudly displaying her T-shirt which declared to the world, "A woman needs a man like a fish needs a bicycle."

Henry walked out to the edge of the raised redwood patio and looked over into what must be the backyard of the city councilman. He saw the built-in barbecue, the lawn chairs and tables, all quiet now, and the hole in the hedge where Pangbourne must have coaxed the unsuspecting boxer dog.

The lemonade was taking quite awhile, he had just decided, when he heard a soft cry coming from the kitchen area. He hurried through the house and swung open the door to the kitchen. Mrs. Pangbourne was sitting at the small kitchen counter with her hands covering her eyes.

"Are you all right?" he asked.

After a moment she uncovered her tear-streaked face. "Yes, I'm all right," she said and tried to smile, then took the five-page letter out of her lap and passed it silently to Henry. It was Pangbourne's small careful handwriting,

Dearest Sylvia,

I have to write this to you because I don't think I could put it into the correct words in a conversation quite yet. At least not with you. So I'm asking you to read this, all of it and then we'll talk.

It seems to me this whole strange series of events started around two years ago when you dragged me out to see that play at the state university, "Who's Afraid of Virginia Wolfe?" The play made a profound impression on me, and for months afterward I tried to analyze just why.

It's very disconcerting to see yourself portrayed on stage, I've decided. To see all your cleverness and little jokes reduced to the futility they so richly deserve.

Perhaps it's just a normal result of the aging process, but all the goals of youth have either been met or surpassed and yet they have left no sense of satisfaction or fulfillment for me. Philosophically, I had always subscribed to the absurdity and futility of life; but I didn't expect its truth to strike so quickly and so profoundly in my own life. What had I accomplished? Plate tectonics? Our geological association? They both would have been developed very nicely without me. And now I find myself being outdistanced by the young turks coming along in earth science. In order to keep on top of them I find myself resorting to bluster and threats and I can feel myself becoming a caricature of my former self.

Perhaps I should take some pride in having contributed to the general accumulation of knowledge. But then, I ask myself, knowledge for what? So a few oil companies can make more educated guesses about where to drill? So our technology which feeds blindly on itself can grow bigger? Has it all brought us closer to the better life? To the quality, the heart and substance of it all, whatever that might be? I think not.

This is just a smattering of the thoughts that have been going through my mind, all of which pointed up the futility and the overriding absurdity of life, and man's futile efforts to make sense out of it all. If life itself was absurd then why shouldn't I be absurd and live my life for any shallow, fleeting pleaure that comes along? If life was one monstrous joke then I would turn that same joke back on life and anyone that got in my way. But it wasn't enough. A joke is not enough to hang your life on. There had to be something more.

You'll be surprised to know I even toyed with your Christianity at this point. Like Kierkegaard, I reasoned if man is in fact a rational being in an irrational world, then what was needed was a blind leap of faith into the arms of a nice fairy tale, like Christianity, that would answer all your questions and rub a salving balm on all your war wounds. But try as I might, this kind of faith seemed to be not a solution but the greatest absurdity of all, underscored ironically by the ubiquitous sight of its founder dying on the cross. The life of service and turning-the-other-cheek was too far removed from the great Ralph Pangbourne to stomach. Especially when my sex glands and my pride seemed constantly to be working in opposition, and my sense of logic so easily overturned that applecart of faith.

I hope you're still reading. Anyway, this is all part of the muddled mess I took with me on the ocean voyage. I intended to do some deep thinking and come up with some rational philosophical treatise of my own that would allow me some rest. The ocean is a good place for that. The unrelenting movement and power of the sea beneath you and the long star-filled nights on watch, totally removed from civilization, gives a person a magnificent chance to clear the mind for a bit of original thinking. My own "beagle voyage," as it were.

But who was I kidding? Try as I might, I always ended up on the same circular treadmill of the absurdity of life. Out of sheer spite I was driven to taking out my frustrations on one of the students on board. One of the lads from my own university, it turned out, was a Bible-quoting creationist and was beginning to get on everyone's nerves with his scriptural literalism.

I mention him because of the heightened irony of it all. Near the end of the expedition, when I was still feeling my frustrations and was far from anxious to get home, we were doing some casual diving in the clear Mexican waters and I happened to draw this Bruce boy as my diving partner. We were going out of the survey sub's airlock with headgear and air tanks just for the fun of it. But it was during that one brief dive that I found my answer. Not an answer I was looking for but an answer in excess of anything I could ever have anticipated. Now let me be very specific here about this sequence.

Near the end of the dive I found myself getting tired and I was about to signal to Bruce that I wanted to go back to the sub. But before I got his attention, I found I was having trouble breathing, and then almost immediately I experienced a strong pain in my chest and arm. Realizing that I would be passing out very shortly, I did the only thing people, even experienced divers, seem to do in that situation: I panicked. I ripped off my mask for a good breath of air, but of course there was none to be had. The last thing I recall, Bruce was trying to force his own mouthpiece into my mouth.

Then in an instant all my pain and anguish was gone and I found myself in what I can only describe as a tunnel, and there was a tremendous rushing sound, something like a train without tracks racing along either beside me or inside of me. I remember wondering what that strange rushing sound was doing under water since submerged sound waves didn't normally act that way. And I found I could see very clearly without my mask, yet I still seemed to be submerged. The light coming from the end of the tunnel was unbelievably bright, yet it had no painful effect on my senses. And it allowed me to see or experience sights I never realized were there before, almost as if there were whole new color spectrums. And through it all I had a sense of well-being. No fear, no pain. No, saying only that is not enough. I can't find the words to tell you what it felt like. The closest I can come to it is *wonderful*.

Then there seemed to be someone with me. Some person or a presence with me inside my brain. (The time sequence of these events are probably jumbled because time as we know it didn't seem to exist.) I remember looking down on my diving partner and it was only then I realized I was having an out-of-body experience, for Bruce was pulling my lifeless body back into the sub. This presence wanted me to see this for some reason. I remember saying or thinking to the presence, this couldn't be real because someone had scrawled the words "Old Score" across the bow of the boat and I knew no such sloppy paint job existed on the real sub. (It wasn't until my return and recovery that I found one of the young scientists on the trip had in fact painted the phrase "Old Score" on the sub *before* our dive while we were waiting to be submerged.)

And the presence let me know I had a choice about returning or not returning to that lifeless body. It seemed the choice was up to me. It was then I thought of you, dear. I thought of the first years we were together with all the promises and hope and love we shared then. I even smelled the varnish that used to permeat our old garage apartment where we first lived, and how you refinished old furniture and sold it so I could get through my doctoral program. (I guess it's true about your life flashing before you at such times.) And I thought of the shabby way I've treated you these past years. I seem to have taken a delight in harming anything in my life that was tender or loving or helpless and dependent. Not that you were ever helpless, but that loving spark we had between us needed care and nurture. And it was that something I seemed to feel needed rejection, perhaps because of the rejection I felt within myself. Whatever the reason, I knew I had to come back because of you and change all that. And instantly I was back inside my own old body.

I tried at first to dismiss it as a dream, even though I knew it wasn't. (A dream is limited to what the dreamer knows or can imagine.) But this went far beyond any dream sensation I'd ever known. Then, when I learned about "Old Score" and realized I could only have seen that name while I was out of my body, for there was no time when I could have seen it while in my body, I realized the true significance of what had happened. Man has a spirit, or a self, which is separate and apart from his body. This to me was overwhelming, absolutely overwhelming. It devastated all my old convictions. For if man has a spirit, a something or other which is beyond the random chance of evolution and cause and effect and death and everything else we scientists say we know, then it's a whole new ball game. Man can't be measured or predicted. Man can't be weighed by any balance known to us or that ever will be known to us.

And what of the source? Oh, God in heaven, what of the source? Perhaps our bodies came by chance from some primordial slime on the slopes of a volcano eons ago, and I'm no longer sure that is so. But where did the Self come from? No chance amalgam of molecules made that. Yet I know it had a source. Where did it come from? Nothing can come from nothing. Where, I screamed at myself, did that spirit I now knew existed come from? There could only be one source.

I was overwhelmed by the realization that God existed. This conviction settled on me not by any kierkegaardian blind leap of faith but by the sheer weight of reason, and I was dragged, kicking and screaming, into His presence, His world, His universe, His understanding.

And once this one central fact was recognized, the whole philosophical dam I built for myself was broken and everything gushed out. If there is a God who somehow created us, then it is logical that He would care about the way we conduct ourselves. And if He cares how we conduct ourselves, it is reasonable that He would influence us, touch our lives, show us the way. And since He has already broken into this sterile system of physics and chemistry we call our world by creating us, what is to prevent Him from doing it again? And again and again? What barrier remains? If one miracle has been perpetrated, why not all of them? The raising from the dead, the loaves and fishes, everything that points to a just, loving, caring God, for I'm convinced this is what we have. The humble man that climbed the hill was right all along.

And as if I needed more assurances, Bruce had brought along several religious books for our ship's library. And while we were cruising home my eye was attracted to one of his titles. It's a book called *Life After Life* and it documents testimony of people like myself who have had this threshold-of-death experience. (I have it here at the office. Remind me to bring it home for you to see.) Their stories were unbelievably similar to my own. The tunnel, the bright light, the overpowering sense of well-being that is almost universally described by the grossly inadequate word, "wonderful."

Perhaps this last element is the most amazing of all for it shows that every last vestige of my old belief is gone. I've never told this to anyone before, but the thought of my own death always struck terror in my heart. My greatest incentive to excel, I think, was always the thought of death and nothingness overcoming me. Like a desperate marathoner, I felt activity of any sort put off the day of the "grim reaper" when nothing can or could be done. But now even this last anxiety has been wiped away. I have no trace of fear for that moment we all must face, but I'm now honestly looking forward to it. What point in resorting to cynicism or despair now? We aren't alone either now or on the other side.

And as for the time left on this side, whatever that might be, I have much to do. The first will be to restore our relationship, if that is still possible. Perhaps we can have a new beginning even now. Is it too late for us? And there are a host of others whose pardon I must beg for one reason or another. It'll be great fun watching their faces. They'll be dumbfounded. I really must learn to smile more simply. I caught myself smiling in the mirror yesterday and I came across as a bald satyr of some sort. Everyone will still suspect me of ulterior motives.

And after this conference, if you're not teaching summer school, I'd like to take the Amtrak up the coast, just the two of us. I seem to get a heightened pleasure out of just the normal sights and sounds of life now. I've just returned from six months on the Pacific Ocean, but I look at it now as if I'd never truly seen it before. Maybe we could stop off at Big Sur again. Remember the stone and glass motel we liked so much?

I've just read over what I've written here and I find I haven't said what I wanted to say about our relationship. (It seems I can babble on about everything else but that.) But I want you to know I love you and am sincerely sorry for the way I've acted toward you. And I'm waiting to hear your answer.

Love, as never before,
Ralph

When Henry looked up, Mrs. Pangbourne was stirring a pitcher of lemonade and waiting for the frozen concentrate to dissolve. Suddenly the crime investigation and his own problems seemed a million miles away.

"It's a beautiful letter," he said.

"Yes, isn't it," she said softly. "It's unbelievable. I didn't know such things could happen to middle-aged men."

"Yes, it's possible." Henry knew.

He looked for signs of another breakdown but nothing came. Like the first time he met her, she was controlling her emotions and she made a small production out of lemonade serving. After forcing a sip she folded the letter and returned it to its envelope, then, "It appears I've lost him twice, doesn't it? But this time my life . . . " She studied her glass and waited for the right word. "This time, at least, it leaves my life livable."

The lemonade ritual over, she walked Henry to the front door.

"I suppose you came here looking for proof of collusion among the professors regarding the Bruce student, didn't you?"

"Yes, I did," Henry admitted.

"Would you like a word of advice?"

"Yes."

"Don't pursue it. There's no love lost among the teachers, but when they're confronted from outside they have a way of closing ranks in a hurry. I know. I've seen it before."

261

"Thank you. I think I had almost come to the same conclusion."

After he started the station wagon Henry looked back into the old house. He could make out the silhouette of Mrs. Pangbourne still standing in the hallway rereading her letter.

She was right he decided. What could be gained by pursuing it, except to further alienate his son.

On the way home Henry couldn't resist swinging by the Navy yard to see what had become of the Precursor. He didn't even get by the gate. Ensign Shirley was on duty again but he seemed to be too busy with paperwork to chat with his old friend Henry. Apparently that door in Henry's life was now closed. With a trace of a smile on his lips he breathed a deep sigh and headed the station wagon toward the airport.

Chapter Twenty-Seven

That night Henry dreamed he was calling to his son. But he could see Philip only in profile. His face was affixed to a coin and the coin was imbedded in a glass cube and the cube was behind the heavy glass in a jewelry store display case. No matter how hard he called, Philip's position stayed the same.

Henry spent the better part of the next two days in his traction bed. Fortunately, the girls had not pestered him with questions once the heart attack news was spread abroad and assimilated and Philip had been cleared of all charges. That was enough for now. Perhaps forever.

On day one Henry was feeling poorly of spirit. The injustice of it all and the fact he was suffering in silence about Philip's part in it were not his only problems; he'd held such a strong conviction he was involved in the whole matter because it was the will of God that he be there. But he'd been frustrated at every turn, and in spite of his best efforts there had been no exposure, no fulfillment. Things happened just as if he'd never been there. So much for his manifest destiny, he decided. He licked his wounds and tried to relax his back with a little positive thinking, but no prayer. God, he decided, had let him down.

But by day two he was thinking differently on the matter. While things had not turned out as he expected he had been the instrument through which Sylvia Pangbourne had learned the truth about her husband's conversion experience. Could it be that had been Henry's true mission? If so, it was most assuredly true, God's ways are not man's ways.

Mid-morning on day three Henry came downstairs declaring he felt "fit as a fiddle" and persuaded Valery they should have a brunch on the patio. But that was the day the San Diego letter arrived and before the scrambled eggs were cold on his plate Henry was back in bed flat on his back.

It was from Mabel Culpepper. She and her admiral husband had known the Garretts in Washington and now they had moved to the San Diego area for their retirement years.

"I saw this article in the morning paper and thought you should have it for your scrapbook. You two must be very proud of your son to reach such a position so early. I didn't recognize him with the beard at first. It seems like only yesterday when he and our Petey were in junior high together. Petey graduated Annapolis last year and is now stationed in Greenland with some hush-hush operation you, Henry, no doubt would understand. I'm sure you're very proud of Philip. Please remember us to him and don't hesitate to drop by if you're ever down San Diego way."

Enclosed was a small newspaper article and picture of Philip:

> Philip Garrett has been appointed to an associate professor chair at El Rio University. The announcement was made this morning by Dr. Wendel Hazard, dean of the physical science

division of the univeristy. "Philip Garrett has demonstrated a remarkable grasp of the physical sciences, both as a researcher and as an assistant to the teaching staff during the past school year," Dr. Hazard said, "and it is a pleasure to welcome him to our university in this important capacity."

Mr. Garrett is in the doctoral program at El Rio and plans to continue his thesis work during the summer months.

"Well, isn't that remarkable," Valery said, pleased as she could be. "This will make all the difference in the world. Dear Mabel, so nice and thoughtful of her to think to send this. Now once Philip settles in down there he'll soon be rid of his wild ideas about overturning the establishment and all, since he'll now have a piece of it himself. And such a position too. Aren't you proud of him, Henry? This will certainly change his feelings toward you, don't you think? Nothing like settling in and knowing where you're going in life to get your attitude about things put right, I always say. Henry, what on earth's the matter with you?"

"I guess I got up a bit sooner than I should have."

"Oh, Henry, on such a happy occasion too. I do wish you'd let me call the doctor."

"No need," Henry said rising. "He'd only prescribe the traction."

She moved to his side and started walking with him toward the stairs. "Well, how much longer do you think this is going to take before it clears up?"

"I don't know, dear. We'll just have to take it one day at a time."